Standing Up

Tales of
Struggle

Ellen Bravo &
Larry Miller

PRAISE FOR STANDING UP

"Ellen Bravo and Larry Miller bring to life how ordinary people find the strength to stand up to fight back and build the community they need to sustain them. The book is funny, powerful and inspiring." — Karen Nussbaum, former director of 9to5 and of Working America

"Into this small novel are packed shocking, terrifying, inspiring and deeply felt lives of the unsung and marginally employed." — Jacquelyn Mitchard, author of *The Deep End of the Ocean*

"From the first page, Ellen Bravo and Larry Miller organized us into readers who couldn't put *Standing Up* down! Worker actions and victories are celebrated with truth and determination." —Sue Doro, Editor/Publisher *Pride and a Paycheck* Magazine

"What a wonderful story of class, class struggle and regular people. Bravo and Miller have written what feels like a merged memoir and novel. The story is about struggle and change, but also about joy and humor." — Bill Fletcher, Jr., author of The *Man Who Fell Out of the Sky* and *Solidarity Divided*

"Great storytelling about standing up to injustice, filled with hope and powered by love and human interdependence. We see the anatomy of stand-ups: courage bolstered by support, where we tell each other, "Yes, you can," and tell our oppressors, "No, you won't." — Ai-jen Poo, author of *Aging with Dignity*, director of National Domestic Workers Association and Caring Across Generations

"So much fiction is about escape and fantasy, but these powerful tales of struggle will enrich our real and daily lives." — Gloria Steinem, activist and author

"Lyrical snapshots of resistance and solidarity at the workplace—hospitals, factories, banks, schools. Told with warmth and humility, these poignant stories provide roadmaps for readers fighting racism, sexism, and homophobia at their jobsite or in their home. A must read for anyone serious about working for change in the world and for anyone who loves a great story. It will be a wonderful addition to the curriculum for teachers in high school and college classes."
— Linda Christensen, author of *Reading, Writing and Rising Up*

"The characters in this book face injustice but together find ways to fight back with wit, rage, heart—and a good dose of laughter. If you've ever worked a low-wage job, you'll love the creative ways Bravo and Miller's characters take on the bullies, bosses, and bureaucrats who stand between working people and the respect we deserve. — Jennifer Morales, author of *Meet Me Halfway*

"Standing Up describes the small indignities and larger practices that play havoc with workers' lives. It captures the process of convincing oneself and others to take a risk and speak up and the personal epiphanies that can result. It's like a cookbook for activists from two senior organizers happy to share."
— Jane LaTour, author of *Sisters in the Brotherhoods: Working Women Organizing for Equality in New York City*

"A gem of a playbook that centers the voices of workers challenging all levels of inequity, privilege and power. I invite union staff, union members, organizers and all students of labor to take this novel journey." — K. C. Wagner, Co-Chair, Equity at Work, The Worker Institute at Cornell

Standing Up - Tales of Struggle, Copyright © 2022 by Ellen
Bravo & Larry Miller

All rights reserved.

Library of Congress Cataloging-in-Publication Data:

Bravo, Ellen, Miller, Larry, Standing Up – Tales of Struggle

1.. labor union 2. Union campaign 3. Social justice 4. Women's
rights 5. Gender equality

6. Civil right

Cover art by Della Wells

Book design by D. Bass

Published by Hardball Press, Brooklyn, New York

ISBN: 978-1-7344938-9-4

www.hardballpress.com

info@hardballpress.com

DEDICATION

To the real-life Sam's and Vanessa's, Annie's and L.C.'s and so many others in our lives who have stood up to injustice and reminded us that the power of the people is greater than the people in power.

And for our sons, Nat Miller and Craig Bravo Miller, who fuel us every day with their love and their ability to make us laugh.

Contents

The Slowdown

"Good Lord almighty, what is *that*? What the hell *is* that?" Eve's screech was loud enough to reach the foremen's office. She jumped three feet back from the sorting table as the two foremen came hurtling in.

"That's human flesh up in there!" Eve pointed to the jumble of hospital linen. Sure enough, a gelatinous chunk of something purple had rolled out of a sheet onto the table. "Where's those gloves you promised us? I ain't touching that." Eve yanked her head scarf off and wiped the sweat from her face.

Nick Turner had just emptied his cart of laundry onto the table. It was his first day on the job. He had no clue what might be in the bundles of soiled, bloodied sheets that poured out of the chutes into the carts he was now in charge of. All he knew was his task: fill the carts, push them to a loading dock and onto the flatbed of a truck. The stench was so bad, he couldn't bring himself to look too close before driving across the street, backing the truck up thirty feet and unloading everything here at the laundry. But Eve's scream drew Nick's glance right to the fleshy piece that threatened to roll off the table. He twisted his head so the others wouldn't see him gag.

"Welcome to hell, otherwise known as Grady Hospital laundry room, man." Jonas kept his voice to a whisper as they backed their empty carts out of the room while Eve continued to holler. This co-worker was only twenty, same as Nick, but he'd been working here for two years and had the muscles to prove it. Jonas was showing

1

Nick the ropes. "I believe you already met our illustrious bossmen, Bob — he's the short one who's outta breath from running across the hall — and Billy-Bob, the one whose mouth runs on its own motor." They could hear Billy-Bob ordering Eve and the other women to get back to work: "There's nothing to worry about, ladies, certainly nothing to yap about. We don't pay you to stand around and have hissy fits."

Nick wasn't sure whether these were their actual first names or just what the workers called them, and he didn't know how to ask. Billy-Bob had given Nick his initial tour of the worksite. The twenty-minute orientation ended with the foreman looking out over the laundry rooms like a lord surveying his estate. "There might be chances for advancement here," he confided, thumbs hooked into his belt. Two white foremen, over thirty Black workers, and one new white boy. Nick knew what "advancement" meant.

It was 1970 and the youth culture had called him — music, love, and most of all, rebellion. In late summer, Nick and three of his Milwaukee buddies decided to quit their jobs and plunge into the counterculture. The others got a beat-up van and headed out to San Francisco, but Nick chose a Greyhound to Atlanta, mindful of the advice of Mr. Adebayo, the high school history teacher who helped him connect the dots between napalm in Vietnam and fire hoses in Selma: "If you want to fight the power, go South, not West. Go to the bowels of the struggle." Nick hoped to get a job in a factory, but the hospital was where he found an opening. Little did he imagine how much like an assembly line it would turn out to be.

He tried to describe the set-up to Sam Kingston, his first Atlanta friend. Sam, all legs and elbows and deep-set eyes, had gotten on the bus in Chattanooga, where he'd been visiting his grandma. In exchange for sharing Nick's joint at the rest stop, Sam helped him get the downstairs apartment in his building. The rent was $50 a month. Nick would be making $64 a week before taxes.

"You the whitest white boy I ever seen," Sam told him after he got the job, pointing to Nick's jeans. "Even your patches have patches. Why you want to work in an all-Black department?"

Nick stuffed his hands in his pockets and made a mental note to go to the Army-Navy store for some new jeans. "I figured I'm old enough to learn a thing or two," he said.

When Nick came home that first night, Sam was waiting on the stoop, long legs sticking out on the sidewalk. "So, my man, what'd you learn at school today?"

"A lot, actually." Nick had spent the bus ride from Grady adding it up. He told Sam about his cousin, close as a brother, who OD'd last summer and lay in a coma for two weeks before coming to. "I visited him at the hospital every night," Nick said. "Never gave one thought to who washes, dries, folds, hauls what must be thousands of pounds of stuff — sheets, blankets, towels, all those doctor's scrubs, you name it. And I sure never thought about what was on all of it."

Sam motioned for him to sit down and handed over a joint. The guy's hands looked like they belonged to someone much older than twenty-four, covered with callouses from the Tramson packaging plant where he worked. "What do they do with patients who got something contagious?"

"That's the thing." Nick took a long hit. "If a department has a diseased patient, they wrap their sheets and gowns in a bundle and write 'contaminated' on a strip of masking tape. And guess what? We handle 'contaminated' materials the same way we handle everything else. No gloves, no masks. Nada. Today I swear to God, some body part came out of a sheet I'd just dumped on the sorting table."

"Damn. What'd y'all do?"

Nick leaned back on his elbows. "Honestly? I tried not to throw up. But the women who do the sorting, they

3

brought the foremen in and gave 'em hell. These ladies have the worst job in the laundry. I heard the bosses keep a list and make sure to assign it to the women with the sharpest tongues." He pictured Eve, not much older than he was, slapping sheets onto the table and giving the foremen the evil eye.

Nick kept hearing the voices of those two bossmen, a deep drawl he had to remind himself not to make fun of. In the few weeks he'd been in Atlanta, Nick had met a number of white youth with similar accents hanging out on the Strip on Peachtree Street. But in the foremen's mouths, that voice sounded disrespectful and ill-mannered. Maybe it was the constant smirk their words slithered through.

***

In no time Nick fell into his routine with Jonas at Grady. After hauling linen to the laundry, they'd pick up the batches waiting in their carts and take them over to the elevators and down to the main floor. There they'd push the carts over to the washers and line them up, ready to spill their contents into the hands of two guys who untangled the heavy mess and maneuvered them into washing machines, or moved the even heavier wet clothes to the dryers. The next part of the operation belonged to the women, some ironing every garment and others folding them, edges sharp as military garb. The whole process resulted in baskets of clean and folded laundry sorted for delivery to the various hospital floors.

Nick found it easy to strike up conversation with the five other men as they worked side-by-side. Once they realized Nick was not a practicing Georgia redneck, preferred Johnnie Taylor to Waylon Jennings and listened more than he talked, they started to warm up to him — except one older guy named J.T. who kept his distance. Sam laughed when Nick told him about it. "It ain't about you, man," Sam said. "The only white folk that guy knows

4

are the ones who cut off his power or lock up his kid. Give it time."

On Fridays, the guys stopped at Jim's on Auburn Avenue, cashed their checks and had a few drinks over plates of oxtails and greens. Occasionally a couple of the women joined in. When Nick asked Eve why she and the others didn't come by, she snorted and gave him a quick shove. "Somebody's got to tend to the kids, baby."

"My mom always had me watch my little sister," Nick told her. "When I whined about it, she'd tell me, 'God may have forced women to bear children, but every human being can help raise them.'"

Eve looked up at him and nodded. "You listen to your momma."

Friday night conversations at Jim's became Monday morning jokes, discussions about everything from politics to sports, and some high-level bullshitting — what his co-workers called "selling wolf tickets." The first time he heard that, Nick thought someone had lottery tickets and asked Jonas how much they were. Jonas leaned over, put his hands on his knees, and howled with laughter. "Good thing you got me to school your Yankee-white-boy-no-street-sense ass," he said.

That was hardly Nick's only schooling. He learned that most of the women came from southern Georgia, towns he'd never heard of like Lumpkin, Tifton, Eastman. A few came from Calhoun County in Alabama. Athalia had moved to Atlanta to get away from picking cotton. Once there, she helped two cousins leave the fields, all of them now at Grady. "Here comes that cotton we picked," Ahalia would say. "No getting away from it, no kinda way." She liked to greet Nick by dangling a little hand-sewn bag of snuff. "Just try a pinch," she'd say.

The more he became a regular, the more he heard about people's lives back home and their hopes and dreams of living in bustling Atlanta. Simple goals of survival, sullied by the low pay and demeaning treatment from Bob and Billy-Bob, not to mention the danger they faced each day.

"Doctors and nurses have that gear to protect them from the filth and disease around here," Eve would say. She looked a lot younger after work, without the bandana and the side-eye. "We want the same."

When Nick sought Sam's advice, his friend delivered a crash course in labor rights in a southern state. Sam was part of a Black workers' group in Atlanta that was trying to get something going in a couple of workplaces. "Georgia is what they cleverly call a "right to work" state, which means we got very few rights at all," he said. "You won't see a lot of unions down here like they got in Wisconsin. But we do have the American Federation of State, County and Municipal Employees. Most of Grady is unorganized, but your laundry area is in AFSCME."

Nick reached for his billfold and pulled out a union card. "I'm a step ahead of you. Remember I told you about Emmanuel Jackson? Great guy, everyone looks up to him. Turns out he's a union rep and he signed me up today on lunch break. Then he took a Polaroid of me holding up my union card to mail to my dad — a twenty-two-year member of the International Association of Machinists Local 629." His dad's forehead folded into a dozen creases when his son left for Atlanta, but Nick knew he'd be beaming while he flashed this photo around to all his pals.

Sam raised his right hand for a high five. "Good man. Means y'all should get some backing if you make a move."

***

For weeks, Nick observed the union representative Emmanuel talk about taking action, how he'd steer his cart from person to person, listening to ideas as he stooped to help someone fold a sheet. Right after the incident on Nick's first day, Emmanuel and Brenda, the other union rep and a Grady long-hauler, stayed after work to

6

talk with the foremen about safety equipment. "They told us we'd get an official reply really soon," Emmanuel said. "Officially, management is keeping their mouths shut."

The urge to do something was spreading like cattail seeds in the wind. Emmanuel and Brenda called a short meeting at Jim's that Friday to put together a plan. Brenda stopped by each woman's station, urging them to join for at least half an hour. "Halloween's around the corner," she told them in a voice raspy from cigarettes and grief. Nick learned she'd lost a son to the streets and a grandbaby to a fire. "Ain't nothing scarier than coming to work here every day."

Soon as they gathered in the back of the bar, complaints started flying. "I'm turning myself into a pretzel trying to get assigned anywhere but sorting," one woman said. J.T. hated how the foremen dogged Athalia, the oldest person working in the laundry. Eve gripped the table so hard, she almost spilled her Hennessey. "All that sex talk from Billy-Bob, that's gotta stop."

Brenda presided over the discussion. "If we stick together and stay strong, a lot of what goes on in the laundry can change. We need to start with health protection."

Emmanuel produced a spiral notebook and they drew up a list of demands as folks shouted them out: "safety gloves — I don't want that shit on my hands." "Masks so my lungs don't give out on me." "How 'bout some aprons and coveralls, fresh ones every day?" "We need some of that antibacterial soap." "No more raw flesh surprises — they gotta separate out the contaminated laundry and body parts." Brenda added a demand for the hospital to begin hiring Black managers.

"And not just any Black folk," Eve said. "They gotta know how to treat workers with respect."

Seven people volunteered to serve on the committee that would organize the effort. "I'm in," Nick told them. Eve raised her glass. "Me, too," she said.

7

The AFSCME local sent a rep to accompany Emmanuel and Brenda when they met with Bob and Billy-Bob, a reminder that the workers had the legal right to hand over their demands. The meeting lasted less than ten minutes. As Brenda reported, "Same as before. All we got from those two were growls, scowls, dirty looks, and five little words: 'We'll get back with you.'"

Two weeks went by with no answer. "That's it," Brenda said. She called a committee meeting that night at Jim's to decide the next move.

Sam had told Nick from the start that the group would have to be careful about a strike. "The hospital would fire all y'all in a hot second and everybody knows it," he said. "There's plenty of people out here need work. The union at Grady is still too weak. But your committee'll come up with something." Sam grinned and gave Nick a quick poke in the shoulder. "And when they do, be on the lookout. Those bossmen are gonna call on you to remain loyal to your kind."

As Sam predicted, the group agreed they would not call for a walkout. Instead they decided to go with Emmanuel's suggestion: "I say we do a secret slow-down," he said. "We don't announce nothin'. We give the appearance of business as usual. But when the bossmen ain't looking, we develop a little molasses in our veins." He demonstrated by dropping a napkin and taking a full minute to bend down and pick it up.

Since there were only two supervisors, they could never watch everyone at once. The focus of the slowdown would be at the front end of the work, so the majority of women doing the folding under the constant eye of the foremen could stay at their normal rate — each would take extra care to iron sharp creases or produce straight folds.

Nick and Jonas were in the thick of it: The key to slowing down was the pace of clearing the laundry that dropped from the chutes. Jonas led the way, picking up

8

the corner of one sheet at a time and carrying it to the other side of the cart in front of him. Nick added a couple flourishes of his own: starting with an item at the bottom of a heap, or trying to flick one sheet from the chute rather than letting them all topple out at the same time. The guys at the washers adopted similar techniques. Emmanuel created a system of alerts for all of them that changed twice a day — humming a certain song, a whistle, a bang, a series of claps, to signal the impending arrival of Bob or Billy-Bob.

In just two days, laundry was backed up to the fourth floor. When nursing aides and candy stripers opened the chute doors, they were packed full; sometimes linen would fall out on the floor.

"I wish you could see the place," Nick told Sam that night. "Complaints started coming to the laundry by lunchtime. Bob and Billy-Bob went nuts. They were running around trying to figure out what was going on. They started following those of us responsible for cleaning out the chutes. But all they saw were people busting their butts. When those two weren't looking, the chutes were overflowing with dirty laundry. I'm telling you, Hollywood could hire these workers. They played dumb so smart, you wouldn't believe it."

Bob and Billy-Bob tried to clean up the piles of laundry themselves, but they couldn't catch up. They were getting calls from more departments as the laundry backed up to higher floors. Their jobs were on the line. Those working in the laundry couldn't see the drama going on elsewhere in the hospital, but they got an earful from the foremen, who made it sound like patients were lying on bare mattresses.

That night at Jim's, Brenda and Eve filled them in on the whisper campaign going on among the women. "If shit starts, we'll be ready," Brenda said. "They mess with any of you, we shut it down."

Joining Nick and Jonas on cart duty was the newbie, Zekia. On the third day of the slowdown, the foremen tried a new tack, selecting particular individuals for mandatory overtime. Nick wasn't surprised they started with Zekia. They knew the guy had lost his job at the Coca-Cola plant for yelling at a foreman on the shop floor.

Billy-Bob and Bob told Zekia to work the chutes on one side of the hospital by himself. They followed him everywhere, yelling at him to work faster until he finally snapped at them. They fired him on the spot.

The rest of the crew heard the news the next morning as soon as they got to work. Emmanuel went to the bosses to ask what happened. They told him Zekia was fired for being "insubordinate."

Zekia was a warning shot and everybody knew it. The bossmen wanted Emmanuel to make it clear that everyone had to get back in line or they would all be fired.

Emmanuel and Brenda held a quick conversation with the committee in the alley during break. Brenda laid out her plan. As she delivered just-washed clothes to be ironed or folded, she would bend close and remind each woman about their promise to stick together. Nick and Jonas would rally the men.

One by one, the entire laundry crew walked to the middle of the folding area in front of the bosses' office. Bob and Billy-Bob came running out with their jaws flapping to order people back to work. Emmanuel crossed his arms over his broad chest and made the announcement: "Zekia doesn't work, we don't work."

An hour went by as they stayed gathered there while the bosses kept disappearing. They were running back and forth across the street to talk to their manager, a big guy with a bald head who Brenda called "Mr. Clean" since "he like to have these other fools do his dirty work."

At one point, Nick went to use the bathroom. Billy-Bob was waiting for him in the hallway afterwards. "Hey,

Turner. What are you doing with *them*?" he whispered. "You're one of us."

Nick silently blessed his neighbor for anticipating this move. He shook off his wet hands, the bathroom always ran out of paper towels — they'd have to add it to their demands. "Give Zekia his job back," Nick said. Billy-Bob spun on his heel and took off for his office. Nick jogged back to his co-workers.

"Hey, everyone, guess who wanted to chat with me outside the can — Mister Billy-Bob." Nick grinned and repeated the conversation. For the first time, J.T. gave him a nod.

It wasn't long before Mr. Clean himself came striding into the room. "Where's his white horse?" Eve whispered.

Mr. Clean held out both his arms as if to gather them all in an embrace. "My people, my people," he said. "Talk to me. I know we can work this out. After all, every one of us shares one mission here — quality patient care."

Jonas mumbled under his breath. Eve shoved her bandana into her uniform pocket. Nick knew they were all bursting to reply to this bullshit, but they had agreed that Emmanuel would be their spokesperson. "Our demands were clear weeks ago," Emmanuel said. "Quality patient care depends on a healthy workforce. We've added a new demand to our list — we want Zekia back. He doesn't work, no one works."

Mr. Clean agreed to meet with the committee while everyone else remained in the folding area. Bob was chewing so hard on his pinky, Nick wondered whether he had any fingernail left at all.

Brenda and Emmanuel did most of the talking. "How can we have dignity on this job and we can't even get soap or gloves to keep our hands clean?" Brenda said. "Or aprons to keep the blood and feces off our clothes?" Emmanuel made the case for Zekia: "He's a hard worker

11

and no one wants someone riding them every minute. We can't go back to work unless Zekia does."

Mr. Clean said he needed time to discuss the issues with Bob and Billy-Bob. As the committee members went back on the floor, they could see the manager frantically making phone calls. Bob and Billy-Bob were huddled in a corner. Clearly the matter was going up the chain to the top brass.

After another hour, the manager got Brenda and Emmanuel to come back into the office. Eve had planted herself at the front of their group. No one moved from the folding area. Finally, Mr. Clean came out to address them all.

The manager's announcements were brief: Zekia could come back to work the next day. The hospital would immediately provide plastic gloves and aprons for the haulers and sorters. He planned to meet with the committee within a week to discuss additional safety and health measures.

"And hiring Black managers!" Brenda added, waving an unlit cigarette. "And respect."

Mr. Clean nodded. "Now I need you all to be a team with me here. We have to get that backed-up laundry taken care of, even if I need to see every one of you in here on Saturday. Are we good?"

Eve and Brenda started a snake dance back to the folding tables. The other women lined up behind them in single file, weaving in and out of the tables as they each took their place. When Athalia got back to her spot, she surprised everyone by letting out a booming, "Thank you, Lord, and thank you, committee!"

Nick couldn't wait to tell Sam, but his neighbor must have had a long meeting or a hot date. Nick smoked a J and listened to Voodoo Child by Hendrix over and over: *I stand up next to a mountain and I chop it down with the edge of my hand.* He was filled with a spirit he had never quite felt before. He couldn't tell if it was the weed or just the pleasure of victory.

The next day everybody quickly got to work. No one talked a lot as they performed their tasks, but every now and then you could hear whistling. Athalia kept up a steady hum.

"It's like everyone was a little lighter," Nick told Sam that night when they finally caught up.

"That's pride, man." Sam said. "Burns up so much less energy than rage."

The Rockefeller Eight

Atlanta, June 1971

Every time he moved his right foot forward, Nick could feel the egg in his pocket, a small oval protected only by a thin handkerchief. He walked as slowly as he dared without calling attention to himself, more worried about how to keep the egg from busting than what would happen if they got arrested for egging a billionaire warmonger.

He first learned about the protest in an article in *The Great Speckled Bird*: "While we were getting tear-gassed and billy-clubbed fighting against the war in Vietnam, David Rockefeller was growing richer off it. Some argued the U.S. had to wage war to make the world safe for democracy. Rockefeller wanted to make it safe for Chase Manhattan Bank. This capitalist behemoth is bringing his message to the Atlanta Chamber of Commerce banquet on Friday night. Let's give him a Hot-Lanta welcome."

That night Nick went to the meeting of the Hell No! coalition. The original name was "Hell, No, We Won't Go," but at some point before Nick moved to Atlanta, the group underwent an intense debate about what to call themselves. Some insisted draft card burning was an important blow to the war effort. Others argued it was great for privileged kids who could afford the risk, but not an option if you were poor or working-class, especially if you were Black. Eventually they reached a consensus to shorten the name and broaden the mission. The group now said "Hell, No" to the war in Vietnam, to imperialist greed, racism, sexism — and a long list of other ills.

Three dozen people showed up at a Unitarian church to plan the protest outside the Candler Hotel, where Rockefeller was scheduled to speak that Friday night. Afterwards, people broke into affinity groups to work on picket signs. Nick was settling in with some magic markers when his pal Danny Sugarman pulled him aside. "A few of us in RYB are going to the park to plan a little more personal welcome. You down?"

Danny, who looked like he was still in high school with his small frame and shy grin, had been trying to get Nick to join the Revolutionary Youth Brigade since they first met at a Grateful Dead concert in Piedmont Park. Despite the group's support for Fred Hampton and Black liberation, they were virtually all white and the leaders were almost all male. Nick hung out with them from time to time but backed off any larger commitment.

Danny and Nick joined four other guys already at a picnic table around the corner from the church. They bunched up at one end but threw a couple backpacks on the rest of the table to keep anyone else from joining them.

"You know Rockefeller and his buddies will never see this demo, right?" Danny leaned in from his spot on the end. "Security's going to sneak them through a private entrance. They won't hear a thing."

"What do you have in mind?" Clay was twenty-seven, the oldest and most educated of the RYB folks Nick had met. He pulled on a lock of hair slipping from an unruly ponytail. Nick noticed the guy always wore a bandana around his neck, ready for tear gas or persistent allergies.

Danny glanced around to make sure no one was near. "A small group of us get inside and make our way to the banquet room after the program begins. I know that hotel, I used to bus tables there in the summers." He pulled out a sheet of paper with a skeletal blueprint dotted with numerous X's. "Here's the front entrance where regular guests go in. That's where the Hell No! folks will be, but security will keep them cordoned off out of view. Over here (he pointed to an X on the side) is the valet parking entrance where they'll take Rockefeller and the other honchos. And that X in the back, that's the employee entrance. I have a buddy who's going to get me a key."

"Far fuckin' out," Clay said, fiddling with his bandana. "How do we get past security at the banquet room, especially since they'll know about the outdoor protest?"

Danny flipped over his piece of paper. "The hall itself has several doors. This one near the back"— another set of Xs appeared at various points around a large rectangle representing the banquet hall — "is for the servers. It connects to the kitchen. But there happens to be another way to get to it without going through the kitchen."

"Your buddy going to help with that?" Clay asked.

"Nope." Danny folded up the paper. "That's on us. I can get us there."

The night air was thick and humid. Clay glanced up at the moths flickering around the nearby streetlight. "What size group, what kind of action?" he asked.

"Eight. Eggs."

As impressed with the brevity of this answer as he was with the ingenuity of the various ways to get inside, Nick said, "So the idea is we get in while Rockefeller is speaking and all lob our eggs at him?"

Danny nodded. "If we can pull this off, the guy will have more than egg on his face. He'll have a lot of reporters asking how much he's profiting off the war."

His voice no more than a whisper, Danny looked around at each of them. "Even if we manage to get into that room, chances are slim we'll walk out unescorted. Two other comrades who couldn't come tonight have told me they're in. That leaves the six of us. I need each of you to say whether we can count on you, knowing there's a risk of arrest. Anyone who can't, no need to explain. Obviously, cone of silence no matter what. But once you commit, there's no backing down."

Only one of the six held off, a young guy Nick hadn't met before who was on probation after serving thirty days for possession of marijuana. "If you do get arrested, just hope they keep you in County," the kid told them. "You don't want them to haul your ass to the prison farm."

Nick had no problem committing to join the action. He was between jobs and eager to speed up the end of this monstrous war. Two years ago, on the night before his appointment with the draft board in Milwaukee, Nick downed several glasses of cheap scotch, the very thing he'd been taught to avoid because it would cause a nasty flare-up of his childhood colitis and ulcerate his colon. The draft board official sent Nick to a proctologist, whose exam was rough but confirmed his condition and gave him a get-out-of-the-draft-free card. The war had already devoured the life of his best friend from high school and several other classmates, along with tens of thousands of other Americans' loved ones and who knew how many millions of Vietnamese, Cambodians, Laotians.

After the group committed to Danny's plan, Nick shared it with his buddy Sam Kingston on the front steps of the building where they each rented a small apartment. No need to swear Sam to secrecy, the Black workers group he was involved with was light years more together than Hell No! or the RYB.

"I'm glad you're not suggesting I join you." Sam had a plate of greens and black-eyed peas with ham hocks which he polished off while they talked. "You get busted—which you will, by the way—they'll give you a hard time for daring to defy the system. They'll hold you a little while for malicious mischief or some shit like that until the ACLU or Legal Aid or one of your buddy's mommas, no offense, bails you out and arranges a fine which they'll get some rich patrons to donate. If the prosecutor or judge crosses a line, you may even get the charges dropped. People who look like me get busted for this? We're talking a charge of felonious assault, maybe even attempted murder. I'd be looking at a long stretch in the state pen."

Nick nodded his head. "I hear you. Just wanted you to know what I'm up to."

Sam bumped his right hand against his heart. "It's all good. Glad you're going after that motherfucker. He thinks we should bow down to him because he gives away a few bucks from the billions he's made off the backs of workers, all while shipping their kids off to war, hoping they'll be pissed off enough at some Vietnamese peasants that they'll forget who's really responsible for them never being able to climb out of the hole."

"Wish I could fit that on my egg," Nick told him.

**

That Friday, several hundred protesters showed up outside the Candler Hotel with an array of posters and noisemakers. As predicted, rows of Atlanta police and hotel security forces with batons raised kept them far from the street and from the hotel entrance. Nick could see the crowd in the distance when he climbed down from the bus, but his group had agreed to ignore it to remain inconspicuous. The last thing they needed was for one of the protesters to yell out, "Hey, Danny (or whoever), where're you going?"

Clay had recruited his roommate to be the eighth person, a gawky guy with long arms well suited for egg-tossing. The plan was for everyone to wear black pants and white button-down shirts like the wait staff, to take public transportation so they wouldn't have any parking to worry about, and to make their way to the back door singly or in pairs, but close to the same time. Nick had worried about some form of betrayal or incompetence on the part of Danny's inside pal, but the key worked fine and no security guards were lurking inside the door. Their team arrived within six minutes of each other; Danny slipped everyone in. Nick, breathing as lightly as possible, was third in line

19

behind Danny, who used hand signals to let them know when to stop, when to swerve right or left.

And then they were directly outside the door to the banquet room. The hallway was empty except for a couple who strolled by arm in arm, giggling at some private joke. Nick couldn't believe it — their group could have been armed to the hilt and gotten away with it. According to the schedule, Rockefeller should have been at least ten minutes into his keynote by now. Danny held up one hand and pointed his finger: go time. Like the others, Nick reached in his pants pocket for the egg which, miraculously, remained intact. He positioned it between the thumb, index and middle fingers of his left hand, visualizing the arc it would make as it sailed toward David Rockefeller's chin.

Nick never saw that chin. Before he could get his second foot inside the door, he was slammed to the ground, egg skittering across the carpet as first his left arm, then his right were yanked behind his back. What felt like a large stick was jammed against his neck, making it impossible for him to turn his head. All around him he could hear a roar of voices, a mix of "Don't-move-a-fucking-muscle" commands in his ear, high-pitched screams from the audience, a voice from a walkie-talkie saying, "He's unhurt, it was only an egg," someone at a microphone on stage urging calm, and Clay's giddy voice on the floor nearby saying, "Danny did it! He got one off!"

Nick was still trying to process it all as they were jerked to their feet and dragged out the door into that same hallway, now filled with cops barking orders, hotel staff running in all directions, reporters shouting questions and popping flashbulbs. The group hadn't planned ahead of time for being escorted out like this, but Danny and Clay began chanting: "No more fascist war!" The other six picked it up immediately, despite police commands to keep quiet. Nick saw that Clay had egg splattered across his left cheek and through his ponytail. A couple others had egg yolk running down their clothes. Nick caught a glimpse of Danny, whose bloodied lip didn't stop him from having a shit-eating grin.

Two police vans shuttled them to the county jail, where fingerprinting and mug shots dragged on for over an hour, according to a giant clock on the wall. "When do we get to make our phone calls?" Clay asked several times. He also demanded someone get an ice pack for Danny's lip. Each time, the five cops in the area enjoyed a good laugh. "How do you think these softies are gonna do at the prison farm?" one cop said repeatedly. "I mean, they seem to like eggs. How they gonna like looking after those cows?" He started a pool on which of the group would be the first to start bawling and call his momma to come get him out. Four of the five cops bet on Clay.

The group spent the night along with a handful of drunks in a large holding cell that reeked of urine, old vomit and rotgut whiskey. Nick tried unsuccessfully to get some sleep sitting upright on a bench with his head against the wall. He had a welt on the side of his neck from the night-stick and soreness in his ribs and hip. Whenever he finally got to take a shower, he imagined he'd see some elaborate bruises. Mostly what he felt was pride to be part of the group Danny had started calling "The Rockefeller Eight."

The next morning, a bunch of cops showed up in front of the holding cell and called their names. One by one the eight were adorned in handcuffs and led out of the jail section to an elevator, where they rode up several floors and were marched to a courtroom. This time instead of an anti-war chant, they took up a call and response: "What do we want? Our right to a phone call. When do we want it? NOW."

The judge, an older white guy with pursed lips, was neither moved nor amused when they entered in this fash-ion. "Unless you want added time for contempt of court, you will stop talking this instant." He glared at Danny, whose mouth was open to begin again "Stand in silence to hear the charges against you."

21

Danny raised his two handcuffed hands. "May I ask a question, sir?"

"You certainly may not." The judge banged his gavel to reinforce his point. "Deputy, do I have before me the eight individuals involved with the premeditated attack last night on Mr. David Rockefeller?"

One of the deputies stepped forward and read their full names. That was the first time Nick realized that Clay was none other than Clayton Seymour Fenwick the Third, son of a prominent Atlanta executive whose family made their fortune processing peanuts.

"All of you have been charged with disorderly conduct, public nuisance, and reckless endangerment," the judge informed them. Nick elbowed Dave and mouthed, "What the fuck?" He couldn't wait to hear an ACLU lawyer at their trial recount the long history of patriots who defied inhumane actions by those in power. Nick couldn't figure out why no one from the ACLU was present. Neither was anyone from Hell No! or the RYB — or for that matter, any reporters. The courtroom gallery was nearly empty. These assholes must have pulled some strings to keep their group from getting attention or support.

"I know you hippie anarchists have zero respect for the law," the judge was saying, after they all entered a not guilty plea. "Luckily, you are not in charge. I assign bail in the amount of $10,000 per person. Given the overcrowding we're experiencing here at the county jail, I hereby remand you to the county prison farm until your trial, which I will set for August 23."

This time Danny didn't raise his hands. "We are U.S. citizens," he shouted. "We have the right to an attorney. We ..."

The judge, face mottled with rage, stood up while pounding the gavel. "In my courtroom, sonny, you have exactly the rights I accord you. Deputies, get this scum out of my sight."

Minutes later the eight of them, still handcuffed, piled onto a green metal prison bus with chicken wire on the windows. To their surprise, they were the only passengers. Guards placed them two rows apart to keep them from talking and shackled them to their seats. As soon as the bus pulled out, Nick maneuvered his body to the side and started singing, "What Are You Fightin' For." One by one the others picked it up and followed with their own favorites, from "Eve of Destruction" to "We Shall Not Be Moved," improvising verses until they pulled onto a dirt road and stopped in a gravel parking lot.

The heat smacked their faces as they made their way to the only structure in sight, a gray, one-story building taking up the equivalent of a city block. A sleek Lincoln town car sat right in front of the entrance. Out stepped a middle-aged woman in a tailored suit, her hair the same auburn color as Clay's, accompanied by a prison official. She pointed at Clay, who was walking between Danny and Nick. "The middle one, officer. He's coming home with me."

"Hell no," Clay muttered, slowing his steps. "I'm not going anywhere. She can't make me."

Danny moved a little closer to him. "It's okay, man. It's helpful to have you out so you can go see those lawyers at the ACLU. Find out why the court's fucking with us and not letting them in."

"I get to decide who's my damn family, and they're not it," Clay said. "I don't want a dime of their fuckin' money. Whatever goes down here, I'm in."

"Use your privilege, comrade." Danny's bottom lip had ballooned from the smackdown, making him grimace slightly when he spoke. "We know where you stand. Let's be honest, we'll all do more good if we're out there organizing. And you can help make that happen. You've seen these cracker guards — we're not trying to be martyrs." He put his handcuffed wrists on Clay's shoulder. "No matter what happens, man, we'll always be the Rockefeller Eight."

The prison official hurried over and led Clay, feet dragging, over to the car.

The remaining seven were herded inside, where guards removed their handcuffs and passed out uniforms, orange striped jumpsuits with "Property of Atlanta County Prison Farm" in giant black letters across the front. Each of them also got a plastic bag to put their belongings in. Overseeing their welcome was a muscle-bound white guy in his fifties who stood at attention and introduced himself as Sgt. Llewellyn.

"It's lunch time, ladies." he said. "Put on your new duds. Cafeteria is this way. Afterwards we'll take you to our penthouse suite and let you know your Club Med activities."

Lunch turned out to be goulash, canned green beans and stale cornbread. None of them had eaten anything since last night so they tore into it. "Not my grandma's cooking," Danny said, "but we'll survive it."

Sgt. Llewellyn and another guard led them to a large room on the other end of the compound filled with what seemed to be a hundred bunk beds. "Sheets and blankets over there," Lewellyn told them. "Find an empty bed and learn how to make it. No maid service here. You missed the regular crews — they go out early morning. For today you'll be weeding the grounds around the building. Tomorrow's Sunday, and even you assholes get a day off so you can reflect on your sins. This is not your typical country club crowd, so you might want to watch your back, if you get my drift. Expect your assignments Monday morning. I'll be back in seven minutes to take you outside and get you your gear."

The group split up and roamed the room, until Danny called out that he'd found a cluster of beds next to or near each other. They each grabbed one and agreed to stay close together both as protection and a show of strength.

By Sunday night Nick and his pals were having discussions with other inmates, Black and white men ranging in age from eighteen to seventy-four, in the areas they were allowed to occupy — the bunk room, the cafeteria, and the fenced-in walkway outside. At first Nick's group mostly asked questions about the work assignments and rules. Although they refrained from bringing up what anyone was in for, inmates routinely asked them that question. Some laughed or shook their heads; a few gave a fist or a thumbs' up.

Nick's longest discussion was with a stocky Black guy with multiple tattoos who people called Toothpick. "That Rockefeller dude, he's the one over Chase bank, right?" he asked Nick, who nodded. "That's why I'm in here. They fucked with my money, opened up accounts I didn't ask for and then charged me penalties on them. When I went to complain, some white lady called the cops on me, said I was 'menacing' her. I been here seven months, still waiting for trial. So thanks for making me smile today."

"That sucks man," Nick said.

"Oh, it ain't just me," Toothpick said. "Mosta the brothers hang out here a long time and get the roughest assignments. We got our own name for this place: Atlanta Plantation."

Sam Kingston's words about unequal justice echoed in Nick's head.

After lights out, Nick and the others compared notes. From what they could tell, many of the inmates were awaiting trial for disorderly conduct, public drunkenness, or loitering. "That just means being poor or homeless," Danny said. A few had charges of battery or larceny. Nick relayed what he learned from Toothpick, who had also warned them who to stay away from, including a few people locked up for indecent exposure, and two KKK wannabes who called Danny and his buddies "pinko pansy Jew-boys."

25

Although Llewellyn said work duty started early, none of them was prepared for the four thirty a.m. wake-up alarm, which blared over a loudspeaker right above their bunks. No wonder that cluster of beds had been available. After a quick breakfast, guards herded them outside next to a row of five flatbed trucks.

Sgt. Llewellyn put a wad of chewing tobacco in his cheek. "Any of you fine gentlemen ever milked a cow? I'm not talking grabbing titties here. I need someone who knows how to scrub the teats without getting kicked in the head or the balls by an angry cow."

Around him Nick could see his buddies tensing up. Danny ducked his head and was swallowing hard.

"I can do it," Nick said. "I have a lot of cousins and they all live on farms."

"Thanks, man," Dave whispered. "Talk about taking one for the team."

Llewellyn grinned and spit out some of his tobacco. "Awright, boy, you've got you a job." Llewellyn assigned two other white guys to jump with Nick onto the back of one of the trucks, which took them straight to the barn at the top of the hill. Their instructions were to meet up with an Officer Dewey, who was nowhere to be found. Nick led the others, who had never been on this detail before, to scout the barn and holding pens. Before long a pickup truck pulled up and a white-haired, potbellied man slid out from the front seat.

"I heard one of you fellas has actually been on a farm," he said. Nick stood up and introduced himself.

"Okay, Turner, watch me now." Officer Dewey positioned himself beside the closest cow and pantomimed the motions. "The hardest part is washing the teats. You grab her tail high up. You push it away from you till she can feel it. You push your shoulder against her hip to get her off balance and you reach down and scrub those teats. If you don't use enough force, she'll kick your teeth out."

One of the guys took two giant steps back. Dewey laughed. "Don't shit yourself. Your part's a lot easier. You and your buddy will be hooking up the suction cup to the teats. Just turn the machine on and suck her dry. It only takes a couple minutes."

Dewey had Nick ready that cow so he could demonstrate the suction cups and how to pour the milk into a stainless steel container, which one of the two helpers was supposed to carry to the milk house at the end of the barn. "You just empty it into the vat to be homogenized, and then bring the container back to be filled again. And tell you what. If you three do your job, I'll leave you alone."

It had been a few years since Nick had actually touched a cow, but the procedure was familiar. Even though he didn't have to, Nick helped the others carry the containers back and forth. He loved the familiar smell of the milk house, the feeling of being surrounded by nature, the soft nuzzle of the cow.

Once they finished the morning milking and clean-up, Nick and the others were free to hang out, play basketball on a wire hoop in the yard, fill up on fresh milk and broken Nabisco cookies, a donation from the nearby plant, until they had to do the second round of milking at five o'clock. That first day from the barn they watched the other trucks driving back to the housing unit. Everybody doing fieldwork got off two hours before the milking crew did. But the fieldwork turned out to be ten hours of back-wrenching labor. Nick's buddies came in filthy, exhausted and famished. "Man, did I ever call that one wrong," Danny told Nick after he heard about his day. "They're busting our balls and you're at summer camp."

It took five days for Clay, using his mother's connections, to cut through the bureaucracy. Turns out the ACLU had been filing habeas corpus motions since the moment the eight were arrested. They'd finally gone to federal court to sue for violation of the Fourteenth Amendment. That action, boosted by some heat from a Fenwick corporate lawyer, got the charges dropped altogether. Sgt. Llewellyn delivered the news after dinner that Thursday. "Looks like you ladies are free to go," he told them.

As the prison bus pulled up to take them back, some of the other inmates came out to say good-bye. One of the farm crew yelled, "All power to the people." A guy Danny had spent a lot of time with shouted something about imperialists and their running dogs. Nick noticed Toothpick making his way to the door of the bus.

"Free all the prisoners," he said, folding his enormous hand into a fist. "Start with us."

Down Yonder Agin' the Wall

Atlanta, 1972

Forget fingernails on the chalkboard. Nick Turner never experienced a sound as jarring as the shaker, the monster of a machine at Grinnell Steel that clamped down on the steel flanges to get rid of all the extra sand. Assaulted by that noise his first morning, Nick scanned the open floor for the source until his eyes settled on what looked like a gigantic set of jaws. The clanging felt as violent as a tornado. He had to wait for it to stop before he could ask the guy next to him what the hell it was.

In his seat on the bus headed to the plant, Nick had been focused on two things: He would finally be part of the industrial working class, where workers made essential things — in this case, the metal parts that connected huge sewage and water pipes — and could put a hurt on the economy if they went on strike. He was itching to be part of some kind of organizing here. Also, he'd be earning two dollars and forty-five cents an hour instead of the buck sixty he got in the laundry at Grady Hospital. By the fall, he hoped to have enough to purchase a used car, maybe a Chevy. He already had a list of what he'd need to keep it polished.

But standing inside the plant that February morning wiped out any thought but one: What the fuck had he gotten himself into? The pounding might let up for sixty seconds every few minutes, but the smell of burnt oil penetrated everything all the time. Nick's throat felt raw almost immediately. He soon realized it was from the steel filings that filled the air, along with coke and sand dust from burning all that scrap metal. It took a few days for him to notice

29

the holes in the roof, maybe eight or ten of them, each the size of a silver dollar. On a good weather day, sunbeams filtered through and lit up every minute particle floating in the air in front of him.

Those holes took on a new meaning the days that it rained. Nick laughed the first time he saw the forklift driver put a garbage bag over his coat. Soon Nick stopped laughing and wished he'd brought one himself.

What most worried him was hearing people cough throughout the plant. The company made a big deal out of protective gear, but all that meant was hard hats and goggles. No ear plugs, and definitely no masks. In the locker room his second week, Nick heard two guys talking about coughing things up. "My daddy had the black lung," one of them said. "Don't matter we're above ground, that's coal powering the blast furnace. I'm gonna have to get out of this place before long or it'll take me, too."

Nick thought about the factory his dad worked in back in Milwaukee — well-lit, airy, a solid structure. And a place where white workers far outnumbered Blacks. At Grinnell you'd see white foremen and some whites in the higher-paid jobs in the shipping dock or inspection. But most of the guys on the floor were Black, doing the dirtiest and the hardest jobs. One position in particular, what they called the card room, was filled with older Black men packing the sand into a frame with a tool that looked like a one-armed jack hammer.

"Man, those guys look like hell," Nick said to Connie, one of the first people he got to know on the job. At thirty-two, Connie was a decade older and an inch or so taller than Nick, but unlike Nick's scrawny self, Connie had the look of a bodybuilder. Normally he had a smile that wouldn't quit, but for this discussion, his face went blank.

"Every one of them came off the chain gang," Connie said. "They get paid by the piece, so they bust their ass every day. Job like this is the only thing open to 'em."

Whatever happened, Nick promised himself he would hang in, at least for a while. He refused to be some weak-assed white boy who couldn't tough it out. His parents were pressuring him to come home to Milwaukee and go to the technical college. "It's time to get a real skill and make some money," his dad told him. Nick had his mind set on learning a different set of skills.

His official title at Grinnell was "helper." The word made Nick picture girls in pink stripes playing bingo with his great-grandma in the nursing home up in Baraboo, Wisconsin. Here it signaled that he'd get various assignments and go wherever he was needed. Some days that meant shoveling filings into bins or spilt sand into frames; other days he'd help move those frames into the ovens or unload the ovens when the sand was baked.

After they'd been eating lunch together for a couple weeks, Connie gave Nick an earful about how pissed off the bosses must be. "I'm sure they intended to advance you, man," Connie said. "But you here eating with us, just breaking their hearts. You done. No boss job for you."

Nick's buddy Sam Kingston, who lived in the apartment across the hall and worked at the Tramson packaging plant, described realizations like this as "a chink in assumptions about white loyalty."

Sitting with them most days at one of the outdoor picnic tables was L.C. Carbin, who brought his own fold-up chair. At close to 250 pounds, L.C. was usually assigned to help in the card room, where he lifted one end of 200-pound boxes of sand and moved them to racks across the room. L.C. shook with laughter at Connie's assessment about the bosses.

"The other day this young man asked me where he could find a tool he needed for a job," L.C. said. "I told him, 'down yonder agin' the wall.' Our Nick asked me to repeat myself twice and then he couldn't stop laughing. 'That's some Southern shit,' he said. I just smiled and let him know, 'You in the South now, boy. I know you rarin' to cause some good trouble, but you might have to take it a little slow."

Nick and L.C. were hired on the same day and dispatched together to get their physicals. At the doctor's office, Nick had been flabbergasted to hear the nurse send them off to different waiting rooms. Every person in the room he landed in was white. The wait was less than twenty minutes. L.C. didn't get out until two hours later. Nick asked if this was some hangover from Jim Crow.

"Oh, you thought that was over?" L.C. replied.

Nick was determined to bring the issue to the union at Grinnell. Maybe it would be an opening for some type of action. Sam Kingston said the local was a branch of the Steelworkers, but with none of the international's backbone. Still, it gave them a place to start. L.C. rolled his eyes but agreed to go with Nick to the loading dock to see the local union president, a guy named Cal.

"Hey, if you don't like it, see your own doctor," Cal told them after hearing the complaint. "The company's not making you go to this one."

"But he's the company doctor," Nick said. "That gives them a big leg up. The union should fight to break all ties with them."

"Like I said, you're free to choose another doctor." Cal nodded without looking at either of them and began to raise the forklift platform. "I gotta get back to work."

L.C. didn't seem the kind of guy to say, "I told you so." In this case, he didn't have to.

This wasn't the only sign that any struggle at Grinnell Steel was going to be a slog. Nick saw it when he first asked Connie about the lunch situation. Day shift went from seven to three-thirty, with a whopping twenty-seven unpaid minutes for lunch. Some eighty workers were batched into five lunch slots. There was no designated room, just two big picnic tables near the locker area with a couple of vending machines. The company set some tables outside as well, and a lot of people took their food out there, except for the coldest days, just so they could breathe a little fresh air and hear each other talk.

Connie said folks had been trying to add fifteen minutes from their paid time as long as he'd been there, which was close to four years. Management wouldn't budge. The company had also been promising to do something about the roof and the air quality for even longer, but never delivered. As Nick got to know Connie better, he began to feel him out on getting something going, a petition maybe, or demanding the union hold a big group meeting.

"Here's what you gotta understand, Turner." Connie always folded his napkin under his thermos before he talked about serious things. "You're not going to get that here for a long time. There are lines of people waiting to get these jobs. What looks like ball-busting work and holes in the roof to us are get-out-of-debt cards to them. Yeah, we got a union. But these crackers ain't gonna back anything we do. Our guys got no trust and no expectations. They come with a lot o' hurt." He glanced around their table. "Everybody's got a story."

Nick bit back a comment about Fred Hampton, "dare to struggle, dare to win." The last thing he wanted was to look like a naive white kid with nothing to lose, he'd been in that movie before. When he raised the dilemma with Sam Kingston a few nights later, his buddy broke into a grin.

"Take your time, man," Sam said. "Don't romanticize the struggle. Over at Tramson, folks have been building connections for years. Your dad wants you in school? This is your school. Soak it up while you look for opportunities."

Nick learned a lot more about patience, and about courage, from L.C. The guy was in his early forties but had as many tales as if he'd lived seven decades. One day at lunch L.C. started describing what it was like to grow up in Alabama. "We knew we were in for hard times when my momma made us chicken feet soup for dinner, when my cousins moved in and shared the beds we were already sharing, when I was given my older brother's clothes as my Christmas presents."

"How'd you get to Atlanta?" Nick asked. L.C. licked the barbeque sauce off his fingers and settled back in his lawn chair.

"I grew up in a small town. My daddy was a share-cropper, dirt poor and miserable. He worked himself to death. My momma passed the year before and my brother'd already lit out, so I took over when I was still a teenager. Believe it or not, I was skinnier than you, but tough as an old boot. I made up my mind to run away, even though I was in debt to that motherfuckin' landowner. Everybody was. Slaves without the chains."

L.C. held up one of the naked ribs. "I kept asking myself how I was going to fool the boss. Took me over a year, but then one day I figured it out. I took the mule that was on rotation loan to till my four acres. In the barn I plied her shoes off and nailed them on backwards. When I was going, they thought I was coming." L.C.'s dimples lit up, but his tone stayed dead serious. "I rode that mule out of Alabama all the way into Georgia. And when I got to the outskirts of Atlanta, I tied her to a tree up on a hill. Walked the rest of the way to Peachtree Street. That sucker ain't seen me since."

Courage wasn't just about facing snarling dogs and water hoses, Nick thought. He tapped L.C.'s beefy arm with his fist. "I'm glad you came here, man," he said.

In those lunchtime conversations, Nick listened for people's hopes and also the things they most worried about. There was a lot of talk about Vietnam. The guys Nick got arrested with at an anti-war protest some months back urged him to bring folks to their marches. L.C. and the others hated Nixon. "Anybody tells you they're not a crook," L.C. said, "for sure, that there's a crook." They all felt Vietnam was a rich man's war. But they saw the protesters as a bunch of hippies. Connie was pissed that the news had talked for weeks about the shootings at Kent State and gave barely a mention to what happened at Jackson State down in Mississippi. The war wasn't going to drive Nick's co-workers to take action.

What did grab people's attention was what Sam and his co-workers were doing over at Tramson, where it was common knowledge that a faction of the Klan ran the union. That August, a rank-and-file caucus of more than two hundred Black workers started a wildcat strike. They had three demands: an end to racial discrimination from plant management and from the union, a pay raise for the dirtiest jobs, and immediate health and safety improvements. Sam supplied news clippings and leaflets, which Nick passed around to whoever was at lunch. He got Connie and L.C. to come to the first community rally. Even those who didn't come were talking about it. Black workers made up half the workforce at Tramson and ninety-nine percent of the strikers. "Ain't never seen a time when workers walked out over race, not here in Atlanta," Connie said.He and L.C. took turns putting a flyer for an upcoming parade on the bathroom mirror. Whenever somebody ripped it down, one of them taped up another. The day the strikers marched down Auburn Avenue, Nick counted at least eight of his co-workers there, two with their wives.

For Nick, one great thing about the Tramson strike was the number of women leaders. He missed having women at the job. He missed the women he worked with at the laundry in Grady Hospital, making time for meetings despite babies and housekeeping and who knows what else, leading the slow-down, taking on the risk despite all they had to lose. He wondered whether these pamphlets he was reading about the industrial proletariat really took women into account.

Nick especially missed seeing Eve every day. Slowly they'd begun hanging out after he left the laundry. He usually saw her one night a week, sometimes on the weekend. He was fond of her little guy, Titus, now almost four years old. From time to time Eve fixed him a plate of food to bring to work. Otherwise Nick packed a sandwich or ate vending machine chili out of the can. His co-workers loved to give him grief over his eating habits. Even so, the guys at Grinnell vastly improved the quality of Nick's life by doing two things: sharing recipes, and taking him to Bish's.

Bish was no taller than five feet six, just a bit of hair on each side of his head and an apron around his neck that was always covered with barbecue stains. Every day, Bish would cook an assortment of soul food on a wood-burning stove. For a dollar and thirty cents, you could get two meats, three vegetables with cornbread and a small bottle of Dr Pepper, all wrapped in the scent of a campfire. Nick tried to catch a ride there at least twice a week. Since the trip took ten minutes each way, Nick learned to gobble his food and pack up what was left for the car ride back to Grinnell.

L.C. ribbed him endlessly. "If anything ever happened to Bish, if he closed that restaurant, young Nick would starve to death."

Bish lifted Nick's spirits, but the recipes and cooking tips transformed his life.When he expressed surprise at how many of the men cooked, Connie gave him a talking to. "You call yourself hip, but you bought the bullshit. You just assume Black men are deadbeats, don't cook, don't look after their kids."

"I never said anything about kids," Nick said, hearing the defensiveness in the rising pitch of his voice. "And growing up I didn't see white guys cook, either." He knew Sam could cook but mostly he ate on the run. Still, much as Nick hated to admit it, he had absorbed messages about Black men shirking responsibility. "I'll work on it," he told Connie.

He was certainly happy to follow his co-workers' recipes. After a while Nick started to bring in food he'd made himself and share it around. One day he brought chitlins that Eve left for him. He added his own touch by smothering them with barbecue sauce, placing them in tin foil on the outside frame of the molding oven and letting them simmer for over an hour before sitting down at one of the tables outside.

Someone passed the chitlins to Slim, a hard-bitten guy in his mid-thirties who often sat at the same table at lunch. Slim didn't have much to say to Nick since a day early on when Nick mentioned Savannah as a place he wanted to visit. In a flash, Slim threw down his napkin and grabbed his plate. "I ain't talking about that town," he said, and he walked off.

Connie took Nick aside afterwards. "Don't take it personal, man. His brother left one day to drive to Savannah to see family. They found his car in a swamp; no one ever saw him again." Connie never took his eyes off Nick. "A lot of us have somebody who disappeared like that."

Things changed after Slim devoured those chitlins. He stood up from the picnic bench and saluted Nick at the other end of the table. "Damn, what the hell is a white boy teaching me anything about chitlins? You put your foot in them with that barbeque sauce, Turner. I live and I learn."

That weekend, Nick saw Slim at the march to support the Tramson strikers.

The person who taught Nick the most about food, not to mention a lot about life and struggle, was Irma Jean, L.C.'s wife and greatest joy. The first time L.C. invited Nick to his house for dinner, Nick saw it as a test to see if he was for real. "Irma Jean wants to meet you," L.C. said. "She seldom leaves the house." Nick was already familiar with her cooking, since L.C. often brought a plate to work and gave Nick a taste. He also knew she was legally blind and ten years older than her husband.

L.C. greeted Nick at the door. Standing in the dining room was a tall woman wearing dark glasses and a bright blue sundress, the front dusted with bleached flour. "This here is Irma Jean," L.C. said. Nick reached out his hand and told her what a pleasure it was to finally meet her. She pulled him in and gave him a gentle hug.

"L.C. has told me what you guys talk about at work," she said. "Called you a young soldier in the fight for freedom. I wanted to meet you myself."

When Nick asked if he could help set the table, they wouldn't hear of it. "You're the guest here," L.C. said. "Just have a seat. Hope you don't mind we drink out of mason jars."

Nick laughed. "My dad's family are all farmers. I've been drinking out of these my whole life." They sat down to a feast of flavor and aromas: fried chicken, fried tripe, turnip greens, macaroni and cheese — "and certainly not from a box," Irma Jean pointed out — fried corn, sliced tomatoes and cornbread. L.C. had told Nick stories about Irma Jean's struggle to regain her eyesight, with no success. But she never complained about it. "I have some vision problems, but I'm not blind," she told Nick that night. "I can cook and I can clean and I can see you sitting there. And I can see L.C., my beautiful, dark black hunk of a man."

Nick held up his mason jar of strawberry kool-aid. "No exaggeration, Ms. Irma Jean, this is the best meal I've ever had. May I learn to cook half as good as you, and may I find a love close to what the two of you have."

On his third visit, Irma Jean told Nick how she lost her sight. It happened during a fight with her former husband. "He abused me," she said, her voice calm, fists in her lap. "Well, time came I wasn't going to take it and I fought back. He hit me full force in the back of the head with the butt of a gun. I was out for days. When I woke up, I couldn't see. That man was a drunk and should be in prison, but nothing came of it. These white folks don't care what happens to a Black woman."

Over the next several months, Nick often wound up at their bungalow, with its well-tended lawn and simple furnishings. They welcomed him to neighborhood gatherings and holiday parties, where people taught him to play bid whist. Once when Nick thanked Irma Jean for being so generous, she shushed him. "I always wanted a passel of kids," she told him. "Too hard with my first husband and too late with L.C. Glad to have you around."

L.C. continued to be a good friend at work as well. One day after Nick finally got his car — a 1959 VW beetle, not a Chevy, but his, free and clear — he drove L.C. to Bish's, radio blaring James Brown and Chaka Khan. On the way back, L.C. yelled out the window at some young woman walking down the street: "Hey, ugly girl!" Nick launched into a lecture on the need to respect women. "You wouldn't want someone shouting at your sister or Irma Jean like that, would you?" he asked. Nick figured they knew each other well enough for him to speak his mind.

L. C. didn't say much. A few days later, Nick drove back to Bish's, this time with Connie and Slim along as well. On the way back to work they saw a group of young women walking down the street. L. C., who was riding shotgun, spun around to address the others in the back seat. "Hey, now, don't make fun of those girls, you hear me? Turner won't like it. He thinks all women are pretty."

Nick let the other men mock him the rest of the ride, until they got inside and the shaker made it impossible to hear. There would be other opportunities to make his case. He'd gotten a lot better with patience since he'd been at Grinnell. He gained new insight into what strength and leadership look like. Above all, he was learning that organizing had to be based on friendship and love. Change, he knew, was down yonder agin' the wall. It might take a while, but change was gonna come.

Dirty Tricks

Baltimore, tip of the Chesapeake Bay, 1974

"He *what*? You bullshitting me?" Moss knew A.D. was a mean, sick motherfucker, racist as a Georgia cracker, but hurling a kitten into the coke oven was beyond the pale, even for a psycho like that.

"You and me been knowing each other since junior high," Harry told Moss. "I don't bullshit. I saw A.D. shove that kitten down the exhaust chute and watch it squeal as it melted." He shivered, his skin covered with a shift's worth of coal dust. "I seen him stand over the chutes, just staring down at the burning coals reflecting on his face. Made him look like Satan."

The young white guy, Nick Turner, took off his hard hat and dragged his fingers through his matted hair. "Don't tell Drew," he warned. "He might just kill that asshole. You know he takes care of those cats like they were his kids."

The three of them were supposed to be heading from the cooling room to the shower, but that story, on top of the heat, had taken everything out of Moss, and seemed to have done in the others, too. No one moved from the bench. Moss lowered his voice. "We have to draw the line with A.D. If it wasn't for his uncle, he'd 'a been fired a long time ago. I say we fuck with him."

"What you got in mind?" Harry asked. He'd already shed his protective clothing and was peeling off his shirt. The gold cross he always wore was stuck to his chest hair. "You know Preach tried a dozen times to give the guy some Jesus — A.D. won't go anywhere near him."

"We should drive him crazy," Moss said. "The dude is always high, fucked-up high. He brags about smoking angel dust mixed with weed."

"Is that why they call him A.D.?" Nick had only been at the Bethlehem Steel plant at Sparrows Point a little over a year. A few months back, Moss walked in on Nick chewing out A.D. in the break room. "Don't think because I'm white you can talk that racist crap around me," Nick was saying. Also, somewhere this white boy had learned to cook him some soul food.

"Yup. I say we mess with his head." Moss grinned at Harry. "You remember that Hitchcock movie, *Gaslight*? The one where Ingrid Bergman's husband makes shit up so she'll think she's crazy? Smoking that mess makes you paranoid."

Harry held up his hand for a high five. "If we can do it without getting caught, I know a bunch of folks around here would enjoy the hell out of harassing that honky. Uh, no offense, Nick."

"None taken," Nick said. "I'm in."

A week later, Moss was taking a break in the cooling room when Harry brought in some news. "Drew said two more of the kittens are missing. It was A.D., I just know it."

Moss wiped the sweat from his forehead. "OK, it's time. The other day I overheard A.D. bragging about screwing black women and how they like it rough." Moss thought of last night with Letisha, her hands warm on his face, her laugh soft on his shoulder as one of the kids interrupted them. He wanted to scream.

"I had to fill Drew in," Moss said. "He kept shaking his head and told me something just as bad that happened that last winter storm. Drew was working with Joy on the ground crew. Said there was a freezing wind and it was below zero. Him and Joy was shoveling coal off the rails below the catching cars, on battery #3. They got so cold they went into the porn shack out there to get warm. Joy had never been inside it before."

Harry pulled his cross out from under his shirt and held it. "I feel dirty every time I go in that place. I like sex, but that's sick. You can't even put your head back, naked women pics all over the ceiling. It's pathetic."

"So Joy leaves right away," Moss said. "A.D. and two of the regulars are sitting there, and one said, 'What's her problem?' Drew told them she's probably uncomfortable with all this ugly porn staring her in the face. A.D. howled with laughter and said, 'That bitch? She's a ho.' Drew said he looked A.D. straight in the eye and told him, 'You sick ignorant fuck, you're not part of this conversation.' A.D. shut right up. You know everybody's afraid of Drew."

"I think A.D. and the regulars in the porn shack do a circle jerk when nobody's around," Harry said. "So what did Drew think we should do?"

Drew had shown Moss and Harry the ropes when they started at the coke ovens four years earlier, a big step up in pay from the shoe factory they worked in after high school. They had nothing but respect for the guy. Drew read like crazy, everything from the daily news to murder mysteries, had a deep understanding of black history. Typically he didn't give his opinion unless asked. But when he did, people listened. "That dude coulda been somebody in politics if he wasn't addicted to the ponies," Moss told Harry. "Gambling ate up his house and his family." Now Drew lived by himself in a small apartment, taking off occasionally to go to the track. Moss covered for him whenever he left the job early.

"He told me he'd been thinking about some dirty tricks. Called 'em DTs," Moss said. "Things we could use to fuck with A.D. Every week, or every few days, we do a new DT."

43

They decided to start the next day. Moss brought together his main guy, Harry, a couple long-timers he could count on, and Nick Turner.

Their first dirty trick was making wanted posters with a picture of cute kittens — Harry found some in the latest issue of *Jet*. At the top it read, "Wanted: information on who's maiming and torturing the battery cats and kittens. Reward for anyone giving information that leads to the parties guilty of these heinous and criminal acts." It instructed people to place information in the envelope labeled "Cats," tacked to the bulletin board in the cooling shack on battery #2.

Moss and the others wrote multiple unsigned letters and put them in the envelope, accusing A.D. of murdering the kittens. They assumed A.D. would get into the envelope, see that he was being fingered and destroy the letters. They were right. Each time A.D. was at work, the letters would disappear.

The group turned to other DTs: simple things like putting hot sauce on the sandwich in A.D.'s lunch bag, writing about the kitten-killer on the bathroom stalls, making sure that when he was assigned to shovel the steps alongside the conveyor belts, dead rats would stream by him. "Fewer cats, more rats," Moss told the others. "Somebody has to call it out."

Most days Moss had A.D. on his mind, but one Thursday morning in July it was so hot when he left his house in East Baltimore, his thoughts were only about the temperature. The tar smell of the mills was already strong halfway through Dundalk. As usual, he pulled into the parking lot at Sparrows Point around 6:10 am.

Walking from the lot through the front gate to the locker, Moss knew he was truly entering an inferno. Everything around him was the same brown-rust color: the buildings, the roads, the puddles, areas where there

44

should be grass. It looked like a post-nuclear apocalypse, including falling ash.

Moss pushed open the locker room door. Scores of men were getting dressed for the day's work, while others were taking showers after finishing their shift, trying to scrub the coal dust and coke soot off their bodies. Moss pulled on the long-sleeved shirt and long pants that would give double protection from the heat and soak up his sweat. Over that he added a flame-resistant jacket and pants, along with flame-resistant gloves. His shoes were steel-toed work boots. He grabbed his respirator, a hard hat with protective shield, and wooden clogs to keep his soles from igniting and burning the bottoms of his feet.

Moss hoped to get assigned to the ground crew, but no such luck — next to his name on the board was the usual, lidman. As the temperature passed 100 degrees, the temperature on top of the coke ovens would rise to over 130 degrees.

Moss was already sweating heavily under his protective gear. He stopped by the "cooling" room - a place that seemed cold only because of the heat outside. He put a jug of water and his lunch in the old Amana refrigerator and climbed up the second flight of stairs to the top of the ovens. Waiting for him on the last stair was the foreman with A.D. "With the heat this bad, I'm splitting lid time between the two of you," he said.

A.D. turned his back on them. "I can't believe I got stuck in this hell," he said. "I'm going first." Moss went back down to the cooling room.

Not more than twenty minutes later, A.D. came barreling in, sweat dripping off his face and neck. He pointed at Moss with his chin. "On you. Hot don't begin to describe what it's like up there."

Moss finished dropping coal into the first round of ovens and went back to the cooling room to hand off the next round to A.D, but the guy was nowhere to be found. Soon, the coal operator started blowing the horn for a lidman to return. The foreman ran into the cooling room to get someone up top.

"It's A.D.'s turn," Moss told him. "Damned if I know where he is."

"You go back up and I'll find A.D.," the foreman grumbled. "Just call me a goddamn babysitter."

Moss told himself he wasn't going to do the whole run, even if he had to walk off the ovens. A half hour later, as he stood on the battery looking thirty yards through the smoke and flames toward the other end, Moss saw what looked like a man floating across the ovens. He did a double-take and realized no one was there. All these years, he'd just laughed when oven workers described seeing a ghost they'd named "Joe." Moss ran down to the cooling room and told the other workers there, who broke out laughing. One of the older guys told him, "Boy, you just got Joe'd. Your body gets stretched like that, you start to hallucinate. And you can blame it on that asshole, A.D., for leaving you up there too long."

By the end of the day Moss's underwear, his layer of clothes and protective gear were dripping wet. He could barely drag himself to the locker room. When he got there he just sat on a bench for half an hour, until he got the energy up to take a shower. He had nothing left in him to think about DTs.

After two days off, Moss was ready to focus again on the pleasures of fucking with A.D. He got Harry and Nick together to see if they had any recon on the dirty tricks. Nick said he heard A.D. asking guys in the cooling room what they thought might be wrong with his car. He described a noise he was hearing that would get more intense as he sped up and he couldn't figure out what it was. Nick took out his comb and whistled a long high note.

The three of them fell out laughing. Moss had orchestrated this. Using liquid nail, they glued a harmonica just inside the bottom of the front grill of A.D.'s car while it was in the parking lot. They wrapped the harmonica in duct tape to hold it for the six hours it would take for the liquid nail to bond and dry. Moss had tested whether this would work by holding the harmonica out of his own car window. Sure enough, as he picked up speed the harmonica started to whistle. The higher the speed, the more shrill the sound.

After two months, their DTs were working. Drew assured them no more kittens had disappeared.

As the summer wore on, A.D. started missing more work, and then he was gone for two whole weeks. Once again he showed up with his job intact, acting crazier than ever. His uncle was a few steps up in management and everyone figured he protected A.D., no matter his behavior.

But this time, when A.D. returned, the craziness in his eyes was worse than ever. He talked to himself constantly. His co-workers could smell liquor on his breath, which he was mixing with whatever drugs he was consuming.

Moss assumed A.D. would be paranoid enough to leave the young cats alone, so they held off on any more DTs. They checked under his car; the harmonica was gone. Moss took down the envelope from the bulletin board. From what they could see, A.D. had become well aware that he was being watched and was laying low.

In mid-September, Moss was working second shift on battery #3. He was making his way to the cooling room when he saw a lightning storm in the distance approaching the Bay. He heard shouting from the crew cleaning the grounds — one of the guys had dropped his broom and started walking towards the Bay. It was too dark to see faces, but in his gut, Moss knew it had to be A.D.

The foreman got there before Moss did. "It's A.D., man!" somebody yelled. "The guy was out of his mind all shift. He was humming, talking to himself and then he started saying something about 'killing motherfuckers.' We saw the lightning storm coming. A.D looked up and just headed towards the Bay. It was pitch dark, and that's the last anyone saw of him. I think he just stripped down and started swimming towards the storm."

Moss leaned over and put his hands on his knees for support.

"All right, guys," the foreman said. "Get back to work, all of you. There's protocol for this. I call the cops, they call the Coast Guard."

Half an hour later a group of police cars, lights full on, came streaming through the coke yards with an ambulance beside them and headed to the water's edge. A Coast Guard boat was moving slowly near the shore.

The next day, one of the lidmen standing on top of battery #3 told Moss and the others he saw them pull a body out of the water. Everyone knew it was A.D. Moss got Harry and Nick, and they went to the area where Drew was working.

Nick flung off his hard hat. "Tell me we're not responsible for that fool killing himself."

"I was up all night thinking about it and here's what I know," Moss said. "What we did had nothing to do with A.D. swimming into a storm. I'm not gonna lie, it gave me some personal satisfaction to fuck with the dude, but my conscience is clear. We got him to lay off the savagery toward the battery cats. When he stopped, we stopped."

Drew took off his own hat and held it against his chest. "A.D. was not destined to live in this world. He didn't respect himself or anybody else. And he sure didn't respect any women, particularly Black women. On top of that, he mixed angel dust with coke with liquor and anything else he could shove in his body. None of you have anything to feel guilty or bad about."

"I need to make peace with it," Harry said. He had his cross wrapped around his hand. "Preach wants us to gather tomorrow at the end of the shift at the spot where they pulled him out of the water. I'd appreciate it if all of you would be there with me."

Nick nodded his head. "Out of respect for you, man, not him," he said. The others agreed to come as well.

The next day at the end of the shift Preach had assembled a dozen workers near the shore of the Bay. They stood in a circle. Preach pulled out his Bible and started reading. *"Acts 3:19*: Repent, then, and turn to God, so that he will forgive your sins."

Preach looked up from his Bible toward the men in the circle, "We do not know what went through this boy's mind as he faced death. We can only hope that in his moment of desperation he asked God for forgiveness. It is not our role to judge, but only to believe in the Lord's forgiveness and benevolence toward all of his creations."

Moss slipped a pint of Jack Daniels out of his jacket, poured a taste on the ground, and took a drink. "Here's what I think, Preach. Racism kills more than Black folks. Carrying that much hate has got to tear you up inside."

Nick bowed his head. "Amen to that,"

Moss passed the bottle around until it was empty. He threw it towards the Bay. Everyone watched it shatter on the rocks.

I'm Paying for My Meal

Baltimore, 1974

Nick had no idea how long he'd be living in Baltimore. He hadn't thought about where he'd look for work if he got laid off from Bethlehem Steel. He still hadn't decided whether or not to get a dog. The one thing he was sure about was that he wanted to fall in love, this time forever, as Stevie Wonder would say. He wanted someone to share long talks and private jokes and kids in footie pajamas smelling of baby shampoo. From the moment he noticed her at a Dump Nixon Coalition meeting, Nick had a feeling that someone was Sophie Reznick.

The coalition was large, maybe seventy-five or so at most meetings. There were dozens of people who came and went who Nick couldn't have identified. But Sophie grabbed his attention the first time she stood up to speak. She struck him as a Jewish Joan Baez — a cloud of wavy dark hair, bold eyebrows, a smile so powerful, he immediately wanted to be the one who prompted it. When he finally talked to her two weeks later, he could see her eyes were blue. As he got to know her, he realized they changed colors to reflect her emotions. They got grayer when she was angry, greener when she was turned on. He wanted to always be the person responsible for that green.

The first night, Nick noticed things he rarely paid attention to: her silver jewelry, tight bell-bottom jeans, the giant belt buckle she wore with confidence on her slender form. And then he heard her speak. She didn't preface her comments with, "that's so reactionary" or "that would be a disastrous mistake" or any of the usual openers when there was some conflict in the group. Instead, in a voice that was insistent but respectful, she said, "When we talk, people need to see themselves, in language they recognize."

She didn't say her name and she left as soon as the meeting was over. Nick asked several people about her, including the wife of an old friend. "That's Sophie Reznick," Sue told him. "I know her from Woman Up." And then, anticipating Nick's next question, Sue nodded. "She came to Baltimore after an unhappy marriage. I think she's finally ready to date."

At the next week's meeting, he intended to sit near Sophie, but she arrived just when the meeting started and took a seat in the back. He spoke and later so did she. He recognized her voice and turned around as she mentioned the people she worked with at South Baltimore General Hospital. "What would make this rally something they'd want to come to?" she asked.

As the chair was wrapping things up, Sophie leaned over the two people sitting next to Nick and handed him a folded piece of paper. He flipped it open. "I think Sue's trying to fix us up," she'd written. Scribbled, really. "Feels like junior high. Why don't we just go out? I'm headed for vacation, so how about a week from Saturday, August 10th?" At the bottom was a phone number and a street address in South Baltimore.

Nick lurched out of his chair and saw that Sophie had not waited for a reply. She was already at the door. By the time he ran through the hallway to the main entrance of the church, she was halfway down the block. "Hey, Sophie," he yelled. "Hold up a sec!" She turned and waited, a smile spreading across her face.

He had to tighten every facial muscle to keep from grinning like an idiot or acting like this didn't happen to him all the time. "A week from Saturday?" Nick said. "I can do that. I'll pick you up at seven o'clock, okay? And how about right now — do you have any time to hang out?"

Sophie checked the Timex on her wrist. "Actually, I have to run. My roommate's boyfriend is cheating on her. I know it and she still doesn't. I asked him to come over before she gets back from work so I can have it out with him: He has to tell her the truth or I will. Sorry about that." She flashed her smile again. "But looking forward to the 10th. Seven o'clock works."

Before Nick could say another word, she whirled around and speed walked toward an old Chevy across the street. He had to scramble for a moment to remember where he'd parked his own car. "All right!" he whispered. "Here we go."

All week Nick thought about where he should take her. He wanted it to be somewhere downtown so they didn't have to spend too much time in the car. He preferred a club with music so they could dance — he fancied himself a passable dancer, enough to look somewhat cool, anyway — but not too much noise so they could talk. His roommate suggested a place called The Laughing Frog. Nick drove by one day to scope out the best way to get there and the easiest place to park.

When Saturday finally arrived, Nick had to work first shift. The day was hot but not too humid. He passed kids splashing in an open hydrant, squealing with joy as the water burst over them. He stopped at a car wash and then spent a good half hour scrubbing his fingernails and making sure there was no coal dust in his pores or the corners of his eyes. A couple months back he'd gone out with someone who actually recoiled when she caught sight of his hands and made an excuse to end the date early.

He was too nervous to eat much, so he just heated up some leftover pork roast and boiled potatoes while he went back and forth on what to wear. He didn't want to overdress, that's not who he was. But he also wanted to show her tonight was special. He decided on a button-down shirt and cotton slacks and took his time ironing them.

Nick arrived at Sophie's house ten minutes early. He drove around the block a few times and parked in front, ringing the bell at six fifty-five. When she opened the door and gifted him that smile, Nick wished he'd brought flowers. Wherever she'd gone on vacation, she'd picked up a deep tan. He tried not to stare at the bare spot, also tan, between her top and her slacks.

"C'mon in," Sophie said. "I just have to grab my purse." Her place was one of those old South Baltimore row houses, full of funky furniture.

"I was thinking we'd go to a club," Nick said. "You ever been to the Laughing Frog?"

"Oh," she said, purse in hand. "I just assumed we'd go out to dinner."

Nick fumbled with his keys. "No problem. Let's stop to get you a bite and then we can try this place my roommate recommended, good music, not too loud."

Sophie seemed surprised when he opened her car door, but otherwise she was relaxed, directing him to a Greek diner a few blocks from her place. Nick tried to keep the conversation casual, although he was desperate to know if she was still in love with her ex. He decided to share some stories about his job and ask an open-ended question: What brought her to Baltimore?

"Fleeing a bad marriage," she told him.

Whatever relief he felt that she was not pining for some other guy vanished as he listened to what she'd gone through. It was a painful story of lies and deception by a guy who'd made her put her own education on hold so she could subsidize his, hidden a gambling addiction, and then blew whatever opportunities he had on poker and ponies and who knew what else. Nick hated to think what details Sophie must have skipped over in this quick telling. Last fall, a close cousin persuaded her to move here and helped her rent the place in South Baltimore and find a job typing cardiology reports at a nearby hospital. The cousin also steered Sophie to Woman Up, where a weekly support group opened a whole new way for her to view the world and an appetite for activism.

Nick worried he'd stirred up old hurts, but Sophie seemed okay. She ate her entire meal, some sort of Greek casserole. As he reached for the check, he noticed she'd pulled out her wallet.

"What are you doing?" he asked.

"I'm paying for my dinner," she said. "Why?"

He tripped over his words. "I don't know, I mean, people don't usually do that."

Sophie looked him in the eye. "Sure they do."

The women he'd dated in Atlanta were bold, but this was new to Nick. He nodded, handed her the check, and prayed he hadn't looked like a backwards fool.

The Laughing Frog was just as he hoped, lively but not packed. They found two tall chairs at the bar and angled them toward each other, talking about their families and dishing on a couple of the self-proclaimed leaders at the Dump Nixon Coalition. At some point the conversation came back to Sophie's ex.

"I'm just glad I found out before we had kids together," she said. "It's over. He's out of my life."

Nick almost crossed himself with gratitude. Not wanting kids would have been a deal-breaker.

When they sat down, Nick signaled the bartender and bought the first round of drinks. Sophie ordered a sloe gin and orange juice, which she sipped through a straw. Nick finished his tequila sunrise within minutes but waited for her before ordering another. As she paid for the next round, Sophie asked the bartender if her drink had a name, and then turned beet red beneath her tan when he told her it was called a slow screw. Later Nick would try to describe this phenomenon to his roommate. "Most of the time she's really smart and thoughtful. She schooled me on feminist basics. And then she has this side that's really naive, like she's been away from civilization for a while. Which, in a sense, is what happened to her."

He asked her to dance. Her hand in his was deliciously soft, no dirt, no calluses. After two fast songs, the band played Gladys Knight's "Best Thing that Ever Happened to Me." He pulled Sophie in closer. Her hair beneath his chin smelled amazing, like sun and apricots.

Back in front of her place, they lingered in the car for a few minutes before Nick walked her to the door and bent down for a quick good-night kiss. "Have you ever been to the beach at Rocky Point?" he asked. She had not. They arranged to meet there the next day.

He would take it slow, give her plenty of room, prove himself worthy of trust.

***

Sophie grinned every time she thought about the look on Nick Turner's face when he ran down the block after reading her note. As she told her women's group the next night, it was somewhere between, "Is this present for *me*?" and "Why can't I open it right now?" He'd pulled together a cool facade, as if women asked him out on a regular basis, but Sophie was certain this had been the first time it happened to him.

She had no hesitation about making the first move. Sue from Woman Up pointed to Nick when Sophie first came to the Dump Nixon Coalition and made sure to mention that he was single. What a word. "I'm single," Sophie had told herself over and over after she finally left Bo. "What was I before, double?"

As she tried to get a look at her whole self in the small bathroom mirror, Sophie worked on swallowing her nervousness. Eight years. That's how long it had been since she'd been on a date. She and Bo starting going together junior year of high school. All the rules were different now, thank god. But how to meet guys? And how much to tell them about her previous life? No one had caught her eye at the hospital. The ones she'd encountered who weren't married or living with someone were too young or too old or too obnoxious. Clearly, she was ready for something. "I don't know if I want a big-time relationship," she told her women's group. "A fling would be nice."

Until then, Sophie'd had only one fling, a guy she got stranded with at the airport two months after she left Bo for good. Her favorite cousin in Baltimore sent her a ticket to check out the city. When the flight was cancelled, Sophie prepared to spend the night in the terminal. The guy sitting next to her, who had bought her a glass of wine after the first delay announcement, suggested they share a room in the airport hotel, his company was footing the bill. She only knew his first name. Later she told her cousin, "I figured it would do me good to have had more than one sexual partner. The guy seemed like he did this kind of thing a lot. Maybe I'd learn a thing or two."

"And did you?" her cousin asked.

"Yup." Sophie held up her wine glass. "I learned frequency doesn't equal competency."

Nick Turner seemed a better choice. He certainly was cute, tall, with an easy smile that crinkled his eyes, a mustache that looked like it would feel really soft against her cheek, and what appeared to be a very nice ass. She liked the way he operated in these meetings. He usually had something to say, but he didn't yammer on and on like some of those guys. It was mainly guys, almost all of them white, who did the talking. He didn't call people names, which seemed the norm in that room. He didn't hide that he was passionate, but he didn't pretend the fate of the country depended on agreeing with him.

So unlike Bo. All that time wasted.

Sophie sighed. Her women's group warned against this kind of thinking. "Forgive yourself, figure out what you learned from it, and move on," was how someone put it about bad choices in men. The best advice she'd ever gotten. Now if she could just remember to do that.

Nick arrived at the door five minutes early, but she was ready for him. She smoothed her navy blazer, worn over a crop top that ended a couple inches above the waistband of her jeans. This was the first time she'd ever had a tan belly, thanks to a week in Ocean City at a neighbor's rental. Maybe it would make her look a little worldly.

Her date stepped inside while she grabbed her purse. He'd dressed up in a wide-collared green shirt, freshly ironed, as if he were going to a club — which, it turned out, is exactly what he had in mind. Sophie assumed they'd be going out to dinner. "Let's just stop on the way and I'll get a quick bite to eat," she told him, as he opened her car door. She could picture his mother drilling that into him.

They went to a Greek diner she knew that had only a handful of guests. As she ate, Nick told her stories about working in the coke ovens, and asked how she wound up in Baltimore.

She decided to give him the short, factual version. "I was getting out of a bad marriage. High school sweethearts. He had a tough home life, needed to get away from his father, convinced me to get married right after graduation so we could be on our own. I had planned to go to college, but I put it on hold to support us so he could get a degree in broadcasting. That wound up taking five years. He wanted to be a sports announcer, told me that's why he had to spend so much time away from home, claimed he was watching high school games, a place to start."

She paused to take a bite of her moussaka. "And where was he really going?" Nick asked.

"Mostly to the track. Sometimes to poker games or places that do sports betting. By the time I figured it out, he'd gotten us deep into debt." Nick's face registered sympathy, not shock.

"If you ever watched soap operas, you know the rest of this story. Bo swore he'd change, started going to meetings of Gamblers' Anonymous, got a job to help pay off the debt, handed over the finances to me." No need to go into details of the lies or the fights or the clawing her way out. She told Nick briefly about filing for divorce, taking back her name and connecting with her cousin here in Baltimore. "She really saved me, that and Woman Up."

Sophie had wept with shame the first time she told this story over the phone to her cousin. She'd been embarrassed, but also enraged when she shared it with her women's group, where she took in other people's horror stories and finally began to think of herself less as a sucker and more as a survivor. This time, she felt somewhat detached as she spun out the highlights and polished off the rest of her dish.

When Sophie opened her wallet, Nick put his hand on her arm. He seemed as puzzled with this custom as if she'd started speaking Greek.

"What are you doing?" he asked, his own billfold in hand.

"I'm paying for my meal."

"You can't do that," he said. "People don't do that."

Sophie took out a ten-dollar bill. "I do," she said, as if she went on dates all the time. "Many women do." So much for feminism 101.

And yet, she had to admit he was a good listener and seemed genuinely interested in her life. When she asked what it was like working in the coke ovens, he mentioned several guys he loved there, and also arguments he was having over pornography in the break room.

At the club he was kind and funny. She'd been terrified of having to order a drink and expose her total lack of sophistication. A friend from the women's group advised her to get sloe gin and orange juice. When Sophie asked the name of the drink, her friend said it was called a slow screw. "Oh, please," Sophie told her. "You want me to go out with this new guy, have the bartender ask what I want, and I'll say, "A slow screw, please.' No way I'm falling for that trick."

After she put in an order for the sloe gin and orange juice, Sophie asked the bartender if the drink had a name.

"That's a slow screw," he said, leaning over the bar. "And if you put a little Southern Comfort in it, you'll have a slow, comfortable screw."

Sophie ducked her head to hide the blush that surely went all the way to the bare strip on her belly. Nick took his hand and lifted her chin. "May I have this dance?" he said. The night ended at her doorstep with a sweet kiss that woke up something long dormant in her body.

The next day, Nick arranged for them to meet at the beach over in Rocky Point, where two things happened that sealed the deal. Their blanket was near an old water fountain. Nick got up to get a drink and noticed three little boys nearby who were too short to reach the spout. "Hey, buddies," Nick said. "Need a hand here?" One by one, he gently picked them up and held them as they drank their fill. Well, she thought. This was a guy who loved kids.

Then at four o'clock, Nick explained he had to get back to help a friend move. "Her boyfriend likes to smack her around," he explained. "The guy works on Sunday evenings as a bouncer somewhere. She made a plan to get her stuff together and get herself and her son away from danger. She has it all figured out, just needed someone to help her haul stuff and give her a ride to a shelter. I hate to end our day now, but I'll make it up to you."

Okay, Sophie thought. Maybe this would be more than a fling.

***

That Tuesday Sophie rode to the meeting with Sue. Nick was waiting outside the church where the coalition met. This time he didn't worry about being cool. He let his grin spread across his face and ran over to meet her. "I'm so glad you came," he said. "Really glad." They walked in together, found two chairs next to each other, left a few minutes early, and wound up at Sophie's place after Nick offered to give her a ride. Neither said much on the short trip there.

Once inside, Nick stood in the living room and made an effort to look around at the furnishings. His hands felt too big to fit in his pockets; he placed them on the back of a chair. "Really good to be here," he said.

Sophie flung her purse on the side table and moved to the stairs. "I'm going to my bedroom," she said, without looking back over her shoulder. "Let me know if you care to join me."

Setting Straight the Orthopedist

Chicago, mid-May 1980

If she stayed completely still, moving only her eyes to watch *Family Feud* or whatever else was on TV while the baby slept and Nick was out romping with Jake, Sophie could pretend she was just taking a little rest. But the instant any of those elements changed — Elly's wake-up squawk, Nick's loud whisper as he unlocked the front door — pain shot from her lower back down her leg as if someone had inserted a syringe filled with agony.

Day six with no improvement. Maybe they'd need to suck up the debt and get her to an orthopedist.

"Hey, babe, we're back." Nick dropped quietly to his knees and brushed his lips against her forehead, having learned the hard way that any move could set off a muscle spasm.

Jake bounded in the door, then switched to an exaggerated tip toe until he got close to Sophie's make-shift bed on the floor. He plopped down on his butt, lifted a sweaty hand and laid it gently on her cheek. "We sawed ten bloomies, Mommy! They're everywhere!"

The guilt flooding Sophie crowded out the back pain. Looking with Jake for the first signs of spring, so late to arrive in Chicago, was one of her favorite pastimes. Now she didn't want to hear about it. She wanted Jake to leave her be, the baby to shut up and her breasts to dry up already. Two days earlier, Nick suggested moving to formula so he could keep Elly with him and take care of the night-time feedings. Sophie felt only relief. What kind of monster mother had she turned into?

Guilt had gotten her into this fix. From the minute Elly was born, Sophie worried Jake would feel neglected. So last week they planned an outing to Lake Michigan. While Elly slept, Sophie and Jake searched for shells and ran with their pinwheels. "Look how it's flying, Mommy!" Jake squealed. "Fly *me* now!" Pinwheels on the sand, Sophie grabbed Jake's hands and whirled in a circle, exalting in her power to astonish this little guy — until her back said, "Not so fast, lady," and they both collapsed in a heap. That evening her neighbor Minnie, an LPN, brought over an icepack and gave Sophie a talking to. "You know that giant belly you had up until six weeks ago? You think maybe it put a little strain on your back? Didn't your doctor ever talk about that?"

Savvy Sophie, always questioning authority, analyzing the ways the system is rigged, marching and meeting and voting against injustice, had treated her doctor like a god. She posed no questions, had no expectations that an ob/gyn should care about more than a patient's reproductive organs. Sophie wasn't just a bad mother. She was a bad activist.

Minnie suggested she see an orthopedist. But Nick's layoff meant health insurance stopped at the end of April. That was the bad news. The good news: He was home full time and caring for all of them.

"Don't worry, Mommy," Jake was telling her now, "I'll help with the baby 'til Daddy brings her bottle." Two months shy of three years and he was ready to step up. Before Nick arrived, Jake made silly faces for Elly and tickled her toes, and then banged the baby's arm with her favorite rattle. Elly's screech launched a muscle spasm in Sophie's back that threatened to engulf her. Enough of wise little Jakie. Sophie was ready to smack him.

She couldn't stand herself.

Nick darted in, grabbed Elly in one arm and Jake, now a mess of tears, in the other. Sophie felt around for the ibuprofen and popped two in her mouth, sucking on the straw of the water bottle Nick had left for her. She could hear him and the kids in their back bedroom, but she couldn't make out whether Jake's noises were cries or giggles. Guilt would have to wait its turn, pain was in charge for now.

The small publisher she worked for had sent her some kind of plant that would probably be dead in a week, given the lack of light in their downstairs flat. Her boss was one of three laid-back guys who published several neighborhood papers and a couple offbeat journals. They couldn't afford any paid leave for the staff, they said, but hey, Sophie and the other young women assistants were welcome to bring their babies to work, as long as they got their tasks done. And so she'd strapped Elly to her in a baby sling and gone back after four weeks because she felt fine, she was a workhorse and her family needed the money. Nick's layoff had been announced at the end of week three.

"They knew we were getting ready to strike," Nick told her. The Teamsters local at the hot water heater plant was fed up with cuts to health insurance and lower wages for new hires. "Management figured a few weeks at piddly unemployment pay and no insurance would sober us up."

Sophie turned her neck from side to side. Their duplex in Logan Square didn't have great light, but it did have a front stoop and a kind of backyard and a park not far away and a lot of neighbor kids. She didn't love the living room, but it was the only one with enough floor space for her to stay flat on her back.

As she lay there waiting for the ibuprofen to kick in, Sophie fought off images of a woman she knew who always carried a special orthopedic cushion and would only go places that had hard-backed chairs. No matter what it took, Sophie was determined to heal and not face a lifetime of restrictions and pitiful glances.

She stroked Elly's infant seat and tried to move her thoughts to a place of gratitude. At least they'd had insurance to cover Elly's birth in a modern hospital. When Jake was born in Baltimore they had none. Sophie had enrolled in a clinic that offered mostly free obstetric services with a young, idealistic doctor who'd done a great job. Not his fault the only hospital willing to take his patients was a strict Catholic institution where the sole decoration on the walls was a giant cross. In between contractions, Sophie yelled at Nick to stuff it in a drawer. The doctor had instructed them to find something beautiful to focus on. Sophie kept her eyes on the metal crank used to adjust the head of the bed. It was so old, some of the metal had scraped off. She imagined it as an etching.

The background music to that time in their lives was the snarling voice of a debt collector who began harassing Sophie to pay a parking ticket Nick got once in New York and tossed in the trash. At first, she took the time to explain the situation and the fact that they'd never received a single notice to pay the ticket, just the letter announcing that a collection agency had taken over the debt which, she pointed out, had ballooned to twenty times the cost of the original ticket. On the third call, as the representative proceeded to threaten her, Sophie lost it. "What do you want from me, money we don't have? The heating oil we can't afford? My unborn child?"

"You're hysterical, ma'am," the guy had said. "I'll call you back when you've calmed down."

Sophie hated that "ma'am." The next time he called, she informed him that the person he asked for had passed away. "But you sound just like her," the guy said. "I'm her sister here to help with the arrangements," she replied. He must have known she was lying, but he never called again.

Okay, this wasn't the direction Sophie meant her thoughts to go in, although getting that asshole off her back was something to be grateful for. She was also grateful they'd come to Chicago soon after Jake's birth to find better jobs and be closer to Nick's family in Wisconsin, and in driving distance from her folks in Cleveland.

Just as she felt herself drifting off, Jake ran in and lay down beside her. "Daddy says I have chicken pops," he said. "Wanna see?" He lifted up his shirt to show a chest peppered with red dots. Nick trailed him with a container of baking soda and a Goofy finger puppet. "Hey, little man, let's give Mom some more time to sleep. Goofy wants a bath with baking soda to get rid of his chicken pox, and I told him that's just what you were going to do." Nick mouthed "Sorry" as he shepherded Jake out of the room.

"What's next," Sophie said out loud. "An eviction notice? Encephalitis?" She rolled onto one side so the tears wouldn't pool in her ears.

Late that afternoon, she heard Nick pick up the phone in the dining room. "Got it, thank you. And health insurance'll kick in as soon as I'm back?" Sophie watched him nod and turn to her with a big thumbs up. "I'll see you for the 7:00 shift tomorrow." Next call was to Minnie, who referred them to an orthopedist who practiced at the hospital she worked at. Thanks to Minnie's magic, they were able to get an emergency appointment for the next day.

Sophie scoured her brain for the right metaphor for this kind of situation. Yay, she could go to the doctor. Ugh, how would she get there and who would watch the kids while she was gone? "I got you, my love," Nick told her. Ten minutes later he'd worked it all out: Minnie's husband would take her to the doctor. Minnie offered to handle the kids.

The orthopedist had an office right on Michigan Avenue. Parking would cost $18 just for entering the garage. Sophie insisted on being dropped off and picked up an hour later. "It's sitting that does me in," Sophie said. Minnie's husband had a passenger seat that reclined almost to horizontal. "I'll be fine if I have to stand for a few minutes in the doorway."

The first thing Sophie noticed about the office was how quiet it was. Not empty — there were six or seven people in the waiting room, all with books or magazines in hand. What they didn't have were any children, unlike the doctors' offices Sophie was used to. The carpet was so ridiculously plush, shoes didn't seem to make any sound here. Minutes after she checked in at the desk, Sophie heard her name called. A nurse guided her to a patient room where she could get an x-ray and remain supine until the doctor came in.

Beneath his white coat, the doctor wore not scrubs but pleated black trousers. On his feet were fancy wingtips, a word Sophie knew only because someone in the office had written a piece about them as a status symbol. As the doctor walked in, he glanced at his watch, something gold with a large face. "Good news," he told her. "It is a herniated disc, but the location and size is such that you shouldn't need surgery. A week flat on your back should do it. And when I say flat, I mean flat. Pillow under your knees, not under your head."

Damn, Sophie thought. The nurse had asked about sleeping with her head on a pillow and must have ratted her out.

"Think of it as a vacation from chores of any kind. I'll write you a script for some painkillers. Get your mother or your housekeeper to take over and you just focus on you."

Sophie's mother had been checking in every day, but no need to ask, she'd used up her one-week vacation to help out when Elly was born. The lawyer she worked for couldn't find his desk without her. Sophie's dad couldn't get off either, and really, he'd just be bugging her every two minutes about how to do this or where to find that. Nick's mom would have done it, bless her heart, but she'd shocked them all by dying right before Elly was born, and Nick was still grieving her loss. As for the housekeeper, whose idea of a joke was that? She and Nick didn't own this house, and there'd be no keeping whatever they did own unless Nick could hang on to his job.

The doctor was out the door before Sophie could formulate a reply.

Minnie turned out to be the savior. She worked evenings and arranged to have Nick bring the kids to her house for two of those days. She had a toddler who hadn't yet had chicken pox and was eager to get her exposed. Minnie wouldn't take any money. "Hey, you're helping my kid build immunity for free," she said. She knew a second neighbor who would help for cash on the other days. Two different friends offered to pick up groceries.

Somehow they made it through to the weekend. Nick was exhausted from building hot water heaters by day and handling ice packs, dinner and baby duty by night. Except for one cursing outburst after he spilled an entire can of formula ("That's a lotta bad words," Jake told him) and one bandaged finger from a mishap at work, Nick was a trooper.

"I'd like to say when I'm back on my feet I'll wait on you hand and foot," Sophie said, "except I can't figure out what that expression means. But I have a few things in mind."

Jake's chicken pox crusted over nicely and he was able to go back to pre-school the following week. Sophie continued to pay the other neighbor to watch Elly while she returned to work half time. Her boss set her up in a special ergonomic chair with a cushion that Sophie vowed she would outgrow. Minnie gave her a set of back-strengthening yoga exercises, something the doctor hadn't bothered to mention and likely had no clue about.

Sophie was scheduled for a follow-up appointment at the end of May. A co-worker was going to give her a ride from work and she'd take the bus home from there. "I'm only going to the orthopedist to set him straight," she told Nick.

"Good one, love. But don't hold your breath." Nick was entertaining Jake by folding diapers and seeing how high a stack they could build before it toppled over.

"I just want the satisfaction of saying my piece," Sophie told him. Slowly she lowered herself down so she could snuggle with Jake, who was still giggling at his falling towers.

"You got this, babe," Nick said. "I believe in you."

"You got this, Mommy," Jake said, carefully placing a diaper on her head. "I believe you."

On the day of the appointment, Sophie found her moment right after the doctor finished his exam. He held out his elbow so she could pull herself up, and she did not let go.

"I wanted to give you some feedback," she said. She could feel the air conditioning on her back where the hospital robe stayed open. The doctor didn't look her in the eye, but at least he didn't peek at his watch.

"Please don't assume your world is *the* world," Sophie said. "Most people have no housekeeper. Our mothers may work and not be able to get off. My husband and I had to scrape and borrow and beg to buy me that week of rest. You don't have the power to fix it, but you can at least let patients like me know that you see it."

The doctor nodded and drew back his arm, adding a notation in her chart. "I'll keep that in mind, Mrs. Reznick. You're good to go."

"It's Ms. Reznick," she called, as the door swung shut behind him.

Nick was already home feeding Elly when Sophie walked in from the bus stop and described what happened. "Ah, you got the nod and the note," Nick said. "I bet it says, 'Beware, difficult patient.'"

Sophie reached out her arms so Nick could settle Elly in her lap. The baby didn't seem to care, as long as the bottle went with her. "There's probably a whole set of acronyms that only the doctors know. Maybe 'COW' for 'Crabby, Opinionated Whiner.'"

Nick said, "I think 'CUB' is more like it. 'Cranky, Ungrateful Bitch.' Then they put it in the system to share with all the other doctors."

Sophie grinned. "Make it into a tee-shirt," she said, as Elly blew a milk bubble and dribbled on her mother's arm. "I'll wear it with pride."

The Listening Session

Milwaukee, February 1982

When she heard about the so-called "listening sessions" at work, Sophie had no illusions. "Smoke and mirrors," she told Nick. "The wet dream of some public affairs guy, hoping to make the phone company look hip with a 1980's version of the suggestion box. Still, you have to admit the format is interesting. Apparently Mr. Schmitz leaves the room and so does his secretary. There'll be two easels with a big pad of paper and there'll be fifteen of us at each session. We get to write any questions we have anonymously, and then he comes back and answers them."

They were in their room folding Elly's diapers after getting both kids down, radiator gurgling in the background. "I can see it now," Nick said, balling a diaper in his hand and pressing it to his heart. "Mr. Schmucks comes in, reads the grievances of his workers, tears at his hair" — Nick raked his fingers over his own head — "and then he jumps up and orders an immediate halt to all the asshole Big Brother rules. They institute paid sick days and they pay you what you're worth. Boom."

Sophie grabbed the diaper and swatted his now wild hair. "Hush. Schmitz'll be an asshole and nothing will change. I'm still excited to see what the other women are going to write. Maybe we can stir up the pot a little, take something to the union."

***

The conference room was arranged with four tables in the shape of a rectangle. Sophie showed up five minutes early and found most of the others already seated.

73

The back table was full and the only open chairs were at the side tables near the front. Apparently Vice President of Administrative Services Ernest Schmitz and his secretary, ensconced at the head table, would occupy that entire side on their own. Since management had played up the anonymity factor, there were no name tags. Sophie knew only that they were all admin, plucked from word processing, billing, customer service and who knows where else. A quick look around showed they were all women, as expected. But the rest of the demographics were skewed: Mostly older, almost all white. Sophie had been hoping for a younger, hipper group.

She pulled out a chair next to a woman with big curls who smelled of hairspray and Doublemint gum. Sophie tried to read people's faces, but most kept their eyes on the black, orange and green magic markers grouped on each table. She didn't see anyone she recognized until 8:30 a.m., the designated start time, when an Iranian woman named Mitra slipped in—they sometimes rode the same bus. Mitra took the only remaining chair across from Sophie.

Mr. Schmitz, whose three-piece suit sported a gold watch chain, pulled out the watch and cradled it in his hand in a gesture Sophie could only describe as tender. The announcement of the listening session hadn't mentioned that the department head delivered a speech before leaving the room, but Schmitz plunged right in without greeting them in any fashion, or even bothering to stand up.

So much for tenderness.

"I've been at the phone company since before most of you were born," he declared. "During that time, the quality of the American worker has steadily deteriorated." Mitra, who appeared to be in her early 60s, folded her hands and placed them in her lap, where Sophie imagined them turning into fists. "I speak to my counterparts in other industries, and all they hear are whiners, complainers, people who want to call off work because they stubbed their toe or got a crick in their neck from watching too many porn films. And don't even think about asking them to step up and pitch in if we're behind or you'll hear, 'You made my back hurt. I'm gonna file a grr-riev-ance.'" He pronounced the word as if it were three syllables.

Two seats down from Mitra, a woman in a navy sweater coughed quietly into a handkerchief.

"Many of you, I'm sure, are doing an admirable job here," Schmitz continued. "We work very hard on our screening process. Still, I wish you could have accompanied me on a recent trip to Japan. Now *there's* a work ethic to aspire to." He paused to glance at his timepiece. "So, let me tell you how this session will flow."

While he spoke, Sophie watched with horror as most of the women turned into bobbleheads, nodding through his insults, his patronizing instructions and his grandiose exit from the room. Her heart lurched. And then she witnessed a transformation as unexpected as Mary Poppins belting out a string of cuss words. As soon as the door closed, these same women started breathing fire. One after another they dashed to the easel pads armed with those magic markers, scribbling pent-up outrage on the ivory-colored paper. The woman in the navy sweater was the first one up on her side. "WHY AREN'T WE ALLOWED TO BE SICK FOR FIVE YEARS?" she wrote in all caps. A redhead at the other easel, breathing heavily through her mouth, used an orange marker to ask her question: "Is it true that supervisors can listen into our private calls even on the pay phones?"

In a small notebook, Sophie jotted down as many of the questions as she could. She couldn't imagine Mr. Schmitz producing a record of this session, and she wanted one of her own.

- "Why do we have to make coffee but managers don't?"

- "Why do we have to measure the width and length of every project we type?"
- "Why did my co-worker get told at 4:30 on a Friday that she was being transferred Monday morning all the way out to Brookfield? Will that happen to me?"
- "Why does management treat us like peons?"

The sole Black person in the room, a woman whose smile Sophie remembered from the personnel office, filled half a page with bold green cursive: "Why are there no Black people in upper management?"

Sophie waited for an opening to add her own question: "Why do managers get flexible hours and we don't?" She was still smarting from being told she couldn't make up the fifteen minutes she missed last Tuesday when Jake's school bus was late — was she supposed to leave a five-year-old alone at the bus stop? Candace, her supervisor, had spelled out the rules: If you knew in advance that you had to schedule a doctor's appointment during working hours, you could make up the time. But they couldn't allow people that latitude if they didn't give advance notice.

"Sorry, Candace," Sophie told her. "I would have, but the bus driver forgot to alert me that he was running late. And I've tried to train my kids to notify me when they're going to wake up with an ear infection, but honestly, they just can't get the hang of it."

The women added their questions in silence, as if the Big Brother they worried about could listen in through the walls as well as the phones. Sophie observed the red-head exchange a few muffled comments with her neighbor. Mitra pushed back her chair to offer cough drops to the woman in the navy sweater.

After fifteen minutes, Mr. Schmitz and his secretary returned to the room. He hadn't introduced her, but Sophie thought she saw "LuAnn" something on a steel-plated name tag on her lapel. Most of the attendees had settled back into neutral faces. LuAnn carefully tore each sheet of questions from the easel pad and placed them before Mr. Schmitz, who took his time pulling glasses from his pocket. The charcoal frames matched the color of his suit. He wiped each lens slowly with a piece of cloth before placing them on his slightly florid face and arching his eyebrows at the first question.

"Hmm, we're starting with an earth-shattering question." He did a mock drum roll with his knuckles on the table. "Who makes the coffee? I gotta say, I'm perplexed why this is an issue. It wouldn't bother me."

Said the man who'd likely never made a cup of coffee in his fucking life, Sophie thought. No surprise, the room contained no refreshments of any kind.

On the question of measurements, Mr. Schmitz seemed to offer a modicum of sympathy. "I can see why that might seem annoying," he said, pulling off his glasses and looking around the room. "If you don't have the perspective of the company's overall performance needs. That's a management task. But we do need to know what kind of output we're getting in each department. It's what keeps the Bell system on the right side of the bell curve."

His chuckle at his own joke became a laugh out loud when he came to the question on eavesdropping. "Ma Bell is mighty powerful, I admit, but let me assure you, she hasn't got time to listen in to your calls when you check in on your kiddies or set up a little hanky-panky on the side." Someone — Sophie couldn't see who— let out a small gasp. The redhead who'd written that question slumped in her seat.

Any pretense of "I'm your buddy and we're in this together" disappeared with the question about sick time. "We take excellent care of our people," Mr. Schmitz declared, as if he'd been asked about the nutritional content of food in the cafeteria. As the woman in the navy sweater held her hand to her neck, Sophie wondered whether she was trying to soothe her throat or prop up an aching head.

Schmitz's voice rose to a shout when he saw the question about the transfer made without input or warning. "I can't believe someone is talking out of turn about someone else's situation when you haven't the slightest idea what all went into that decision." The woman next to Sophie jumped slightly in her seat. "Outrageous! You should have asked your supervisor and kept any discussion to yourself."

A middle-aged woman in the right back corner, headband askew, raised her hand. "That was my question," she said. "I did ask my supervisor. She told me it was, and I quote, 'none of your damn business' and never to mention it again."

Mr. Schmitz took a deep breath. "Let's move on," he said. He plowed his way through the next set of questions, summarizing each in a few words until he came to Sophie's, which he read aloud, glaring first at the sheet of paper and then at all of them. He looked like a man who longed to hold a cigar between his fingers and wave it around.

"Whoever wrote this, listen up. We expect our managers to be available 24-7, every day of the week. They make this job a priority when they step up, and as a measure of our appreciation, we allow them some wiggle room if they need it." Next came the pause where he would have dropped the growing ash from the tip of his cigar. "Obviously we couldn't keep our operations efficient if we allowed that for the front line workers. Abuse would be rampant."

Sophie hadn't planned on saying a word in this gathering. She'd applied for the job last year when they moved to Milwaukee from Chicago to be closer to Nick's dad. One of them had to get something with health insurance and Sophie typed a hundred words a minute. Nick took the first job he could find, making labels with toxic glue. But he was on the list for an opening at GE with a union and benefits, and then she'd be able to get out of this mind-numbing place, try to get hired by a women's group or a community organization. Still, a hand went up and a voice spoke out, and Sophie realized they both belonged to her.

"Does this mean that mothers of young children can't be managers at the phone company?" she asked. "Because clearly they can't be available twenty-four seven every day of the week."

Mr. Schmitz rose slightly from his chair, his cheeks and forehead now a bright scarlet. LuAnn ducked her head, either out of fear or to hide a smile. Sophie hoped it was the latter.

"Young lady, I'll have you know that the phone company prides itself on its excellent representation of women in management. It's insulting to every one of them to suggest otherwise."

Sophie thought of Candace, mother of three, so grateful for the opportunity to move from taking dictation into the supervisor slot that she didn't dare let on if she found any of the rules unreasonable or unfair. Sophie had overheard Candace's frantic whispers to whoever watched her little ones, even though personal phone calls in the department were strictly prohibited. "Did you try a time-out?" she'd said. "OK, just let him have the jelly beans."

"We seem to be running out of time," announced Mr. Schmitz, without pulling out his watch. "Let me answer one more question and then, as you know, my door is always open. Contact LuAnn if you would like to schedule an appointment." Sophie was unaware of anyone who'd actually attempted to do that. She noticed the scowl on the face of the Black woman from personnel. Her question was easy to spot, Mr. Schmitz had slipped it under the rest of the pages.

The final question he addressed was Sophie's favorite: "Why does management treat us like peons?" Mitra had written that with perfect penmanship.

Mr. Schmitz sat back and put his hand to his heart. "Let me give you some important advice," he said, as LuAnn rolled up their precious words and secured them with a thick rubber band. "It's all a matter of how you feel inside. If you feel good about yourself, no one can make you feel like a peon."

"TREAT us like peons," Sophie wanted to yell. "The question was why does management TREAT us like peons." But Mr. Schmitz was already on his way out the door. Sophie scurried so she could walk out at the same time as Mitra. "Thank you," Sophie said. "We heard you even if he can't."

***

That night, Sophie waited until the kids were in bed to tell Nick about how the session went. The Pointer Sisters were playing softly on the boom box. Nick pulled her to him and stroked her back. "GE's gonna happen," he said. "We'll spring you soon."

Sophie snuggled closer and enjoyed the slow circles Nick was making on her back. "I'm thinking about calling that woman on the union's executive council, the one who wants to start a Women's Caucus," she said. This was Sophie's first union job. It was certainly the best paying position she'd had, but the jobs were rigidly segregated by gender and the guys made much more, she was sure. The union leadership seemed oblivious to concerns the women had about disrespect, inflexibility, and sexual harassment. Sophie had been taken aback at her first union meeting when the sign-in table featured bumper stickers that read, "Let a phone man put it in."

"Unlikely we'd get the officers to take up equity or flexibility issues. I imagine racial discrimination is not even on their radar screen. But the transfer-with-no-warning business might get their attention. It'd be a foot in the door."

"Worth a try," Nick said.

Sophie sang along with the Pointer Sisters: "I know we can. Yes we can can."

***

80

Margaret Conway, the first — and only — woman on the union executive committee, was delighted to get Sophie's call and arranged for them to meet with the union president, Harry Johansen, the following Tuesday. "Tell him about the stuff that came up in the session," Margaret advised. "Let's see what he bites on. Pick your battles. He's on the fence about approving the Women's Caucus, so I don't want to piss him off."

Margaret offered to pick Sophie up after work at the 35th Street office and ride together to the union headquarters downtown. Everything about Margaret spelled "no nonsense." She had retired some years earlier, wore her hair short and unstyled, dressed in pants that looked more like trousers, and had likely never put a lipstick to her mouth. Her car was some kind of Ford compact from the 70s, stick shift, uncluttered.She kept the windows cracked.

Harry Johansen was on the phone when they arrived but signaled for them to have a seat. His office was decorated with union paraphernalia, framed pictures of him with various political leaders and multiple hockey trophies, along with photos of a large extended family at a cottage labeled, "Up North."

"Hey, Maggie, great to see you," he said as he hung up the phone and held out his hand. Even seated, Harry Johansen was a formidable presence. Sophie could imagine him towering over the other hockey team's players. "And nice to meet you, Sophie. I've been hearing several reports on these so-called listening sessions. Just a lot of BS to try to kick the union's ass."

Sophie had decided to type up the questions she'd captured along with Mr. Schmitz's responses. She handed a copy to Harry to review. "These women looked meek when he was in the room, but they're full of rage," she said. "I think Margaret's idea of a women's caucus is great." She watched him do a quick scan of her readout.

Harry grinned. "I know our Maggie has a bee in her bonnet to get more gals out in the field. Not that men don't like to see women climbing poles." He didn't seem to notice he was the only one who chuckled. "So sure, go ahead and encourage 'em to apply. It's a tough job, the tests are a bear. But hey, anyone who has the balls to do it, they're good in my book."

Harry thumbed through Sophie's typed pages. "As far as these points about more Blacks or women in management, I gotta say, the union's job is to protect our members, not move them out of the bargaining unit into the corner office, aina? I'm sure you agree, Mags."

Margaret didn't nod, but she didn't disagree, either.

"And as for paid sick days, it's a trade-off. The guys in the really hard jobs made a choice a while ago — more money in their paychecks, health insurance had to come first.

Sophie cleared her throat. She was quite sure corporate executives didn't see a need to choose between decent pay and paid time off, but this didn't seem the right time to bring that up. She replayed Margaret's advice: "Pick your battles."

"What about this transfer without notice issue?" she asked.

Harry nodded his approval. "Can you get that woman who was transferred to Brookfield to file a grievance? We'd love to go after them on this — but it's hard to get women from that department to take action. Some of them don't even know they're in a union. Others are Timid Tillies. If you can deliver her, we're on it like white on rice."

Margaret pounced. "All righty. Let's start the Women's Caucus. Give me a budget and a part-time staff. We'll bring folks in."

Harry got out from behind his desk and offered Margaret his hand. "Aw-right, Miss Conway. I need to get approval from the executive council. Some of the guys see this as women's lib run amok, another management trick to keep the workers divided. But I'll support you — we'll get it passed. Go do some rabble rousing among these gals. Let's see what you've come up with in six months and then we can assess it."

Sophie hated hearing Harry dismiss Mitra or the woman in the navy sweater or any of the others in that room. Timid Tillies, my ass — *Tormented* Tillies was more like it. This job was where most of them would stay until they retired. Sophie felt a pang of guilt for planning to desert them.

Although the #30 bus to Sherman Park stopped right across the street from the union office, Sophie said yes when Margaret offered to drive her home. "You were just the spark we needed," Margaret said as they pulled out of the parking spot. "They think it's a women's auxiliary, but we're gonna show them a thing or two. Can I count on you?"

Sophie fiddled with her seat belt. "Actually, I don't know how long I'll be on this job," she said.

Margaret pulled a pack of Pall Malls out of her coat packet and put one in her mouth without lighting it. "You don't have to be a lifer to be a hell-raiser."

Sophie grinned. "Okay. There's a real firecracker in my department, and another from that session who ought to be involved. I'm glad to invite them. And I'm in for as long as I'm here."

"It's a deal." Margaret gave two short taps on the horn. "Maybe the union will learn to do a little listening of their own."

The Debate

Milwaukee, 1983

"The Source of Family Dysfunction? Working Mothers." The headline leapt out from the top of the opinion page like a wagging finger. Nick had seen it first and carried it over to Sophie, who was on the couch scrubbing the jelly stain from Jake's Star Wars t-shirt with a toothbrush and rubbing alcohol.

"This Mary Reynolds is a right-wing fanatic," Nick said. "She describes herself as a proud follower of Phyllis Schlafly. Says mothers who work outside the home are to blame for everything from alcoholism to teenage suicide. You could write a great response."

Sophie paused just long enough to read the heading. "Me and any other mom who can stay awake long enough to read a newspaper once we get the kids to sleep, whittle down the stack of dirty clothes, whip up tomorrow's lunches and dig through backpacks for permission slips. Did I mention salvaging a five-year-old's favorite shirt? Just drop it on my desk, please." Sophie angled her head toward the folding table in the dining room stacked with articles, newspaper clippings, and folders labeled "Working Women Surveys" and "Fundraising."

Nick brushed his lips against her forehead. He had the grace not to mention that he'd cooked dinner and been in charge of baths and locating Elly's teddy bear. Sophie's co-workers couldn't believe she'd landed a guy who did things like that. "It's a problem," she told Nick recently. "I can never complain about the ways you fuck up."

Four days a week Sophie typed up legal jargon as a temp for Newman Spiegel and Hastings. Fridays she volunteered with a new group called Working Women United, devoted to winning higher pay and better leave policies for working women. She'd signed up for WWU after reading their slogan on a flyer at the Sherman Park co-op: "My consciousness is fine, it's my pay that needs raising." If she waited 'til this Friday to send a letter to the *Milwaukee Journal*, it might be too late — that was the advice they'd gotten from a state legislator who was mentoring the organization. Sophie would try to compose something tomorrow on the bus if she got a seat and type it over her lunch break. This temp job was a lot better than her stint last year at the phone company. At least no one counted the length and width of every project you typed, or dinged you with an absence point if you weren't there at 7:30 on the dot, even if your kid's school bus showed up late.

That Sunday, Sophie's letter appeared in the paper. "Mothers with paying jobs are mothers who put food on the table, keep the lights on and a roof over the family's head," she'd written. "Last I looked, these are all things children need to flourish."

The following night she got a phone call from a Fran Lewandowski at the public television station. Fran's voice was soothing, like a good children's librarian. "I really liked your letter," she said. "We have a show on Thursday nights at 7:00 called Community Conversations. It's hard to believe we've reached 1983 and still have to debate whether mothers should be allowed to hold jobs, but there you are. I'd like to have you and Mary Reynolds together on the show." Sophie didn't know whether to make some excuse or jump up and down.

"Mary said she'd do it, but only if her husband joined her," Fran added. She and Sophie shared a laugh. "So we'd like you to bring your partner as well. The lone woman on our camera crew told me, 'If this Sophie Reznick has a husband, I bet he'd be up to the challenge of appearing on the show. And if she has a girlfriend, even better.' Will that work?"

Nick needed no persuading.

The show aired live, so they had to arrange a babysitter. As they waited for Shyla to walk over from her house down the block, Jake sidled up to Sophie and put his hand on her herringbone blazer, a hand-me-up from her younger sister. "How come there aren't any boy babysitters, Mom?"

"There definitely are boy babysitters," she assured him. "And you can babysit when you get older. But you're right. Most babysitters are girls because most families aren't like our family. Most dads don't share raising the kids."

"That's what you and Daddy are going to talk about tonight on that show, right?" Jake took after Nick's side of the family, fair and gangly. Only two-year-old Elly, with her dark curls and bold eyebrows, looked like a child of Jewish descent.

Sophie hugged Jake hard. "You got it, Jakie." She'd promised herself she wouldn't brag about her children, but on the drive to the studio she shared this tidbit with Nick. "I gotta say, our kindergartner is pretty advanced."

Fran Lewandowski apologized for what she called the bare bones studio. It looked pretty bustling to Sophie, with two cameras, multiple lights, and a set with two small couches, but she had nothing to compare it to. Fran would moderate from a chair placed between the two couples. As Sophie and Nick took their seats, she was pleased to spot the woman behind one of the cameras and gave her a quick nod.

Don't let me fuck this up, she told herself. She tried to visualize the women who came to WWU monthly meetings, sitting in the church basement bursting with stories of being underpaid and overworked, dissed and groped and made invisible in their various workplaces. *They'll be watching,* Sophie thought. *I'm just talking to my friends.*

Nick grabbed her hand and gave it a squeeze, as if he could hear her silent pep talk.

Mary and Warren Reynolds had arrived early and already occupied the couch on the right-hand side. Everything about Mary Reynolds was tightly bound — her hair, her facial muscles, the hands clasped on her lap. The most charitable thing Sophie could say about her opponent was that she sat up straight, as did her husband, a round-faced man with a swirl of hair completely covering his forehead; Sophie imagined Warren Reynolds calling his wife "Mother."

Sophie wore a charcoal gray skirt and rose-colored sweater with the blazer. "All I have are these flats," she complained to Nick when they were getting ready. She owned two pairs of the same shoe, one navy and one black. On more than one occasion, she'd arrived at work to find one of each color on her feet. "Also I don't know how you're supposed to sit. Cross one leg over the other? Turn your legs to the side?" When Nick said the camera would probably stay on her face, all Sophie could think about was a director who visited her theater class at the technical college. "Your face is fine for the stage," he'd told her, "but don't ever do television. Nothing about your features is diminutive."

No one in the whole world cares what you look like, she reminded herself. *Nick said only eleven people watch this show.*

Fran Lewandowski was introducing them, describing Sophie Reznick as a clerical worker, mother and activist, and Nick Turner as a machinist at General Electric. Warren Reynolds turned out to be an accountant. And Mary, in her own words, was a "housewife and mother."

What an odd word, "housewife," Sophie thought. What was the wedding like? What did the house promise to do? She pinched the chair to keep herself focused.

Mary lit into Sophie right away. "I volunteer three days a week at my children's school. I help out wherever they need me, and often that's in the office. It makes me so angry when a child gets sick and I call the mom and she tells me, 'Oh, I'm sorry, but I'm at work. Can't you just keep him there?"

This wasn't going to be as hard as Sophie thought. "I'm angry too," she said. "But why are you mad at the mom, and not at the boss who'd fire her if she left to pick up her kid?"

Mary used both hands to smooth imaginary wrinkles in her skirt. "A woman's highest duty is to her family, not frittering her time trying to earn money for a fancy car and the latest contraptions for her home."

Sophie pictured Gus the Bus, the 15-year-old station wagon Nick drove to work, and the discount furniture in their house. "Lots of two-parent families live paycheck to paycheck," she said. "And what about all the women who are raising kids on their own?"

She could feel Nick's thigh muscle tighten. He'd probably love to jump in, but she knew he wanted the focus on her tonight. Warren Reynolds seemed content to remain silent. Occasionally he tugged at the sweep of hair on his forehead.

Sophie and Mary went back and forth, arguing over why women earned less money than men ("They choose easier occupations," Mary insisted, until Sophie pointed out people with degrees in early childhood were near the botom of the pay scale); what to do about sexual harassment ("Women who are modest in their demeanor will do just fine in the workplace," according to Mary); whether or not child care was harmful to children ("I love seeing my children learn art and music and other skills we're just not equipped to give them," Sophie said. "Not to mention grasping that they're special but other kids are special as well.") Fran Lewandowski sat back and let them tangle.

A clock across from them indicated the segment was nearly over when Nick finally entered the conversation. He looked directly into the camera. "Men should be so grateful to the women's movement because they've given us parenting," he said. "Even though it's a huge responsibility, it's such a joy. We should just say thanks."

Sophie beamed. This guy had come a long way since their first date when he couldn't understand why she was paying for her meal. A week ago, he'd given a talk at a labor conference about the successful struggle he and the union waged at GE to get fans installed in his work area, the carcinogen they had to use for cleaning up epoxies had already messed up his lungs. Nick titled his talk, "Real Men Won't Get Cancer."

Fran Lewandowski invited them all to stick around and chat afterwards, but Sophie really wanted to get home. Mary and Warren Reynolds looked like they couldn't wait to get their coats on and leave the moral turpitude behind.

It had started to snow while they were in the studio. Sophie brushed off the windows while Nick coaxed the car to a smooth start. As they made their way from the studio back to their house on the west side, they discussed which part of the program the kids would have liked best. Elly probably got distracted, but they were eager to hear what Jake thought. "I bet he liked the bit about the school calling," Sophie said. "I remember how relieved he was when I showed up that time he threw up in the wastebasket."

Shyla and both kids were waiting by the door when they arrived. "I tried," Shyla said, one hand resting on each kid's head. "Really I did. Turns out *Greatest American Hero* was on at the same time." This was Jake and Elly's favorite show — Sophie had forgotten all about it.

"But, Mom, we watched you during the commercials," Jake informed her. "We saw a lot!"

"Good." Sophie moved them all into the living room and unbuttoned her coat. "What was your favorite part?"

"When the words went over your faces at the end." Jake swooped one hand from the top of his head down to his chest. "That was really cool."

Nick gave her a swift hug before walking Shyla home. "So he's not the most advanced five-year-old," he whispered. "But you kicked some serious butt. I know all eleven viewers were really impressed."

Sophie shut the door and closed her eyes for a moment before joining the kids. The dishes were still in the sink and she had laundry to fold. Elly had come home from day care with only one mitten, so she needed to root through Jake's cast-offs to find another pair. But first she'd let Nick's words of praise float over her like the credits. And she'd add a few of her own.

The State Hastens to Say

Milwaukee, 1984

Whenever the Working Women United office closed for "maintenance operations" — the landlord's euphemism for extermination services — Sophie Reznick worked from home. Today she broke up her day by pulling on her parka and walking down to Vanessa Jackson's in the early afternoon, stopping mid-block to admire a pine tree decorated with dozens of early valentines. Vanessa answered the doorbell with the phone to her ear and rage in her eyes. She waved to indicate that Sophie should come in.

"I know my rights." Vanessa's voice was much calmer than the storm on her face. "I got a right to a hearing and I intend to have one. I'll stay on the line while you set it up." Phone still pasted to her ear, Vanessa followed Sophie inside, dragging the long phone cord behind her. They sat side by side on the plaid couch while Vanessa's twins chased each other around the dining room. The older kids were still at school. "Yes, ma'am. Next Monday, February the thirteenth, two in the afternoon. I'll be there."

The two women first got to know each other a couple years earlier, at a block party right after Sophie and her family moved to Forty-Fifth Street. The kids begged for a playdate and the moms slowly became friends. Only after Sophie ranted about Reagan's cuts to public assistance did Vanessa open up about being on welfare.

"Sorry you had to hear that," Vanessa said. She set the phone back in its cradle and tucked the cord under the table next to the couch. "They like to make you feel so small. Wait 'til you hear what my unreasonable request is

93

— an additional one-time supplement of thirty-five dollars to buy more dishes, glasses, cutlery and two more chairs so we can all sit down to a meal at the same time. You know what that harpy said? 'Maybe you should have thought of that before you had all those kids.'"

Sophie laid her hand on Vanessa's arm.

"At the hearing they'll ask me what they always ask, 'Why aren't you working, Mrs. Jackson?' And I'll say, 'Last I looked, keeping five Black children safe, fed, curious and healthy on five hundred nineteen dollars a month in a place like Milwaukee takes more work than just about any job on earth.'"

"Amen," Sophie said.

"Then they'll ask me if I get any money in child support and I'll point out that the file in front of them says clearly that my husband, the father of *all* of my children, was killed by a hit-and-run driver while walking home from Sherman Park library on a Saturday afternoon. I'll remind them, speaking of working, that cops put in very little effort to find the responsible party, and that my husband, despite years of hard work at Allis-Chalmers, had not yet been deemed worthy of a pension."

Vanessa's fingers were splayed against her neck. "You know, I've been to their hearings twice before. They always tape them. But when I ask for a copy of the recording, they never give it to me."

One of the toddlers started to shriek and ran in to bury his head in her lap. Vanessa stroked his soft curls.

"Working Women United has a tape recorder that fits in a purse." Sophie was thrilled to have something constructive to offer. "You can make your own tape."

Vanessa's face lit up against the backdrop of Reggie Jr.'s sobs. "Why don't you come with me? A white lady with a tape recorder? That'll stir up a mess."

Sophie cleared her throat.

"Oh, don't get me wrong." Vanessa lifted Reggie Jr. to her shoulder. "I'll do all the talking. I just want the pleasure of seeing him do a double-take when he gets a whiff of you."

***.

Sophie and Vanessa arrived at the welfare office twenty minutes early, but were instructed to stay in the crowded waiting area until summoned. The room was so warm, Sophie immediately pulled off her parka, but Vanessa sat perfectly still in her polyester coat, hood up, gloveless hands still jammed in her pockets. At 1:59 someone hollered, "Vanessa Jackson!" and pointed to a hallway. Ahead of them a guy in a shiny blue suit made his way to a hearing room with a briefcase tucked under his arm as if he were guarding the nuclear codes. A small woman followed him, hugging to her bosom a clunky, reel-to-reel tape recorder. The woman stopped at the door and beckoned them to enter, pointing to seats at one end of a rectangular table.

The guy, who never introduced himself, had already taken a seat at the other end, where he opened his briefcase and pulled out several items: a case file with a label so large, Sophie could read it across the table: "Vanessa Jackson Case No." followed by a long set of numerals; a ballpoint pen with a matching mechanical pencil; and two well-sharpened colored pencils, one red and one blue. The woman, who also failed to introduce herself and appeared to be his secretary, took a seat to his right, plugged in the recorder and pressed the button.

Sophie nodded at Vanessa and took out her own, much smaller recording device. Vanessa finally pulled her hood down.

Had the hearing official been kind, or candid, or even vaguely professional, Sophie wouldn't have paid attention to the comb-over — the thin strands of hair raked

95

over a third of his enormous dome of a head. But whatever restraint she might have called upon vanished the minute he opened his mouth and referred to himself as "the State."

The official patted the tips of hair on the right side of his head and spoke in the direction of the tape recorder. "This is Monday, February 13, 1984. Representing the State, Case Manager Harold Franklin Grimstad presiding over an expenditure hearing involving Mrs. Vanessa Jackson, Case #B19814266879." He picked up the folder and waved it in their direction. "The State asks Mrs. Jackson to identify herself and introduce her com-pan-ion."

Vanessa unbuttoned her coat. "I am Vanessa Whitley Jackson," she announced in a loud, clear voice. "And this is my neighbor, Sophie Reznick. She directs Working Women United."

The official held out his hand to signal to the secretary to stop recording. Vanessa pulled a gas receipt out of her pocket and scribbled something on the back before sliding the paper over to Sophie. "Told you," it read. The official, who appeared to be in a trance, did not glance their way.

"What's he doing?" Sophie wrote back.

"Humpty Dumpty needs time to figure out his next move." Vanessa scrunched up the receipt and put it back in her pocket.

A clock on the wall ticked loudly while the official sat with his hand extended for several moments before nodding to his assistant, the apparent cue to push the start button again. "The State hastens to say that clients are not permitted to bring in a recording device," he proclaimed. "We will not be able to continue this hearing until you remove it."

Sophie kept her eyes on Vanessa, who crossed her arms tightly across her chest. "You have a tape recorder," Vanessa said. "You want to document the meeting. So do we."

The official grabbed the red pencil and marked something in Vanessa's file. Without looking up, he tapped the pencil against the table. "Nothing in our policy papers provides for clients to have recording devices. The State once again asks you to remove the recorder or we will discontinue this conversation."

Vanessa wasn't much taller than Sophie, but her posture and long neck made her tower in her chair. She raised one eyebrow. "Does anything in the policy papers *prohibit* a client from having their own tape recorder?"

Again, the official held out his hand to order his secretary to pause the recording. He began to click the button on his ballpoint pen. Sophie slipped a small notebook out of her purse, opened it to an empty page and set it between her and Vanessa. "HD needs yoga," she wrote.

Vanessa drew an egg beneath those words with stick figure legs in lotus pose. Sophie struggled not to laugh. Then Vanessa turned the page.

"Show time," she wrote.

Another minute passed. Another nod. Humpty Dumpty patted his tie. "The State hastens to add that the client has proven herself to be intractable. The meeting is ending at 2:13 p.m."

Vanessa jumped to her feet. Sophie's tape recorder continued to whirr. "This is Mrs. Vanessa Jackson, officially requesting a copy of the policy papers of the Milwaukee Wisconsin office of Aid for Dependent Children. If you fail to send them to me by the end of the month, Working Women United will get an attorney to appeal this ruling to your boss and hold a press conference."

Sophie bit her lip to keep herself from grinning as she nodded several times.

"I figure reporters like that kind of story," Vanessa said, "a lawyer surrounded by a bunch of moms and their kids on those nice steps outside."

Without a word, Humpty Dumpty swept his paraphernalia into his briefcase and left the room. The speed of his getaway made his jacket flap, but his hair did not move. His secretary, eyes glued to the tape recorder, removed the plug from the socket and followed in his trail.

***

As they rode the bus home, Vanessa asked for the notebook and reviewed her drawing. "I hope I didn't overstep by making that declaration about the press conference," she said in a low voice. "I've been to that little room you call an office, with the sidewalk sale furniture and a few hungry mice. But HD has no clue about that. For all he knows, you have a mighty network that will storm his office. What he knows for sure is, he's got no grounds to stand on."

Sophie laced her fingers together and stretched her arms above her head. They couldn't get a hundred people to storm an office, but they could wrangle twenty for a press conference, especially if you counted kids. "Overstep?" she said. "Are you kidding? I loved it."

Vanessa added one more drawing — an egg splattered on the ground. She closed the notebook and handed it back. "Even if nothing happens, I got a lot of joy from watching him come undone. Someday when those little hellions of mine are in school, I'd like to do that on a regular basis."

***.

On March 3, while the twins played with their new Star Wars figures — a gift for their third birthday from Sophie's kids — the doorbell rang. Sophie salvaged Jabba the Hut from under the rug as Vanessa greeted the mail carrier and signed for an envelope. "It's a certified letter from Humpty Dumpty," Vanessa said, tearing it open. She held up a check and started to laugh so loud, the other children ran in from the back of the house where they'd been watching TV. "Well, lookie here. Thirty-five U.S. dollars payable to Mrs. Vanessa Jackson!"

Sophie pumped both fists in the air.

"I'm surprised they didn't make it payable directly to Goodwill," Vanessa said. "To make sure we don't go overboard, you know: No silver. No china. No padding on the chairs." She folded the check in half and stuck it in the pocket of her flannel shirt, one that had likely belonged to her husband.

"And what did the State hasten to say?" Sophie asked.

Vanessa turned the envelope inside out. "Looks like we left them speechless."

Should Banks Care about Kids?
You Bet.

Milwaukee, June 1986

The woman across the booth from Sophie was small and sturdy, eyes the color of eggplant.

"The bank pays peanuts." Rosa Arellano's bangs didn't cover up the worry lines on her forehead. "They lure in single moms by offering health insurance. Today we got a memo saying they realized they'd been 'overly generous'" — Rosa drew swooping air quotes to indicate these were their actual words — "and could no longer underwrite this cost. We'll each have to fork over ninety dollars a month. Starting immediately. They said they were informing us on a Monday so we'd have time to 'prepare.' (More air quotes.) "Ninety dollars is almost a week's take-home pay."

In between gesturing, Rose kept stirring her coffee, even though there was no sign of cream or sugar. "I want to get the story out," she said, laying the stirrer on the saucer. "They're bat shit about avoiding bad press."

Since Sophie Reznick joined Working Women United, talking to women about standing up for themselves was her favorite part of the job. Helping them realize the risk involved was the worst part, the one that tightened her throat and sometimes caused a twitch near her eyebrow. Once she officially became WWU staff two years ago, Sophie participated in a weeklong training with a senior organizer at the national office. Some of what they discussed she'd already learned by what she called fucking up and they called on-the-job training. She'd also picked up a lot from her husband Nick's experiences. "Be honest, don't sugar coat or overpromise," the trainer said. "And be clear. The best protection is taking action as a group."

Sophie pulled a pen and a checklist from her tote bag. "Thanks for your courage, Rosa. We can help get a reporter on this — Nina Barber at the *Journal* would be terrific. Do you know her writing?"

Rosa, who looked to be younger than Sophie, maybe early thirties, gave a thumbs up. "I hardly know any reporter's name, but I do know hers. I loved that series she did on the working poor."

Outside the diner a fire truck whooshed by, sirens blaring. Sophie tightened her hold on the pen. "Great. I just want to be sure you realize she'll want to use your name. I imagine the bank won't be thrilled about that. Here's what you need to know: Wisconsin is what's called an at-will employment state. That means if you don't have a union, management can, may, and likely will fire you if they feel like it."

This was where Sophie wished she could say, "Don't worry, we have a fund to help you out," the way Nick's union back in Chicago had a strike fund that helped folks survive during the two months they were on the picket line. But WWU was a non-profit. They were lucky to make payroll for Sophie and a part-time admin.

"If they fire me, they fire me." Rosa fingered the small cross around her neck, the only accessory to her navy skirt and white blouse. "The fact is, they go through with this, I have to get another job anyway. I have four kids. Two have asthma, and all four have this thing where they like to eat every day."

Sophie realized she'd been holding her breath and exhaled. She was grateful Rosa hadn't assumed there was some law that automatically protected you for telling the truth about your employer. It clawed at her insides when people confused what should exist with what did.

With a nod, Sophie turned to her checklist. "Okay. I can call Nina Barber as soon as I get back to the office. Let's talk strategy. And then I want to hear more about your kids and how many are spitfires just like you."

Rosa smiled for the first time that afternoon. She undid the clip that pulled back her dark hair, which fell in straight lines to her shoulder.

The diner, located a couple miles away from South Milwaukee Community Bank, was nearly empty, fragrant with molé and some spice Sophie couldn't identify. Rosa had suggested it as a good place to have privacy. "It's mostly Spanish speakers who come here, and the factories nearby don't let out until five o'clock." The sun streamed through the window, lighting up Rosa's square hands and unpolished nails.

"First, let's figure out what support you have on the inside," Sophie said. "I have some ideas about what we can do outside to back you up."

As Sophie took notes, Rosa answered her questions about the number of non-management workers — about forty-five — and the number she knew personally — two-thirds of those; the number she thought were pissed off about this policy reversal — everyone; and the number she most trusted and could talk to over the next day and a half — five or six.

"Here's what I'm thinking," Sophie said. She'd been brainstorming since Rosa phoned on her lunch break to arrange this meeting. "Nina will want to do her story quickly. There's a large interfaith group we can reach out to who could mobilize some folks in a short period of time. Almost all our members work during the day, but we might be able to get a few people out. You picked a great day to get in touch, we have a board meeting already scheduled for tonight. If Nina interviews you tomorrow and the story drops on Wednesday, we should be able to have at least a dozen people show up when the bank opens, carrying posters and handing out flyers. What do you think of this slogan: 'Should Banks Care About Kids?'"

Rosa's grin lit up the space along with the sunshine. "Wow, you move fast. So your people will give the flyer to customers as they drive into the lot? I *love* that."

"We could ask them to pass it on to whoever they're going to see at the bank." Sophie ripped a blank sheet of paper from her notebook and sketched boxes for blocks of copy as she talked. "The flyer could have that question at the top and under that a really brief description of what happened. Maybe a quote from 'a teller.' Then it can say something like, 'This bank exists because of families in this community. So, of course, banks should care about kids.' We can put a couple bullets directed at the bank managers, like: 'Help staff take care of their loved ones. Reverse the decision to dock a whopping $90 a month for health insurance.'" Sophie looked up to gauge Rosa's reaction. "We wouldn't ask anyone to boycott the bank or pull their accounts, but hopefully bank officials would fear that possibility."

Rosa traced her fingers over the boxes. They discussed practical matters: the best place for the group to stand as customers drove into the parking lot, what Rosa would say to the co-workers she was alerting to the action ahead of time, the value of having clergy present "in uniform," as Rosa put it. Sophie agreed to call as soon as she got through to the reporter, and to come to Rosa's house the next evening, hopefully to meet some of her co-workers and talk specifics.

"I'd also love to meet your kids," Sophie said.

"They're going to like you," Rosa said. "I could tell you're a mom even if I hadn't seen that coloring book in your bag. Truth is, I'm no braver than anyone else. We do what we have to do for our kids."

As she gathered her things, Sophie asked Rosa how she knew to call WWU. "My friend, Soledad," Rosa said.

"She called you when she was being sexually harassed by her boss."

Sophie felt the heat rise in her chest and neck. She certainly remembered the woman. Soledad cleaned downtown office buildings and had a supervisor who would come up behind her and rub against her while she was in a hallway by herself. He harassed other cleaners as well, including a woman in her sixties. Sophie had excitedly told Soledad how to file a complaint with the EEOC, all the better if there were several of them doing it together. "Yeah, I know there's a government agency that takes complaints," Soledad said. "There's another agency that deports you if you don't have papers. We report him to the one, he reports us to the other."

Sophie was mortified that she hadn't anticipated this dilemma. She mailed out a sympathetic note along with two fact sheets: one describing what employees could do, and the other, what an employer was obligated to do, and wished she could ram the paper down that asshole's throat.

Thankfully, Soledad came up with her own plan. She and her co-workers wound up slipping the employer sheet under the supervisor's office door with a note that said, "A working women's group knows exactly what you're doing. If you don't stop, they will take action." She informed Sophie that the guy backed off.

"The ingenuity and the courage — those were all hers," Sophie told Rosa now.

"Hey, you were there for her." Rosa pushed her coffee cup to the middle of the table. "You heard her. You told her she had rights, which she did not know. You sent her the information immediately. And when they took a step, you cheered them on."

Deeply moved by this generosity, Sophie squeezed Rosa's hand. "Once we confront those bankers, I'm recruiting you to get involved with Working Women United."

Back at her desk, Sophie got hold of Nina Barber, who arranged to meet Rosa after work the next day at the WWU office. Then she bustled around getting ready for the 6:30 pm board meeting. Some members went home from work and brought children back with them. Along with snacks, WWU provided a kids' corner and a volunteer who kept them occupied. That night the kids drew colorful posters for the protest; one toddler added stickers with a gleeful "I did it" each time. Someday they hoped to afford a bigger space with a separate room for the kids.

Vanessa Jackson, who lived down the block from Sophie and had recently joined the board, knew folks at the interfaith alliance — her pastor was vice chair — and pulled the phone into a corner to contact him. Before the board left that night, he called back to say he'd lined up five clergy who each said they'd bring at least one member of their congregation. "This is not the start of a joke," Vanessa reported. "They'll have a Catholic priest, a Lutheran pastor, a Baptist minister, a rabbi and an Episcopalian bishop. He's trying to get an imam as well."

The board went through the membership list and came up with twelve people who might be able to make it to the bank on Wednesday morning. Several board members divided up those names to call. Folks suggested other groups to involve and get quotes from for a press release, which they would send out embargoed the next afternoon.

"Remember, we have to keep the action a secret, so we take them by surprise," Sophie said.

Vanessa's daughter, Keisha, who introduced herself to the other kids that night as being "seven and three-quarters," looked up from her poster board. "I won't tell anyone," she said. "I promise."

Sophie's kids were getting ready for bed when she rushed in after the meeting. Elly, hair still wet from her bath, jumped up and down and opened her mouth as wide as she could. "I lost another tooth, Mommy! Daddy made broccoli and I bit down and it just popped out! Some blood got on the broccoli and Daddy said I didn't have to eat it. But Jake had to eat his." Sophie wrapped her girl in a one-armed hug, the other arm beckoning Jake to come share highlights of the third grade field trip to the dairy. Nick leaned against the kitchen wall and winked as Sophie luxuriated in her children's voices and post-bath freshness.

After story time and lights out, Sophie filled Nick in on Rosa's situation and the plans for Wednesday. "I *so* want to nail these guys." she said as they cleaned up the dinner mess. "Any chance you can come?"

Nick picked up a blue erasable marker. "For once, the universe is on our side. The restaurant wants me to do lunch prep tomorrow, so I can cover the kid front when you go to Rosa's in the evening. And Wednesday I don't start til ten o'clock, so I can go with you to the protest. No history class 'til Thursday." He made adjustments on the big calendar they'd hung in the kitchen to track Sophie's schedule, Nick's classes at UW-Milwaukee, where he'd enrolled that January after being laid off from GE, and his hours at the Chinese restaurant. "They hired you because you're such a good cook, right?" Jake asked when Nick got the job. "More 'cause I'm a good chopper," Nick replied.

The next day in the WWU office, Nina Barber set Rosa at ease within minutes. When the reporter asked what her kids thought about their mom speaking out, Rosa reached into her handbag and drew out a photo of the four of them, three girls and a boy. "My oldest daughter and my son think it's cool," Rosa said, caressing their faces. "This one" — pointing to the youngest, who looked to be about three — "was too busy building a fort to take it all in. And my seven-year-old, she's a worrier. She just wants to know we'll be able to keep buying food and not have to move to Mexico to live with my mother."

Nina asked Sophie to put the bank's behavior in a broader context. Between calls to community groups

107

that morning, Sophie dug into the media portion of her organizer training book and spent time practicing sound bites with the communications person in the national office. "We keep hearing that women earn so little money because they lack skills and choose flexible jobs," Sophie told the reporter. "In fact, if you stay home with a sick kid, you don't get paid — where's the flexibility in that? Women earn so little money because they're paid so little money, and *that's* because their skills are undervalued and their caregiving responsibilities are unseen."

Wednesday morning, Elly bounced on her parents' bed at five forty-five to announce that the sun was already up and no rain in sight. Jake trailed her with the morning paper — Nina's article was on the front page. It featured a photo of Rosa in front of a poster in the WWU office that read, "A woman's work is never done, or appreciated, or paid what it's worth." Nick read the article out loud, making his voice louder when he came to Sophie's quote. At the next paragraph, he stopped for a moment and guffawed.

"Oh my God," he said. "Listen to what the lawyer for the bank said: 'It's time, workers realize we run this bank and we can do whatever we want.' Finally, a little truth."

Despite Jake having to hunt for his permission slip for summer arts camp and Elly dripping jam on her shirt and having to change, Sophie and Nick managed to get out of the house, drop off the kids and get to the bank by seven-thirty. This was the final week of school. For the rest of the summer, they'd have to deal with a mish-mosh of recreation programs that started too late in the morning and ended too early for most working parents. The kitchen calendar would get filled in and erased and rewritten multiple times.

Most of the arranging would fall on Sophie — she forced herself to let go of that for now. She needed to focus on Rosa and the three other tellers she'd met the previous night, all of them beside themselves about this financial blow, worried about how they would pay their bills and what would happen to Rosa, and slightly mistrustful that strangers they'd never met would show up to try to pressure management to have a change of heart.

"It makes sense," Rosa said over tea and *pan dulce*. "If the bank gets away with this, it's like a signal to other companies that they can do whatever they damn please. I don't mean that Working Women United doesn't care about us. But it's way bigger than just us." That was enough to win over her friends, an older woman from the same village in Mexico where Rosa was born, a young woman who turned out to be the first Black person hired in a non-custodial position at the bank, and a white woman whose father laid bricks for that bank building. "We look like a Benetton commercial," Rosa said when she introduced them to Sophie. "We also look like the staff who make this bank run."

After taking some time to hear from each of them, Sophie asked the best way to make sure the flyers got to management the next day. The group decided they'd get the other tellers to compile all the flyers they received in one stack, which the three of them would deliver at the end of their shift to their manager. Rosa knew someone in the loan department who she hoped would do the same. All of them expected Rosa to be sent home shortly after she arrived at work.

Sophie and Nick had arranged to get to the bank early so they could greet Rosa as she got out of her car. With a defiant smile, Rosa spun around to show off her best suit,a light blue that complemented her dark skin, and high heels that made her appear much taller than her five foot frame.

"Wow, Ms. Arellano," Sophie said. "You look like you own this place. I've heard of dressing up for an interview but never for a firing. You may just be too much for them."

The various clergy began to arrive with their own homemade signs, several with Biblical verses. Sophie's favorite was from Isaiah: "What do you mean by crushing my people, by grinding the face of the poor?" Other protesters picked up the posters the kids helped make Monday night. The Episcopalian Bishop's robe outdid the others, but all the clergy wore something that made visible who they were. By eight am, when the bank opened, nearly three dozen people were greeting cars as they pulled in; Sophie estimated at least two-thirds of the customers rolled down their window to accept a flyer. Nina Barber was there, along with camera crews from three television stations and a guy from public radio. By nine o'clock, the media was gone, Nick and several others had to go to work, but Sophie and a third of the protesters stayed on until one.

The first call from Rosa came at the end of her shift. "No pink slip, no reprimand, *nada*," she said. "The other tellers delivered the stacks of flyers customers gave them. As expected, they had to hand them to the secretary. Radio silence all around. But, oh my goodness, the rest of us? We were all lit up. Long-time customers were outraged and a lot of them said they were going to call the bank president. Some wrote personal notes at the top of the flyer or in the margins. A bunch of them put 'Yes!' or 'You bet!' after the headline."

Rosa paused for a few seconds to regain her composure. "Whatever happens, they can't take that away."

The second call came at nine-thirty the next morning, from Nina Barber. "I just got off the phone with the bank president. He told me on the record that staff would be getting a $25 a week raise. Claimed it had been in the works all along. No mention of the health insurance, but when I asked, he confirmed that the co-pay was still happening." Sophie let out a whoop and danced around the office. "I hope you know how rare this is," Nina said. "And it makes it very hard for them to fire Rosa."

"At least for now," Sophie said. She filled the reporter in on the customer responses. "We'll stay on it. Glad that you will as well."

Sophie knew Rosa couldn't call until lunch time. The other tellers who'd been in on the planning clustered around the phone with her in the break room. After passing the receiver for several rounds of cheers and thank yous, Rosa came back on the line. "I'll never forget what you said, Sophie. 'You don't always win when you stand up for yourself, but you never win if you don't.'"

For dinner that night, Nick brought home pork dumplings, shrimp toast and pineapple fried rice to celebrate the victory. He even opened a bottle of wine and filled the kids' glasses with grape juice as he toasted his wife, Rosa and the others.

"I know it's just one scratch in their armor," Sophie said. "Maybe if the lawyer hadn't been so stupid, they'd have gotten away with it. And in a way, nothing much changed for the workers. The raise will just pay for the added health care cost. Still, for those women, this was a huge win."

"Savor it," Nick said. "You all just sent a message to women throughout the city: Damn straight, every employer should care about kids." He clinked her glass with his own. "And women aren't the only ones who heard it."

Listen to the Children

Milwaukee, Wisconsin, May 1985

Sophie pulled into the driveway sun-dazzled and drowsy after Saturday afternoon "me time" at Lake Michigan. "Two hours alone with the waves and Alice Walker and I'll be fully recharged," she told Nick, who was happy to watch the Brewers game while the kids played outside. As she turned off the ignition, Sophie noticed Darlene, the upstairs neighbor, gripping the railing on her back porch.

"It's Elly," she announced before the car door even closed. "She's been hit by a car."

""That's impossible." Sophie clutched her tote bag to her chest. "Elly would never go into the street." She was about to protest again when she caught sight of Jake sitting with his action figures at the backyard picnic table.

"It's okay, Mom," he said. "It's only stitches. Dad's with her at the hospital."

On their frantic drive to the emergency room, Sophie learned that Jake had actually witnessed his younger sister dart into the street and get knocked down by a car and then ran home to get his dad. And poor Nick — she pictured him half-crazed when he heard the news, racing around the block with Jake to where Elly lay in the street.

Sophie only began to breathe normally when she saw her girl alive and awake in a cubicle in the ER. Elly gave a feeble wave and a teary smile. What looked like a broken arm turned out to be a splint for an IV. The doctor turned to address Sophie as well as Jake, who was hanging onto the back of the gurney.

"You've got yourselves a tough cookie," the doctor said. "Nothing broken, mild concussion and some bruises, a few stitches back there where she hit her head." Sophie glanced at some of Elly's dark curls strewn on the floor.

The doctor looked like a resident, probably a decade younger than Sophie and Nick. "You're lucky," he said. "Apparently the driver was going slow and slammed on the brakes. We'll keep Elly overnight just to be safe." He showed them the neck brace he'd ordered as a precaution and called for a transportation aide.

The good news and kind voice opened the flood-gates. Sophie, Nick and Jake fell into each other and burst into tears. "I'm so sorry I wasn't there," Nick said, his mouth pressed against Sophie's ear. Despite the air conditioning, his arms and face were lined with sweat.

"Oh, god, Nicky. At least you were home. I was off gallivanting at the lake."

The doctor's reminder that children under ten weren't allowed as visitors spurred them to action. Sophie was eager to whisk their boy away from the smell of disinfectant and the clang of monitors. They decided Sophie would stay overnight, Nick would take her place early Sunday. For now, he'd take Jake for a bite and bring back supplies for Sophie and a surprise for Elly.

Shortly after they got settled in the hospital room, Darlene stopped in with egg salad sandwiches and a beanie baby named Paddy O'Lucky.

"Why does everyone say I'm lucky?" Elly wailed. "This is the worst thing that's ever happened to me!" Her misery increased as various interns came by every hour to shine a flashlight in her eyes. She wouldn't let Sophie leave her side except to pee, and even then Elly demanded the bathroom door stay open.

Around midnight, Elly pleaded with her mother to remove the neck brace.

"That's what will get you out of here tomorrow, sweetheart." Sophie twisted in the chair clutching an afghan Nick had dropped off. "I know it's uncomfortable but it's just for a few more hours."

Elly, who looked tiny in the hospital bed, let out a long howl. "Nobody loves me!" Sophie knelt by the bedside, choking back laughter even as the tears streamed down her face.

On her way out the next morning, Sophie spotted at least three kids alone in their rooms. Her heart seized. She wanted to pop in to each one and offer comfort, but Jake was waiting for her down in the hospital lobby.She found him sitting still in a big chair, his fair hair shorn for the summer, Luke Skywalker clutched in his hand.

"Elly's doing good," Sophie told him, kneeling down to fold him in a hug. "Dad's up there drawing silly pictures to make her smile."

Jake leaned his head back and looked her in the eyes. "You know, Mom, if Elly'd died, I'd have slept on her grave every night for a year."

Sophie wondered where all that trauma lived in a kid not yet eight years old.

They kept Elly home from child care that week. "I wish I could be the one to stay with her," Nick said. But there was no discussion. The Visa bill was overdue, they couldn't afford to lose even one day of Nick's wages. While Working Women United might not pay much, flexibility was part of the organization's DNA.

***

In the weeks that followed, Elly's injuries healed well, but she began having nightmares and clinging to Nick. He didn't see anything out of the ordinary, even when Elly pitched a fit one Saturday when he was about to go fishing up north with a friend. "Take me with you!" she cried, lunging to grab his knees. Nick wound up cancelling his plans. He agreed with Sophie that Elly should see

115

a therapist, but pooh-poohed the notion that her attachment to him was anything unusual.

Sophie ping-ponged from anxiety to resentment to rage. She and Nick embarked on the worst conflict in their eleven years as a couple.

Sophie waited for the kids to fall asleep before having heated conversations with Nick, demanding they both whisper. It was the same argument every time — they could have taped their remarks and hit "play." Once Sophie even wrote out the script:

Nick: "All kids go through periods where they get a little clingy with one parent or the other. She just turned five. This is nothing to worry about."

Sophie: "Thanks for the wisdom, Dr. Spock. I can't believe you don't get this is all about gender. Elly sees you as the competent man who can keep her safe. I'm just an accessory. She doesn't want to be alone with me because she's scared and she doesn't trust I can keep her out of danger."

Nick: "Babe, I really think you're overreacting."

Sophie: "Don't fucking patronize me! This is the problem when you get so much kudos for being an 'evolved man.' You think you don't have anything to learn."

Nick: "So what am I supposed to do, act all weak and helpless?"

Sophie: "How about don't undermine me? When she comes and asks you for soda, check whether I've just told her no. Tune in."

Nick: "Why do you have to blame Elly's fears on me?"

Sophie: "Why do you have to keep missing the point?"

It was Nick who finally broke the logjam. "Remember those handouts you brought home from the conflict resolution training WWU did?" He cupped her face in his hands. "I really liked those. Can we pretend we're Working Women United?"

That weekend Vanessa Jackson, who lived down the block and was the new board chair at WWU, invited

Jake and Elly over for what her family called "burgers and Blockbuster." Nick and Sophie used the time to create their own little conflict resolution retreat. They pledged to listen to each other and summarize what they'd heard, no interruptions, no accusations or labeling. Over the next couple hours, each slipped up on numerous occasions: "Male posturing is not a label, it's a fact!" "Your words may have been all right but your *tone* was accusatory!" "A correction is not an interruption!" Still, by the end of the evening, they had a breakthrough.

"I hear your frustration at being blamed for Elly's feelings," Sophie said. "I really don't want to make you feel that way."

Nick wrote his insights on a large piece of paper. "I hear I can do some things differently, and I will — like not automatically get in the driver's seat, or put up the tents when we go camping."

"You left one off: 'I will not give orders to you and the kids.'"

Nick grabbed a red magic marker and added that pledge, underlining the word "not."

They eyed each other across the placemats. "What's the protocol for post-resolution interaction?" Nick asked, creeping over to her side of the table.

When they walked over to pick up their children, Vanessa was standing at the screen door with a huge grin on her face. "Your shoulders and your hips tell me all I need to know," she said. "Good job."

Madison, Wisconsin, February 1988

Sophie was haunted by the faces of those kids alone in their hospital rooms. "There oughta be a law," Vanessa said when the board discussed it. "So let's figure out how to win one." WWU formed a coalition called Keep Families First. After dozens of rallies and hearings, stacks of petitions, coordinated lobby visits and multiple debates, a bipartisan majority of the legislature passed the Wisconsin Family and Medical Leave Act in early 1988.

Sophie was cheering the news over the radio when a coalition partner in Madison called with the bad news.

"The governor won't sign it," she said. "He insists they send him a different bill, just for maternity leave, no longer than thirty days." Nothing for dads. No leave to care for other family members. No time to heal from a heart attack or stroke. Sophie and the others were furious and held an emergency coalition call.

"Only someone with a wife at home and a full-time housekeeper thinks you oughta hop up after delivery and run back to work," Sophie said.

"Or says babies are the only ones who need care." Vanessa clutched her elbows as she spoke. A year earlier she'd lost a job for missing too much time taking her dad to chemo and helping him navigate the aftermath when he could barely walk or keep anything down. She took a series of temp jobs, got the kids on Medicaid for their health care and relied on prayers for her own. "Tell me we're not giving up."

Shouts of "Hell no!" and "No fucking way!" filled the phone line.

Sophie, hands free thanks to the speaker phone, had been constructing a long chain of colored paper clips, her office stress reducer. "If the governor won't listen to us, maybe he'll listen to children," she said, twisting two paper clips until they were jagged pieces in her lap. "They know what it means to need a parent's cool hand. They see what happens when cancer lays waste to a grandparent." Vanessa's middle child, Keisha, was particularly distraught over her granddad's illness and the outrage of her mother's firing.

The coalition needed kids who had a compelling story and were able to be in Madison on a given day. They quickly found volunteers from the children of WWU members and other coalition partners and asked for a meeting with the governor.

As soon as Elly got wind of it, she wanted in.

By then their adventurous girl had made a lot of progress, and so had Nick and Sophie. Still, they decided to check with the therapist who worked with Elly after the accident. Dr. Robertson gave them her blessing. "What Elly learned in those six weeks with me was that most situations are safe as long as you know the right person to call on or the right thing to do, like staying out of the street or looking both ways," she said. "This adds another dimension. People often need public policies that protect them, and your little girl can help make that happen."Agency. Power building. Sophie was delighted to expand this concept to children, especially a kid like Elly, who'd felt so powerless after the accident.

She could have prepared her testimony at home, but Elly insisted on joining the other children from Milwaukee at the Working Women United office, where they chomped on microwave popcorn and took turns telling their stories as Sophie and a board member typed them up. "It'll be all your own words," Sophie told them. "We'll just edit a little for length."

The governor, citing a schedule conflict, arranged for his secretary of Employment Relations to meet with them. On the ride to Madison, the Milwaukee kids speculated what this guy would look like. They all agreed he'd be white. "Aren't they all?" Keisha asked. Elly was sure he'd have crossed eyes and a shiny head.

In fact, he was tall with a full head of hair and eyes perfectly aligned, fixed on each child as they read their neatly typed words. Nine children in all took their seats around the polished conference table, Elly was the youngest. Also the smallest.

First to speak was Cecilia, a teenager cradling her baby sister as she shared their mother's story of needing welfare because her boss refused to hold her job for more than a week after she gave birth. "I volunteered to tell my mom's story today because I'll be the first in my family to go to college," Cecilia said as her little sister drooled merrily. "I've already been accepted at Howard University on a full scholarship. I don't want to graduate and get a good job and then lose it because I do what most human beings do at some point, have a family."

Next up was Willy, a scrawny redhead from Sauk City who'd been adopted for the first time at the age of twelve. He told the secretary how much he loved having family. "But it's been hard to get to know my new brothers and sister," Willy said. "My mom has to put us to bed right after supper so she can leave for work. The adoption agency said she had to be home during the day, but her job said she couldn't take off."

Willy had been a last-minute addition. Sophie tried to catch his eye and give him a thumbs up, but he was too nervous to lift his eyes from the paper.

Several kids spoke about their parents needing time to care for another sibling—a sister with a developmental disability, a brother with sickle cell, a toddler with a heart condition. Vanessa's daughter, Keisha, was one of two whose beloved grandparent had died: "It was hard enough for us to lose my grandad. Why did my momma have to lose her job, too?"

Those stories had been tough to hear. The secretary, who'd started with his arms folded, let his hands hang by his side. Even harder to listen to were the kids who'd needed care themselves.

Unlike the other children, Elly stood to speak, chin up, curls sliding out from behind her ears. Only her head and shoulders appeared over the table. She remained matter-of-fact describing the accident itself. "It was my fault," she acknowledged, saving her emotion for the two days spent in the hospital, how strange and scary it all was.

"If one of my parents hadn't been there every single second, I don't know what I would have done," she said. "And I just want to ask, Mr. Governor, how would you feel if your kid was in a hospital bed and you couldn't be there?"

Sophie, seated in the corner of the front row so she could see most of the kids' faces, pulled out the kleenex in her purse. She swallowed the images from that day and flashed a big smile at Elly, who nodded but held her lips tight.

Last to go was Zachary, whose mother was active in the interfaith group. Like Elly, Zachary had heard his mom talking about this event and asked to be part of it. He was big for a nine-year-old. Sophie had a hard time imagining him at the age of five, bony and bald in a hospital bed, when he was receiving treatments for stomach cancer. Zachary also stood to read his statement.

"Each time I had a treatment, I needed both my parents there, one to hold me and the other to tell me a story," Zachary said. "There was no way I could have taken those shots otherwise." He lowered his paper and held his hands six inches apart: "That's how big the needle was. But the kid in the next bed had nobody there when he had to go through whatever they did to him. His parents just came at night, one at a time. Back then I didn't understand why. But now I get it. They'd have lost their jobs and their insurance if they missed work."

Zachary paused to look the secretary in the eye and went off script. "I don't remember that kid's name," he said. "But I do remember that he loved the Supremes, especially the song, 'Stop in the Name of Love.' It seems to me that's what we need to do with this law, just stop treating people this way."

The secretary remained standing throughout the presentations. At the end he was smiling but his eyes were also moist as he thanked each of the kids by name, referring to a list Sophie had typed up. "I have to tell you, we're so used to dealing with lobbyists, we forget about the people who are actually impacted by the laws that we pass. So, thank you all."

Sophie couldn't believe the guy openly acknowledged how beholden he was to lobbyists, just as he clearly hadn't noticed her taking down every word he said.

"Does anyone have a question?" the secretary asked, although his body was already beginning to turn toward the door. Much to Sophie's surprise, Elly's arm flew up in the air.

"I do," she said, rising again to her feet and looking up at him. "I just want to know, why wouldn't the governor sign the law that passed?"

This time the secretary did laugh. "Well, Elly, I promise you, he will sign some version of that bill."

The coalition had worked hard to get this meeting and make it go well. At best they'd hoped to get some media attention and maybe some acknowledgement that the governor would consider their request. Never did Sophie let herself hope for an actual win. This statement by the secretary was real news — they needed to run with it.

She leaned over to Vanessa, who managed to be there by trading shifts at the call center where she'd recently been hired. "Senator Plewa said we could use his office," Sophie said. "I'm going to type up a press release with the announcement: 'Secretary of Employment Relations promises children the governor will sign some version of the Wisconsin Family and Medical Leave Act.'"

Vanessa nodded her agreement, short locs bouncing. "Great. I'll round up the kids and get everyone down to the press conference. I've got the snack packs. Too bad we don't have flowers, those kids nailed it."

Senator Plewa had arranged for them to gather in a large, open room with a stage. When Sophie arrived, she noted with joy at least five television cameras and several members of the press corps, along with dozens of people from their coalition partner groups. "Sign-in sheets show fourteen Assembly and ten Senate staff," Vanessa whispered as Sophie went backstage. "Looks like several of their bosses are here as well."

The kids walked onto the stage in an orderly line. A chuckle went through the audience as each child solemnly took their place on one of the red circles Vanessa had laid down. Senator Plewa, a devout Catholic and a Democrat who'd gotten several Republican colleagues to vote in support of the bill, strode to the center of the stage to welcome everyone.

"I've been involved with a lot of legislation," he said. "I can't think of any that touches families more than this one. And never in my thirty-some years in the legislature have I seen children step up like this." He led the audience in a long round of applause.

The kids spoke in the same order they used earlier, each walking to the mike at the front circle to make their statements. When it was Elly's turn, she held her paper with her arms straight out in front of her and swayed slightly back and forth until she came to her direct "and-how-would-you-feel" question for the governor. For that, she stood completely still.

Sophie watched people tear up as Keisha spoke. She was the only one who didn't read her statement.

"My grandaddy got cancer," she said, long limbs taut with emotion. "He needed care and no way was my momma gonna leave him by himself. Her boss should have said, 'What do you need?' Instead, he said, 'You're fired.'" Keisha looked out at the audience. "Please help us stop this."

"There's no way that child is only nine," Sophie whispered to Vanessa.

The tears continued as Zachary gave the final testimony. Sophie willed him to add his impromptu comment about the Supremes, but he stuck to his written statement. Like most of the kids, he was a little taken aback by the number of people in the room and all the flashbulbs.

Senator Plewa paused to shake each child's hand as the audience applauded wildly. "One more thing," he said. "I have a statement to read from the Keep Families First Coalition." As he shared Sophie's release about the secretary's pledge, the room filled with shouts of jubilation. Zachary's mother had snuck out to buy red roses, which she held up to the senator. He handed one to each child.

The kids were giddy on the drive back to Milwaukee, the car fragrant with roses and chocolate milk.

"You did it!" Sophie told them. "You're making history!"

Elly couldn't wait for Nick to come home from his final class so she could fill him in. She flew into her father's arms as soon as he entered the back hall. "We won it, Daddy! The kids did! Everyone said so!"

"Wow, Elly, I'm so proud of you!" Nick embraced her and swept her into the kitchen, where Sophie was boiling pierogi — Elly's favorite. "I just hate that Jake and I couldn't be there." Jake had rehearsal for a school play, Nick had a chemistry midterm. He begged his professor to let him take it early or do a make-up, but no go. This was the same guy who said on day one, "If it's been twenty years since you took high school chemistry, you'll never get an A in this class." Whoever wrote those brochures encouraging laid-off workers to go to college had forgotten to talk to the faculty.

Before Nick unbuttoned his coat, he turned off the stove and eased Sophie over to the table, nuzzling her neck and pulling Elly on his lap. "My amazing ladies. Tell me everything."

As Elly speed-talked her way through a remarkable level of detail, Sophie squeezed Nick's hand and thanked the universe that the two of them had gotten back in sync.

The day after the meeting with the secretary, the Milwaukee paper published an article on page three with the headline, "Children Lobbyists Win Lawmakers' Hearts." Elly was one of the kids quoted.

Another reporter wrote a personal account in the Madison paper detailing her visit to the governor's office after the press conference. "I marched in there with a face full of tears," she wrote. "'Did you hear those stories?' I demanded of his staff. Everyone nodded. 'Well, then, are you going to listen to the children?'"

Nick helped Elly cut out the articles and put them in a frame on her dresser. Jake promised to press the rose petals and arranged them on a special plate next to the frame.

***

In mid-March, the WWU board met on a Saturday afternoon to evaluate the campaign. Bowls of nuts and sliced apples surrounded plates of Sophie's brownies at either end of the big table, with Vanessa's signature rum cake in the center. "Until we finish, all you can do is sniff it," Vanessa ordered. "We need sober minds."

Everyone's list started with the kids: "gutsy," "powerful," "unstoppable." They also praised how the coalition stayed on message and demanded the leave be gender-neutral and include family care. And they hailed Sophie's quick action to turn the secretary's remarks into a press release.

On the other hand, they couldn't get around the fact that the bill itself was really weak. For starters, it was too little time — only six weeks for bonding with a new child, two weeks to care for your own health or a family member.

"Cause, you know, cancer treatment just takes a minute," Vanessa said, "and who needs to breastfeed?"

Of the twelve board members, three would not be covered because they worked for a company with fewer than fifty workers. According to this law, siblings and grandparents weren't family, that applied only to kids, parents and married spouses. Cecilia's mother Faithe said it best: "My girlfriend and I would gladly say 'I do' if the government would just stop saying, 'No, you don't.'"

In big letters, someone added the word "UNPAID," with an asterisk, then linked it to an item in the plus column: People who had accrued any paid time could use that during their leave — *their* choice, not the employer's. This wouldn't mean much for people who had few if any paid days off, but it would make a real difference for those who did. Most of Nick's jobs over the years offered some sick time, but only if a doctor verified that you yourself were ill.

When they finished the lists, Sophie held up a newsletter from NYU featuring an article by a feminist academic who dismissed the bill as rubbish. "This means nothing for most working women," the professor said. "Those who fought for it sold out."

As Sophie passed the clip around among the board members, Vanessa pored over the woman's photo. She was wearing dangling turquoise earrings and a rope of silver and turquoise around her neck. "I lay you odds this woman has never worked side by side with anyone or done any organizing," Vanessa said. "Certainly not with the native women whose jewelry she's all wrapped up in."

Their board had discussed this dilemma many times: How do you know when to compromise? On the one hand, the bill fell way short. On the other, workers like Faithe and Vanessa and the parents of the kid in the bed next to Zachary's at least would keep a job and health insurance thanks to their campaign.

Sophie stopped making her paper clip chain, today all of them red. "Nick and I had a long talk about this once with a guy who'd been organizing for decades in Chicago's Black community. He said it depends on two things: how much power you have, and whether or not the movement goes home. 'If you're getting close,' he told us, 'hold out for what you need. But if you've done all you can for now, ask yourselves: Will we stay connected? Will we keep building power? If so, take the smaller step, but only if it goes in the right direction. Otherwise, this is all you'll get for decades and the suckers in charge will say they delivered.'"

Vanessa got to her feet: "Well, I'm not going anywhere. Here's to building the power it'll take to win the society we deserve — in the name of my father." One by one the others stood and made the same pledge, each on behalf of someone they loved and needed to care for.

Sophie smiled through her tears as she sliced into the rum cake.

***

A month later, Sophie took Elly to the bill-signing ceremony. The Keep Families First Coalition held a press conference beforehand where Sophie and several others spoke, welcoming the new law but also recognizing its limitations. A reporter asked, "What do you say to your opponents who claim this is just a toe in the door, what you really want is fully paid leave?"

Someone passed the mic to Sophie. "I say the truth: We'll keep organizing until no one loses their job or their income because they were there for the ones they love."

At the signing, the governor pointed to Elly and acknowledged the role of the children in getting him to approve this bill. He held out one of the pens he'd just used for the signing. Elly, standing with one leg hooked over the other, cocked her head at Sophie with a look that said, "I know he's a bad guy, but I really want that pen." Sophie grinned and gave her a nod.

When they got home, Elly laid the pen gently on the rose petals and moved the plate a little closer to the framed newspaper clips.

The Stand-Up

Milwaukee, December 3, 1991

Emma hovered by the coat closet, slowly peeling off her parka while she watched Marisol speed walk the aisles of the call center with coupons for an entree at Sanchez Brothers restaurant. Emma admired her friend's boldness: Despite the subversive nature of her mission, Marisol had worn her most conspicuous blouse, the one her mother sent from Mexico, a pulsating red with bright blue embroidery. Her face was beaming.

"Here's an early Christmas present," Emma heard her say to someone at a nearby work station. Behind each coupon in Marisol's right hand was the brief note Vanessa had typed and copied and cut into skinny strips at a local women's group: "At 8:30 stand in place for sixty seconds. Keep working as always. Today CSA workers are standing up." The coupons in Marisol's left hand had no note attached. These she saved for the cubicles they'd singled out — Doris Litzko and two dozen others they either didn't trust or didn't know well enough. So skillfully did Marisol handle the distribution, even Emma couldn't tell which hand was depositing the paper at each stop. Forget lingerie sales — this woman's next gig should be running a shell game.

Emma watched those hands weave through the air for hours the night they planned the stand-up. Two weeks before Thanksgiving, they'd been having dinner at Vanessa's, venting over the latest outrage — Emma's discovery that management could listen in through their headsets even if they weren't handling a call — when

129

Vanessa's sister walked in and wanted to know what they were moaning about.

"Sounds like an electronic sweatshop," she said, after hearing the blow-by-blow of how managers timed and tracked and listened in on every call, imposing quotas on how many transactions they completed each hour. "I thought CSA stood for 'Central States Airlines,' not "Central States Automatons.' Are you chained to your desks? Don't ya'll ever get to stand up?"

"Oh, my God!" Vanessa pushed herself up with such force, her chair nearly toppled over. "You're right, we never stand up in any sense of the word." She shook her head. "Look at me, on the board of a women's group urging sisters to believe in themselves, and I bought this 'you-can't-fight-the-power ' bullshit about my own workplace. Even if it's just symbolic, we gotta find a way to say, 'Enough.'"

It didn't take long for Vanessa to come up with the idea of the stand-up. "We won't be breaking any rules. Everyone will still be working. It's just that, for one minute, we'll be doing it standing up."

Emma glanced at her friend Annie. Neither of them had ever done anything like this before. She felt like the big sisters were about to cut school and were letting the little sisters tag along. "Count me in," Emma said. She couldn't wait to tell her grandmother, who was the whole reason Emma and Vanessa were friends. Grandma attended the same church as Vanessa and asked her to look out for Emma when she started at CSA. "They know righteousness," her grandma would say when friends asked why a Greek immigrant went to a Black church. "And they know how to sing."

"Count me in, too!" Annie uttered the words as she rushed to gather her things. "I hate that I can't stay to help."

Emma hated what waited for Annie at home; her husband kept her on a short leash. They each hugged

130

her and promised to fill her in the next day. Then Emma, Vanessa and Marisol buckled down to figure out the mechanics of the stand-up, especially how to spread the word to their co-workers. Despite their objections, Marisol insisted on taking all the risk.

"Look, why don't you just accept it?" Marisol told them finally. "I'm gone. I'm outta there. At most I'm staying until after Christmas and then I'm opening my lingerie business. They fire me before Thanksgiving, what do I care, the nieces and nephews find a little less under the tree. You know we'll get to more people this way. If a bunch of us try to distribute notes, Doris is gonna notice and wonder why she's not getting one and that'll blow everything. Plus, coupons for my brothers' restaurant are the perfect cover. It's brilliant and you know it."

Emma felt a pang of guilt, but she knew Marisol was right. Days at CSA wouldn't be the same without this badass woman.

Finally, Vanessa came up with a compromise. "What if we let you do it, but we wait until the first week of December? That way it won't be so long before the holidays, if Henderson does go after you." They'd all agreed.

Now, as she shut the coat closet and eyed Marisol in action, Emma worried that they'd been wrong to let her sacrifice herself. Getting to work early seemed like a small gesture of support. If one of the supervisors came on the floor, Emma would try to head them off long enough for her friend to get back to her seat.

But the ruse seemed to be working. The plan included Marisol dropping off coupons for the managers before she began her speed rounds on the floor. By the time Emma sat at her work station at 7:59, a Sanchez Brothers coupon was waiting for her, the little note nestled beneath it. Scooping it into her pocket, Emma plugged in her headset, winked at Annie, who shared the work station, and began the countdown.

8:00: "Central States Airlines. How may I help you?" Emma feels as if she's waiting for the English teacher to hand back a test. That was her best subject in high school. But there's always a chance she didn't do as well as expected. Apprehension edges out excitement.

8:03: As she locates a six a.m. flight from Houston to Minneapolis, Emma's stomach lurches slightly. She's terrified of calling attention to herself, breathing too loudly or making a noise that would give them away.

8:07: Hyper-alert, her ears pick up fragments of other agents' conversations: "That flight is completely booked." "I'm sorry, but you do have to pay full fare for children." "Three o'clock is the last plane leaving Seattle unless you want to take a red-eye." She pictures the front of the plane as a giant eye red from crying.

8:11: The caller wants to know when his wife's flight will arrive but isn't sure what her flight number is or even what airline she's on. Emma notices that third shift has tacked a new cartoon at the top of the partition. Timmy, flailing his arms in the water, yells to Lassie on the shore: "Get help, Lassie!" In the next panel, Lassie lies on a psychiatrist's couch.

8:15: Behind the partition on her left, a chair creaks. As she searches for weekend flights from Omaha to Fargo, Emma imagines the woman behind her trying to re-position her generous body in that child-sized seat.

8:18: The sound of rubber soles marching straight to her chair restarts the motion in Emma's stomach. She whirls around expecting to be face-to-face with Mr. Henderson, only to spot him near his office all the way across the room. Emma turns back to her screen and books the early morning flight to North Dakota. With one hand she reaches for a Kleenex to wipe the sweat from her lip.

8:21: The caller is an older woman going to visit her sister in St. Louis. She's trying to tell Emma about her sister's health. "Can you believe they put a catheter in her and she never asked a single question?" the woman is saying. "She won't see the doctor. I've got to go there right away."

Emma clenches her jaw. *I have my own problems, lady,* she wants to tell her. *Try working for Big Brother for minimum pay and maximum pain. They even track 'unmanned time' in the bathroom, and ding us if we take too long. We're all gonna need catheters.*

Then she thinks of her grandmother, face pinched with worry, talking just like this to some stranger in a store. Emma cringes at the memory of a sharp-tongued clerk complaining about old people wasting her time. Resentment drops like a cat's shed fur. "I'm so sorry I had to rush you," she mumbles into the phone. "Good luck with your sister."

As she disconnects the call, Emma feels her body return to normal. No one is going to turn her into a robot, whatever the consequences. Her grandma had been tickled pink about their plan. "You need this job," she told Emma, who hardly needed the reminder; Dean and his folks were struggling to keep their stationery shop from going under. "But you need your dignity more." Eight minutes and counting.

8:27: Emma picks up a new call. *This is the person I'll be talking to when we stand up,* she tells herself. She'll always remember the date: December 3, 1991. As a child, every year on her birthday she signed her name and the date on the wallpaper just below her bed frame, secret markings for some child who would live in the house decades later. When Emma turned twelve, her mother took the wallpaper off the bedroom walls as a surprise and painted the room a light lilac. Emma would have to make her mark some other way.

8:30: Besides Annie, four others knew about the plan; they would all stand when the digital wall clock moved to 8:30 am. Those folks would try to get their seatmates to stand at the same time and hope others who read the note would follow suit. Emma feels herself rise, her keyboard snug in her left arm while the fingers on her right hand tap the appropriate keys.

"What time do you want to return on Sunday?"

Annie is a microsecond behind her, standing as erect as she can with her eyes on the monitor. Once again Emma hears the chair behind her; this time the noise sounds more like a squeak of surprise.

"Yes, we have room on that flight."

Emma glances quickly to her right. Four more cubicles in that direction and it seems everyone is standing. With her headset on she can't turn all the way but she manages to glance behind to the right. Most people are up, like some glorious version of the Pledge of Allegiance.

"Are you the only passenger?"

There seems to be slightly fewer participants to the left. She'll have to wait for lunch to talk to Darnell, whose station in the back gives him the best opportunity for a count. But it doesn't matter — even if only a third join in, they're on their feet.

"How's seat 10C, ma'am, on the aisle?"

Sixty seconds. That's all the time they were up. Emma borrowed Max's stopwatch that morning in order to have a second-hand. "You just push this button, Mom, right here," he told her. "Try it yourself. It's really simple." Sammy, smelling of maple syrup from the good-luck pancakes Dean made, moved closer to give his advice: "If Mr. Henderson walks by, just pretend you had to stretch."

"Nah, Mom, just stand there," Max said with the certitude of a monk in the body of an eight-year-old. "You're not breaking any rules."

Sixty seconds and then they sat back down. They'd continued their work the same as always, but nothing would ever be the same again. They knew what it felt like to stand up for themselves.

***

"What's next?" Mr. Henderson demanded. "Are we looking at a walkout? A general strike?" He glared at each of his managers.

"Really, Mr. Henderson, there's no cause for alarm." His deputy, Allyson Bartlett, referred to some notes in her hand. "All they did was stand up. No one stopped working. Nearly half the group stayed seated."

"Which means more than half the group participated!" Henderson hadn't recovered from the sight of all those handheld keyboards when Libbie summoned him back into the big room. She'd forgotten to use the code he developed for the supervisors in case of a terrorist attack or out-of-control husband. They were supposed to say, "Code Red." Libbie had simply dialed his extension and sputtered, "Better get back out here. Fast." He'd peeked out from behind his door, expecting to see someone with a gun drawn. Instead, his eyes fastened on all those keyboards, gun-level.

Now, standing at the head of the table in his office, he focused one by one on the managers, none of whom dared to sit down. Allyson, as usual, was trying to keep everyone calm, part of the foo-foo leadership crap she studied in her MBA program. Next to her, Libbie looked as if she'd been confined in a room crawling with roaches. Hazel, who'd been a supervisor for less than a year, kept her eyes on her hands, which were fastened on the back of the chair.

"This happened on my watch and it's going to stop on my watch, do you hear me?" Henderson scanned their faces. "I want to know who's behind it and I want them fired, NOW. Then I want to know why we didn't have the slightest idea someone was working to subvert Central States Airlines and I want mechanisms in place to ensure nothing like this ever happens again. Do you read me?"

"You bet, sir." Libbie had the words ready before the question was asked. "As senior supervisor, I know exactly where to start." Henderson noticed her lipstick was marred by teeth marks on both the upper and lower lips.

Allyson smoothed her notebook page, as if orderliness would solve their problems. "With all due respect, sir, I think that would be an overreaction. First of all, this was a meaningless action. It didn't slow down the work at all. If it was designed as a show of strength, it fell far short. It's getting close to the holidays. I think some of the employees just staged a harmless prank. To respond as if it were a serious and organized effort would give the thing much more credibility than it deserves. Surely it would backfire."

He watched Libbie bite off more of her lipstick. "Wake up, missy," Libbie said. "Some of us have been in this business since before you were born. What we do now is critical. They start with something like this to test us. If we let them get away with it, they'll move on to something bigger to gum up the works. At lunchtime they'll be toasting each other in the cafeteria, calculating how many days 'til the next step. They won't stop 'til they get rid of the call quotas and the monitoring and who knows what else."

Henderson wanted to hear more before jumping in. "They have no next step," Allyson said. "I agree that our reaction now is critical. If we come on strong, we'll drive them ito the hands of someone who does have a next step — a union or some community group. The newspaper will get wind of it. Nothing hurts more than bad press."

He was glad to see Libbie wasn't buying it. "Let's look at the facts," she said, pulling a Sanchez Brothers coupon from her jacket pocket. "Right after that little performance, Doris Litzko stopped by to show me one of these coupons that had been left on her desk. Marisol Fuentes passed them out to us as well. It's her family's place. That must be how the word got out about when to stand up. Doris didn't have a note left with her coupon, but I bet you dollars to donuts the others did. Clearly Fuentes was behind this. She's the one who mouthed off when we

136

introduced the new monitoring system. Some of you may be asleep at the wheel, but I know exactly who her friends are — that Vanessa Jackson, for one, and Darnell Chaney. One of them is probably the mastermind. You know how sneaky they can be."

Hazel looked up from her hands. She tried to pass as management material, dressed conservative, never talked ghetto. Henderson had promoted her after Allyson pressed him to hire a Black supervisor in the Milwaukee office. But he was no dummy; Hazel was always prickly about race. "And who would 'they' be, Libbie?" she asked.

"Oh, come off it, Hazel, you know what I mean. I'm not talking about you."

Henderson cleared his throat. "Let's get back to the issue at hand. I think Libbie has made a convincing case about the Fuentes woman. Who was in the glass cage when this thing started?"

Hazel looked directly at him. "I was, Mr. Henderson." Turned out she'd been the only one monitoring the computers at the time. Just five minutes earlier, Libbie had gone into Allyson's office to review the weekend schedule. Henderson, who liked to check the computers personally from time to time, had been listening to the latest statistical report. His plan was working: Their call volume was up. The Milwaukee office was close to the number two slot company-wide. They'd survive any downsizing.

"Well, Hazel, you're the key person then. What did you see? Who stood up first?"

"Actually, I didn't see anything." Hazel kept her gaze on Mr. Henderson. "I was watching the computers, not the floor. I didn't notice that people were standing up until Libbie ran in."

"Doris Litzko rang me in Allyson's office," Libbie said. "She's one of our most loyal employees. Otherwise we might have missed the whole thing."

"She did exactly what that bunch wanted her to do." Henderson couldn't get over his team's naïveté. "They wouldn't have had the desired effect if only one of the managers caught the show." He paused and pulled at his shirt cuffs until they were perfectly lined up on his wrists. "Are you sure you don't recall who stood up first, Hazel?"

Hazel never withdrew her eyes. "Quite sure, Mr. Henderson."

"Please, sir," Allyson interrupted, "let's move very cautiously on any disciplinary action. What would the charge be? We can't say the action disrupted the work. I checked the monitor. The calls for that half hour are as high or higher than normal. There's nothing in the personnel handbook that explicitly prohibits employees from standing up while they do their work. As you know, our public image is very important. We don't want to give the media an excuse to write something negative about us — not when competition is so fierce for holiday travel."

Henderson bowed his head for a moment. The room was totally quiet. "Allyson has a point," he said. "We will not discharge anyone specifically for involvement in today's charade. What we will do is stay on the alert for any infraction of the rules. I want a list on my desk by the end of today of everyone known to associate with Marisol Fuentes. Then I want the personnel files of each of those individuals. We will carefully inspect those files and lay the groundwork for disciplinary action wherever warranted. We will administer that discipline rigorously and by the book. Is that clear?"

Libbie fastened the top button on her dress, as if to hold in her disappointment over not being able to fire the Fuentes woman on the spot. Hazel returned her gaze to the back of her hands. Allyson kept her face expressionless. Quickly they filed out of the room.

Alone in his office, Donald Henderson sank into his chair. He was back at the Boundary Waters, the summer of his tenth year. He and his father had gone on a camping trip together, just the two of them, so that young Donald could learn to survive in the wilderness on his own. His mission was to make it back to the campsite within twenty-four hours of being left on what he'd thought of as a steep hill with a compass, a canteen and a packet of K-rations. When his father found him a day later than planned, he was barely a mile from his starting place, his face covered with scratches and mosquito bites, and most shamefully, tears.

He remembered his father's sole comment: "On your feet, Donald." He'd gotten up then, and by God, he'd get up again now. He was not about to let a ragtag group of feminazis turn his office into the one corporate decided to axe.

***

For once, Darnell was already seated when Emma got to the lunch table. He called her and Annie the pixie twins; Annie was tiny and fair and Emma, not much taller, wore her sandy hair in a pixie cut. "Okay, ladies," he said, hands clasped across his broad chest, "here's the official estimate: According to our expert counters, Mrs. Sadie Gillick in the west, Ms. Vanessa Jackson in the east and myself in the south, about eighty of these suckers actually stood up at eight-thirty. I know for a fact that at least ten of them had to scratch their butts. Four thought we were having a prayer vigil, and Benny Beinhofer, who started drinking at five forty-five this morning, was ready to give a toast. Yet and still, a lot better than I expected from this sorry-ass bunch."

"It's a good thing you're better at countin' than you are at makin' predictions, Mr. Chaney." Sadie poked the air with her fork; her Irish lilt broke through only when she was really excited or really mad. She turned to Emma. "He thought it would just be the eight of us and a few stragglers here and there. Wouldn't you love to be a fly on the wall in Henderson's office right now? I can just

139

picture him choking on his liverwurst sandwich. You know he brings one every day, makes them himself in the morning, right after he does his calisthenics and reads his *Wall Street Journal.*"

"Jeez, Sadie, how do you even know that?" Emma was always amazed by this woman's inside information.

"My sister-in-law's daughter cleans his office. He's usually still here when the crew comes in. She heard him on the phone telling someone his routine."

"So what's happening with Marisol?" Emma had thought about little else since they sat back down. "Any sightings?"

"She's been plugging away all morning," Darnell said, wiping his mouth with a napkin. "Ain't never seen a lady about to be fired look as happy as she did. I expected her to get up and start testifying in the aisles. Stop worrying about her. She's going to a better place."

Emma opened the dolmades her grandma prepared in a gesture of solidarity. "Did anybody hear what people are saying?"

"Well, Doris Litzko — "

"Please, Sadie, Mrs. Roger Litzko," Darnell reminded her.

"— said, and I quote, 'What was that supposed to prove? That some people at Central States can talk and stand up at the same time? Now if they could only do their job, maybe this office would have a chance of staying open.' I ran into her in the bathroom talking to that dumpy little lady with the rat's nest on her head. But who cares what Doris thinks. She couldn't find her fanny in a hall full of mirrors with both hands behind her back. Benny Beinhofer, on the other hand, told me our little stand-up was the best thing since beer started coming in six packs."

Maybe it was Emma's imagination, but the lunch room chatter seemed more lively today. People were looking around, poking each other and laughing. She wished she could listen in on all the conversations. For now they'd have to rely on snippets in the bathrooms and buses. Her grandma was already asking her what the next step was going to be — as if they had some grand plan. Getting people out of their seats was as far as they'd gotten. Even Vanessa had no clue what they should do next.

Darnell lifted his Coke can in Emma's direction. "Well, ladies, you pulled it off. I know Henderson saw us — he must be foaming at the mouth. If nothing good ever happens again at Central States, I'm glad I lived to see this day."

Emma wrapped her sweater tighter around her body. She couldn't wait to get home and tell her family all about it. "We made ourselves seen," she'd tell them. "We have no idea when we'll stand up again. But CSA has no doubt that we will."

Gratitude

December 10, 1991

Buttoning her cardigan against the frigid air conditioning, Dorothy eyes the girl slouched in the seat next to her. A woman who seems to be the child's mother sits directly across the aisle. She's about to make a call on the airline phone perched on the back of the seat in front of her. Dorothy imagines what a pretty penny that will cost.

"Don't worry, baby, Granma's going to be fine," the woman says, nodding her head for emphasis. She has those dreadlocks Dorothy usually finds so unruly, but these are short and neat. To her, they look surprisingly soft.

"You don't know that." The girl, who Dorothy guesses is about eight or nine, tries to curl into a ball, but her legs are too long. Like a colt, Dorothy thinks.

"I feel it, Alicia." This time the woman reaches her slender fingers across the aisle to take her daughter's hand. "I feel it in my bones."

Dorothy longs for such a feeling in her own bones. She is returning from St. Louis, where her sister Sylvia has some bladder condition she can neither name nor describe. Imagine those medical people shoving a catheter in and sending her home from the hospital, and Sylvia never asking a single question! Dorothy's own bladder aches just thinking about it. Oh, dear, she'll have to ask the girl to let her out.

Dorothy gathers her travel purse and clears her throat. The child doesn't notice.

"Alicia, I think this nice lady would like to get up," her mother says. The girl rolls out of her seat.

"Why, thank you," Dorothy says, nodding in the woman's direction as she hurries to the little lavatory in the back of the plane.

When she returns a few minutes later, Alicia and her mother are both standing in the aisle, the girl's head buried in her mother's bosom. The call must have brought bad news. Dorothy stops in her tracks. She dreads arriving home and finding her own bad news, heralded by a blinking light on the answering machine. Before she left, she'd written down all the questions Sylvia needed to ask at the doctor's appointment, scheduled too late for her to accompany her sister and still make the flight.

She hasn't talked to anyone else about it except the airline clerk who arranged her reservations last week over the phone. A complete stranger, and she was so kind, listening to Dorothy fret and wishing her sister good luck. As soon as she put down the receiver, Dorothy wrote a letter of appreciation to the airline, pulled on her galoshes and overcoat and walked to the mailbox across the park so the note would get out the same day. "Her name is Emma," she'd written. "Please thank her for making time for an elderly woman during a rough patch in my life." Dorothy hoped they had a robust employee appreciation program. Some public recognition. Maybe a small gift.

But wait, the girl's head is up and she's not crying. She's laughing, a sweet, high giggle, and so is her mother, an alto version of the girl's. And look at that, right there in the aisle, the mother takes her daughter's hand and twirls her in a tiny circle, once, twice, three times around, as they celebrate what must have been wonderful news after all.

Dorothy steadies herself with her hip against an empty seat. The mother notices and leads her daughter a few steps forward. With a flourish, the woman waves Dorothy back to her row.

"Forgive us," she says, bowing her head. "Just a bit of foolishness."

"Oh, no," Dorothy tells her. "It was lovely. Thank you. Thank you both so much." She slides into her seat and buckles herself in.

Annie's Stand-Up

Milwaukee, December 3, 1991

For some of her co-workers, the stand-up was a prank. Many experienced it as a rare moment of power. For Annie, it sparked a whole new life.

She didn't know this when they planned it or even when they first got up. But somewhere during those sixty seconds on their feet, Annie felt a shift inside her as palpable as a baby's kick. If she could stand up to her boss at the call center, maybe she could find a way to leave her abusive husband.

First step: put it on paper. As they cleaned up their work station at the end of the shift, Annie passed Emma a note: "I have no idea how or when I'll leave him. But I know I have to, and for the first time, I think maybe I can." Emma pulled her in for a quick hug.

The truth was, Annie never intended to say a word about Bill. Not to her mother, who seemed to know, not to anyone in her church — not after the pastor spent an entire sermon on a wife's duty to make her marriage work and "rise above" any challenges, and certainly not to anyone at Central States Airlines reservation center when she started working there the previous winter. But Emma figured it out the first time Annie showed up to work on a warm day wearing a long-sleeved dress with a turtleneck. Emma's sister worked the front desk at a battered women's shelter and had taught her the signs. Early on Emma brought Annie pamphlets and told her it wasn't her fault. In August she invited Annie to join biweekly dinners at Vanessa Jackson's house in Sherman Park.

Getting away for one dinner was no easy task, not to mention one every two weeks. Vanessa figured out the perfect cover. "Tell Bill you're going to a sewing class at the community center on the near south side," she said. "It's for real, I know someone who goes. You can say they're free and it's a way to save money on stuff you need. It so happens I love to sew. I can whip up something each time, a dish towel, an apron, simple things for the kids." Somehow it worked. Annie's mother volunteered to babysit Dorey, who was nearly six, and three-year-old Daniel, since Bill said he needed early evenings to search the newspaper want ads.

The first couple of get-togethers, Annie had been on the alert for signs of pity and "how-can-we-save-you" syndrome. Emma knew from her sister how common domestic violence was. Turns out Vanessa had witnessed it up close when a neighbor appeared at the door one day with her arm wrapped in a blood-soaked towel, asking for a ride to the hospital. But, hallelujah, these two women seemed to actually like her. Walking into these meals together was like entering a forest in one of Dorey's tales, a place where even the trees were kind.

Still, kindness didn't produce miracles.

A dinner that October was the first time they talked openly about exit strategies. They were seated around Vanessa's big dining room table with the remains of a luscious root vegetable stew and a nearly empty bottle of wine. From the back room they could hear hoots of laughter as Vanessa's youngest, ten-year-old twins, listened to the *Cosby* show.

"Look, I appreciate how much you want to help," Annie told them, feeling a blush move up her cheeks. "I'm not ashamed to talk about it anymore. Really. I'm actually glad you know. This is the one place I don't have to lie about slipping on the ice or tripping over one of the kid's toys." She looked down at her skinny wrists. "It's the one place I have an appetite."

146

Vanessa held up her glass. "Here's to plain talk and some meat on the bones, Annie. Anything you need, if it's in our power, we'll help."

"I believe you." Annie wanted to gulp this in. She'd been on her own since the first time Bill laid hands on her when she was pregnant with Dorey. "It's just — it's complicated. Bill's threatened to take the kids if I leave him."

"Annie, no judge is going to award him custody." Vanessa waved her fork in the air. "He can't even watch the kids when you're at your pretend class."

Annie surprised herself with how steady her voice remained. "He wouldn't. He'd go back home and have his mother raise them. She and his dad live in Houston. Bill wouldn't bother to ask the court, he'd just take them. He's told me that, not when he's angry and hurting me, but other times, when he's calm." She gazed at the fingerprint bruise peeping out of her sleeve. "I can always get over getting smacked around, but I'd die without my kids."

Vanessa's hand formed a fist around her fork. "How could his parents let him do that?"

Annie told them the story that played on a loop in her head after every beating. "Right after Daniel was born, we drove all the way down from Milwaukee to visit them. One night Bill's mom was feeling really sick. I told her to lie down, I'd make dinner. When his dad came in and saw her on the sofa, he started yelling. I tried to explain." That voice, stinking of whiskey and disappointment, was a staple in Annie's dreams.

"He shouted, 'She lies down when *I* say lie down,' and he ordered her to sit up. So she grabbed on to the back of the sofa and dragged herself to a seated position." Annie paused for a moment. "'All right' he said, '*now* you can lie down.'"

Annie registered the horror on her friends' faces. Vanessa was blinking hard: Emma didn't hide her tears as they both got up from their seats to stand beside her.

147

"What about calling the police?" Emma asked so softly, Annie had to strain to hear her.

"He's the father of my kids," Annie said after another long pause.

Just then Vanessa's boys came in to paw through the leftovers. Annie used the disruption to grab the Green Bay Packer blanket Vanessa had made for Daniel, wave her goodbyes and disappear out the door.

December 7, 1991

After the stand-up, Annie finally allowed herself to think about possible ways out. She practiced speeches in the shower, knowing any mention of separation would provoke a verbal shake-down, if not a bodily one. She imagined running away, but couldn't figure out how to do it without the car, which Bill would find a way to trace. All her ideas vanished into dead ends, until Vanessa planted a seed at the dinner celebrating the stand-up.

They were nearly finished eating. Vanessa sopped up the remains of her soup with a crust of bread and pulled her chair closer to Annie's. "Back in the 80s, I had the queen-for-many-days experience of having to use welfare," she said, raising one eyebrow. "The only saving grace was meeting a kickass group of welfare mothers. One of them had a running fight with her landlord. Roaches, plumbing, ceiling leaks — she had it all. She tried talking to him, and then screaming at him, with no success. So one Monday she told him she'd called the Housing Authority and they were sending a team over that Friday. The slumlord cursed her up and down, but he made all the repairs by Thursday afternoon."

"Why didn't she call the Housing Authority in the first place?" Emma asked.

"Actually, she never did call them." Vanessa leaned back in her chair. "It usually took forever to get through. And some staff were plain nasty, more likely to strike you off the list for Section 8 housing than go after the landlord. You never knew what you'd get. But pretending to call worked."

"So you're saying ...?" Annie heard a car trying to start next door, the engine finally turning over.

"What if you just threatened to call the police? If Bill ..." Vanessa swallowed hard and started again. "The next time Bill goes after you, once he calms down, you say you've decided you have to call the cops unless he agrees to let you leave and have primary custody of the kids."

Annie tucked the idea away for safekeeping. Her shower monologues expanded.

December 10, 1991

That Friday night, Bill had a T-shirt with a big rip at the shoulder and brought it to her to mend. Annie, limbs heavy with dread, wanted to delay until after the kids were bathed and asleep, but Bill just grew more insistent. "Let's see what they're teaching you in that class," he said, planting himself right in front of her and thrusting the sewing kit in her lap.

"I'm sorry," Annie said as she fumbled with the needle and kept failing to line up the seams. "It's just, it's hard for me to work well with someone staring at me." Dorey and Daniel seemed to sense something was coming, like arthritis sufferers feeling a storm before the sky turned dark. Dorey took Daniel's hand and scurried with him to the room they shared.

At the click of their door shutting, Bill grabbed Annie so hard, he almost pulled her arm out of the socket.

Spools of thread flew across the room. The shirt and needle landed on his mukluk. "I want to know who it is, you whore!" he demanded, his face so close, she could smell the marinara sauce from dinner. "You no good slut-faced liar. Who are you fucking in those so-called sewing sessions?" He flung her away from him, where she crashed into the coffee table. Hard to say which came first, the pain or the sound of ribs cracking. Definitely not enough meat on the bones.

Annie rolled to her side; her breaths ragged and halting, the throbbing so sharp, she imagined there was a shard of table sticking out. Suddenly Dorey was kneeling beside her. "Did Mommy fall?" she asked. "Should I call 911? We learned how in school."

That brave voice, more than the pain or the struggle to breathe, got Annie to her feet. "It's okay, sweet girl," she managed to say. "No need. Daddy'll take me to the doctor. And Grandma will come get you."

Bill left the car right outside the emergency room door and guided her to a chair while he ran out and parked. "I'll take care of the paperwork," he told her. She could make out only a few words of his conversation at the desk, "legos," "tumble," and a flash of her insurance card. Afterwards — five minutes? fifty?— a nurse came with a wheelchair. She was small, like Annie, but muscular. "My name is Tameka and I'll take you back to see the doctor," she said.

Bill rose to go with them. "We need to take her for an x-ray first," Tameka informed him. "Someone will come get you when she's ready."

While they waited for the x-ray technician, Tameka helped Annie slip off her clothes and gently guided her arms into a hospital gown. The nurse took a deep breath as she eyed what Annie thought of as the ghosts of bruises past.

Tameka crouched down to look Annie in the eyes. "You're not alone," she whispered. Annie kept her eyes open and squeezed Tameka's hand.

"We can keep him out there until the doctor's finished." Tameka's voice was like a cool cloth on a fevered forehead. "Tell me if you want me to make a call to the police, or to a shelter."

Somewhere Annie found the strength for a slight smile. "Thank you," she said. "I have it covered."

When Bill finally was allowed back, the resident declared Annie "lucky," no damage to the lungs, young and healthy, two broken ribs should heal in a few weeks, she could even go back to work if she rested all weekend and did her breathing exercises. On the way home, Bill drove with one hand and held hers with the other. His words rolled into each other: "I'm so sorry/if you just hadn't lied to me/you know how much I love you/you're all that matters to me/no man can live with deceit/this will never happen again, you'll see/I swear/I promise/trust me." When they arrived, Annie let him walk her into the house and bring her an ice pack. Then she delivered the ultimatum she'd practiced, punctuating her sentences with the breathing she'd just learned: "The nurse knows." Breath. "I will file charges unless ..." Breath. "... these two things." Breath. "You let me leave." Breath. "I have the kids."

Dorey and Daniel were already at her mother's. The cab dropped Annie there until Bill could find an apartment.

December 25, 1991

He got a temp job that Monday and a small, furnished place by Wednesday. Annie returned to a house that had been thoroughly straightened, laundry done, fresh sheets on the beds. That night and twice the following week, Bill arranged to take the kids for burgers or pizza with Annie's parents at the adjacent booth. So when he asked to have the kids stay with him for Christmas Eve and bring them back in time for church the next day, Annie said yes.

No one showed up Christmas morning. Bill didn't answer his phone.

Annie's dad rushed her over to the apartment, where a slightly hungover super agreed to let them in. All that greeted them were empty hangers and open dresser drawers. The only trace of her kids was Daniel's Green Bay Packers blanket, which Annie found smooshed up under the couch. As soon as she could summon her breath, her father took her back to call Bill's parents in Houston.

December 27, 1991

"His mother answered." Annie filled in Emma and Vanessa as they huddled in Vanessa's car two days later after work. "She wouldn't say outright that they were there, but I could hear Dorey's voice in the background asking if it was me." This detail always made her choke up.

"His mother pulled the phone into a closet, I think, and said it was all my fault my family wasn't together and didn't I care how much I was hurting my kids … ." Her friends stayed silent, their breath fogging up the car windows.

Annie had called in sick the day after Christmas to try to find a lawyer. Those who agreed to talk to her for free had no good news. "Same answer from all of them," she said. "Unless I have money — a lot of money — they can't do a thing. I don't have a custody decision. No police file, no restraining order. Nothing to prove a dad doesn't have a right to take his kids to see their grandparents."

"What about that nurse?" Emma was leaning over from the back seat, tears silvering her face in the December dusk.

"The lawyers call it 'helpful but not dispositive.' That's a fancy way of saying, it doesn't change a thing. It's not like a rape kit. There are no photos. There is no proof."

Inside that car, Annie pledged them to absolute secrecy and then told them the bare outlines of what she was planning. "I don't know how long it'll take," she said. "Bill's not going to trust me. He and his parents will watch me like a hawk — I'm going to have to put on a good show. But sooner or later I'll find an opening. And then I'll take my children back."

"Oh, Annie," Emma said, sinking into her parka hood. "That means you'll have to sleep with him."

Vanessa took off one of her mittens — she'd knitted identical pairs for all of them — and clutched Annie's hand. "Say your plan works. He'd just come back here and snatch the kids again, and this time he wouldn't buy any reconciliation story. Then what?"

Annie barely moved her lips. "I won't be coming back here."

The words swirled around their ears like the snow shower that had begun outside. The women looked at each other for several minutes. Vanessa was the first to speak.

"You'll need money."

"There's a ring and a brooch my grandmother left me — I'm going to the pawn shop on my way home. And my mother, she feels really guilty that she didn't say something a long time ago. Turns out for years she's been stashing bingo winnings and birthday checks and skimming from the grocery money. She's turned it into fifties and she's sewing it into my raincoat lining. Must be a thousand dollars." Annie's heart filled her chest when she'd seen it.

Houston, January 8, 1992

It took twelve days for Annie to convince Bill she wanted him back and was willing to go down there to live

153

with him. The kids were waiting with him at the gate in the Houston airport when she finally arrived. Daniel's Batman T-shirt barely covered his toddler belly as he waved both arms madly, as if she might not recognize them otherwise. Dorey stood beside him clutching rosary beads. Annie had to bite the inside of her cheek to keep from crying out as she took in the purple shadows under her daughter's eyes. That night at bedtime, Annie rocked Dorey for a long time. "I'll stay here 'til you fall asleep, sweet girl," Annie had whispered.

"It's okay," Dorey told her, "I fell asleep fine. I just woke myself up a lot to pray that you'd find us."

Dorey's bedroom was two doors down from Bill's. Annie would have to remember to call it "their" room. She opened the door to see her suitcase had been emptied, everything hung neatly in one side of the closet where she'd already put away her raincoat. Bill had poured the contents of her purse on the bedspread and left her wallet on top. Annie didn't need to pick it up to know it no longer had the three twenties and a ten her dad had given her before taking her to the airport. As expected, the slots for her driver's license and credit card were empty. Without a word, Annie slid the wallet back into the purse together with her hairbrush and kleenex, brand-new pocket notebook and two CSA pens, chapstick and scrunchies and Dorey's ponytail holders. She put salve on her almost-healed ribs, traded her clothes for a lightweight nightgown, and waited for Bill to return from the den. She had learned by now how to separate herself from her body.

January 17, 1992

Bill found some kind of job in the insurance office his father recently retired from. As usual, as soon as he left for work, both his parents took up their sentinel positions,

154

his dad in a recliner in front of the television, his mother in the open kitchen, where Annie and the kids sat at the table and colored, sang until Bill's father shushed them, read from the few books they'd brought with them and made up stories. The kids were allowed to play in the backyard, which was fenced in, but it had been raining off and on all morning. "Stay put for now," Bill's mother told them. "I can't have you tracking in mud."

"The kids could really use some books and activity sheets," Annie said. "And I could use some guidance on home schooling. I'd be glad to walk over to the library with them, give you both some quiet time."

"It's quiet in the library." Bill's mother finished stirring a pot of macaroni and cheese and brought it to the table. After lunch, she accompanied Annie and the kids to the neighborhood branch, where she made sure Dorey and Daniel — but not Annie — got library cards and picked out books.

Annie felt like a dog hemmed in by an invisible electric fence. One wrong step and she'd be in for a shock. To keep herself going, she carried out imaginary conversations with Emma describing an afternoon jumping in puddles with the kids. At the call center, Darnell Chaney used to call her and Emma the pixie twins. She sure could use some pixie magic right now.

Rapid City, South Dakota, January 30, 1992

The next time Annie had an actual conversation with Emma was from a pay phone at a Dallas airport after the escape. The kids were squashed in the booth with her so she kept it short, promising a letter where she'd tell the details. For now, she gave the condensed version: While Bill was at work, his father got a nasty cut slicing an apple.

The kids were napping. Annie convinced Bill's mother it would be okay to take her husband for stitches, why disturb the children, they'd just cause a ruckus at urgent care.

The second they were gone, Annie made her move. "I'd practiced it over and over in my head," she told Emma while Dorey and Daniel drew pictures from their breath on the glass walls of the booth. "Wake the kids, fill our backpacks with the raincoat and bare essentials I'd crammed into two pairs of sweat pants, take the bus downtown with change I swiped from Bill's father's dresser."

"The bus?" Emma said. "When you were in such a hurry?"

"I didn't want a cab driver who could say where we'd gone." Annie would always remember the weight of the sun beating on their heads, Daniel hanging on her leg and Dorey glued to her hip as they rounded the corner to the bus stop, where, miraculously, a city bus was just pulling up.

"Can you tell me anything about where you're headed?" Emma lowered her voice, as if Bill and his parents were in the next room.

"After we're settled, you'll hear something from my mom," Annie said. "We'll send you letters through her."

Dorey's voice rose in the background. "From all three of us."

January 31, 1993

Annie decided they would celebrate the date they arrived, rather than the date of their escape.

To flee from Bill in Houston, they'd taken a wild combination of transportation — two buses downtown, a train to Dallas, cab to the airport, flight to Provo, Utah, Greyhound to Rapid City, South Dakota. On that last leg, with Dorey asleep on the bus, Annie got off at a rest stop with an antsy Daniel to let him run around and buy a hot chocolate. As they were coming back out, the Greyhound driver was about to take off with her six-year-old daughter and their few belongings. Annie could hear Dorey's screams through an open window: "You stop right now!" she ordered.

"Rules are rules!" the driver shouted. "When I say five-minute rest stop, I mean just that." Earlier he'd announced through a small microphone that he was a retired prison guard. After braking so hard one passenger almost slid out of her seat, the driver pulled the stick that opened the door and barked at Annie to get her brat and her stuff off his bus. "You have till I count to ten," he'd told her, staring the whole time at the road. Her kids clung to each other while Annie gathered their backpacks. They'd had to wait two hours for another bus. In the confusion, Dorey's favorite Cabbage patch doll got left behind.

When they arrived in Rapid City, Annie found a battered women's center that helped her locate an apartment and a job at a hospital admitting office. The hospital had an on-site day care which took a big bite out of her paycheck, but meant she could have lunch with Daniel every day. The shelter also produced an ID for Annie with her new name.

Both kids slept with their mother for the first several weeks. Daniel lost his bravado and didn't speak much for a while, but a Saturday play group at the shelter helped over time.

In the evenings, Annie read the letters they'd pick up once a week from the battered women's center sent by her parents and Emma and her kids and Vanessa, who mailed them to a shelter in Minnesota, where someone put them in a new envelope addressed to the local center in Rapid City.

Annie felt like she was in witness protection.

She tracked down every free attraction in town, found a Boys and Girls Club that taught gymnastics and swimming, and arranged her schedule to take the kids there twice a week. All three of them got a library card and they'd read stories together. And sometimes, when Daniel was off playing with Star Wars characters passed down from Vanessa's twins, Dorey would ask Annie to tell a story of her own. Tonight, after a second piece of anniversary cake, Dorey put in her request.

"Have I ever told you about the stand-up we did at Central States Airlines?" Annie would always start it this way.

As part of the ritual, they arranged themselves on the couch, Annie cradling Dorey's head in her lap. "They had total control over our time and counted it against us if we were even one minute late getting to work or coming back from the bathroom. We never got to stand up and stretch. So we decided we had to do something, even if it was only symbolic. A few people — Emma and Vanessa and Marisol — planned it on pretty short notice. We each got one other person to agree to participate. We'd written a note to give out to the people we knew or trusted. It said to keep working, but stand up for one minute at exactly 8:30 a.m. Marisol hid the notes under these coupons she handed out for her brothers' restaurant. You should have seen her, she was so excited she glowed. But the truth was, until we actually did it, we had no idea if anyone else would stand with us. We'd synchronized our watches, and at exactly 8:30, the eight of us stood up. We all had headphones on and held our keyboard in one arm. We kept on taking reservations."

"And then what happened, Mommy?" This, too, was part of the ritual.

"Emma and I were at a workstation in the front of the room, so we never got to see everyone, but we heard people all around us. For months we'd been complaining about these horrid chairs we had, no support and always creaking. That day I almost got down on my knees and kissed those chairs for letting us know that a lot of people took to their feet. I twisted my neck to each side" — Dorey acted this out in exaggerated fashion — "and I saw standing bodies everywhere. A friend in the back told us more than half the room, eighty people at least, stood up."

Annie slipped her fingers through Dorey's. "Sometimes sixty seconds seems like a really long time. Other times, a single moment whooshes by, and you wonder, was that even real? The stand-up was like that. But it was real, my sweet. I felt something I can only describe as a surge of power."

"What's that mean, Mom?" Annie felt her daughter shiver with excitement, even though she'd heard this answer dozens of times.

"It meant I knew we deserved a better life, and that we had the power to make it happen."

Milwaukee, June 18, 2002

Annie waited until the kids were teenagers to come back to Milwaukee. For years Bill contacted her parents and tried various schemes to get them to reveal Annie's whereabouts. Last year he initiated divorce proceedings so he could remarry. That was one factor in Annie's decision. Mostly she wanted Daniel to be old enough to know what to do if his dad approached him. Dorey had skipped a grade and was ready for college. Marquette accepted her with a full scholarship.

They stayed with her parents until Annie could find a job and a rental in Riverwest. The night they settled in, after a raucous picnic with Emma and Vanessa and their families and after Daniel holed up in his room with a new

159

video game, Dorey put in a request for the stand-up story. This time, when Annie finished, her daughter sat up and looked her in the eye. "Here's a question I never asked before, Mom. What if no one else had stood up? Would you still have been able to get out of your marriage? To come and get us back after Dad took us to Houston?"

Annie placed her hands lightly on Dorey's face. "That's a good question. I didn't know it at the time, but yes, I think I would. We had no way of knowing whether anyone else would join us. The only thing we knew for sure was that we had each other, and that we had to stand up for ourselves. Turns out that was enough."

The Union Makes Us Strong

Milwaukee, 1993

For the third time in ten minutes, Emma unbuttoned her coat and stepped away from the window. She didn't know why she expected Mary Catherine to be on time. If their car weren't on the fritz, Emma would gladly have let Mary Catherine make her way to the meeting by herself.

"How come you got your coat on, Mom?" Sammy was out of breath from practicing karate kicks with his dad and brother in the basement. He'd raced up to use the bathroom.

"Remember I told you the union hired Vanessa? That means our committee can get back together so we can bring in the union and improve our jobs. Tonight's the meeting at her church."

"Right. Well, watch this." Sammy leaned slightly to his left, fists tucked beneath his chin, his right foot darted out from his side into a perfect "L" and pummeled an imaginary foe. "If Mr. Henderson doesn't listen to you guys, me and Max'll give him some of this."

"Whoa, mister. What happened to 'Don't worry, Mom, this is only for self-defense, promise?'"

Sammy lowered his leg. "It would be self-defense. That guy always beats up on you."

Emma pulled Sammy close to her, then leaned his head back to kiss each ruddy cheek. One way or another, she thought, our children feel every blow we take, no matter how hard we try to conceal it.

"You should quit that job, Mom." Sammy's body, always in motion, looked impossibly vulnerable when still.

161

"Don't you worry about me, kiddo. I think this time's going to be different. We got something better than karate kicks."

"What?"

"People power." *For the union makes us strong.* Maybe if she sang it enough times, she'd believe it.

Mary Catherine's horn blared at last. Emma pictured the sound taking solid form in the January night, an icy finger pointing at her door. "Okay, Sammy, that's my ride."

The trip from Emma's duplex on Sixty-Third Street to the church on North Avenue didn't take more than ten minutes. Emma and Mary Catherine argued the whole way.

"I still don't understand why we aren't having the meeting at the union hall," Mary Catherine muttered.

Emma grit her teeth. "Holy crap! For the tenth time, Vanessa thought it would be better to start on familiar turf and I agree." Emma refused to pander to this woman's fear of driving in the Black community. When they first formed a committee to find a union in those roller-coaster weeks following the stand-up, Vanessa had arranged for them to meet in her church. She argued they needed someone like Mary Catherine. "Look, she's from a union family, she's been at the call center a long time and she knows most of the white workers," Vanessa said. "They're the biggest group. We don't get the majority of them, we don't win a union drive. Sure she's complicated — get over it."

The church was cozy and well-lit, still smelling of Christmas pine. Vowing to be nicer on the ride home, Emma offered to hang up both their coats in the vestibule. She pulled off her hat, patted down her staticky short hair and made her way downstairs to the meeting room. Everyone was here tonight, even Maxine from third shift.

"Well, Emma, you ladies sure worked some magic." Maxine handed her a slice of lemon pound cake.

As Emma bit into the soft yellow concoction, her face and shoulders loosened. "This is divine. Did you make it?"

"My daughter. To celebrate the committee starting up again." Maxine's body was all sharp angles, but her manner was warm and welcoming. "So how'd you do it?"

How, indeed. When Rod Huebnor from the National Transportation Union declared them "unorganize-able" and walked away, Emma thought the struggle was over. "Isn't that just like a guy," Maxine had said. "Pulls out before you get what you need."

"You should have seen us — Gloria, mostly." Emma felt like a girl scout who hadn't yet earned her badge. "Gloria sat across from the union president and raised hell about sending us someone with the title of organizer who refuses to listen to the workers. She had two pages of arguments for why the NTU should restart the union drive and hire Vanessa to run it, only this time with all our demands and house visits to win people over. The guy in charge agreed to interview Vanessa the next day. She did the rest."

Tonight, Vanessa had placed the chairs in a U-shape and stood at the opening. Her loops of hair were pulled back in one of her kid's scrunchies. As she started a slow clap, people took their seats and the room grew quiet.

"Welcome back. Ashanti. Shalom." Emma was cheered to hear several voices echo Vanessa's greeting. "I feel a lot of emotions as I look around the room — pride, joy, humility. But mostly I feel eagerness."

"Say it, girl!" Maxine shouted, waving both her hands. Her nails were painted silver with shiny gold stars at each tip.

"We have a big job to do, folks," Vanessa told them, "but we're gonna do it *our* way. Next meeting will be back at the union hall and John Daitsman, a senior organizer at NTU, will join us. I've spent many hours with this guy, and let me tell you, he gets it. We've got a lot to learn from him, but he wants to take his lead from us. He knows we're the experts when it comes to the call center at Central States

Airlines." Emma had heard rumblings about Vanessa's inexperience. This combination was a good move by the union.

Vanessa called on them to share what they learned from what happened. Darnell shuffled in his seat. "I'll tell you what I learned. An asshole's an asshole — pardon my French — even dressed in union clothing. I learned you got to trust your instincts."

Three others spoke before Emma got to her feet. At first her voice was too soft and she had to begin again. "Darnell's right. We all get that Rod was a jerk. But what I learned most is, it's up to us to stop the jerks. I knew he was wrong to drop the equal pay issue, but I didn't say anything."

Emma had thought about this for months but never said it out loud. "I was always afraid Rod would get mad and the union would pull out. That happened anyway, even though we did what he said. He predicted racial conflict if we raised equality. Well, we ran smack into it anyway, only we had no way to talk about it because he never let us do house visits. That's the only way we get unity, and the only way to get enough cards signed to win the union. I should have had the courage to speak up." She looked around the circle. "So, I want to stop being afraid of what might happen and focus on what *is* happening that needs to change."

After several others spoke, Gloria raised her arm. Emma tried to hold on to an image of Gloria squealing with laughter at a poker party when they first set up the organizing committee. But a more recent picture kept intruding: Gloria stretching each finger of her gloves when Emma came over to apologize after Rod blamed Black workers for the union drive falling apart. "You don't like something Rod says, deal with him directly," Gloria told her. "I can take care of myself."

Now Gloria looked at Emma, seated across from her. "I've been pretty bitter about Rod and what happened," she said. "I'd like to break down the mistrust. For me, it's simple — either you got my back or you don't. But I'm willing to try again."

Emma pictured trust as something soft and living. Something you had to feed.

Gloria turned back to Vanessa. "Getting you in this job is just what we need, Vanessa. You helped plan the stand-up, you came up with the idea of an organizing committee, you gave up precious time with your family to work with us even after they fired your ass, and you were dead right about the demands."

Vanessa bowed her head. "Thank you, Gloria. All right, Mary Catherine, I think we just need to hear from you."

Mary Catherine pushed herself up. "I have to admit, as a long-term employee, I'm still not convinced about the wisdom of the equal pay demand. But Emma's right. Mr. Henderson did try to make the white workers think they'd get a pay cut if the lower-tier workers got a raise. People came to me with that. I don't like having people mad at me. But I don't like lies, either."

Emma shifted in her seat to face Mary Catherine. "We'll get better at explaining it. Some people are going to be mad at us no matter what. They'll deal with it. And so will we."

The next part of the meeting was easy. They quickly reached consensus on the platform of the union drive, the same as their original demands: no discipline for legitimate absences, no more being spied on when they weren't handling a call, a raise for everyone and an end to the two-tier wage system. They agreed they'd start with visits to people in their homes. Vanessa had already made a grid for each member to indicate specific people they wanted to visit.

"Folks, we should do these visits in pairs," Vanessa explained. "How do you want to divide up?"

Darnell rubbed his head. "The only way that works. We got to divide up by race."

Emma felt torn. "What kind of message do we send if we do that? It makes it look like white people on the committee won't go to Black workers' homes."

"And will they?" Gloria raised an eyebrow as she looked around the room. Emma wasn't sure she wanted to hear the answer.

Vanessa turned to the chalkboard. "What do we want to accomplish in these visits?"

"We want to win people to the union," Maxine said.

"And that means they gotta feel free to speak their mind," Darnell added. "Get real. Whites are not gonna speak their mind to someone Black. And Black folk sure as hell ain't gonna ask hard questions if some white person's in the room."

Mary Catherine raised her hand. "What kind of questions, Darnell?" she asked.

"Like how we gonna get white folk at CSA to support equal pay for Nee-groes."

"Isn't the point that equal pay will also benefit white workers in Tier B?"

Darnell leaned back in his chair. "Bingo. Maybe the point is, racism hurts whites, too."

After more discussion, the group agreed to have mainly Black pairs and white pairs. Vanessa was also going to enlist Marisol, who'd quit shortly after the stand-up, to help make their case with Latino workers.

Vanessa wrapped up the evening by asking each person to name someone they were holding close that night. "My former seatmate, Annie Stotz," Emma said when it was her turn. "I've been feeling her presence like a phantom limb. She said the stand-up was what inspired her to leave an abusive marriage. Now her courage is what's inspiring me." Darnell placed his hand over his heart. Everyone knew Annie had to flee with her kids. What they didn't know is that Emma kept in touch by sending letters through a shelter that mailed them to wherever Annie was living under some other name.

***

Emma inhaled deeply, eager to prolong the scent of spring in her nostrils. She and Sadie Gillick were poised on the steps of a south side bungalow, waiting to see a new employee, Marilyn Bromlich. Through the open window, they could hear a man arguing with what sounded like a teenage boy. "It's my goddamn TV," the man yelled. "I paid for it, I worked my ass off all day, I'm watching what I want to watch."

After three rings, Marilyn Bromlich came to the door.

"Yes?" The woman fingered charms she wore on a chain around her neck, against the backdrop of a Green Bay Packers sweatshirt. She made no move to unlock the screen door.

"Hi, Marilyn. I'm Emma Pappas and this is Sadie Gillick, from work. Do you have a few minutes for us to come in?"

"What's this about?"

Sadie held out a salmon-colored information sheet. "It's about improving things at Central States. Better job security, better pay, less stress." They'd worked hard on what John Daitsman at NTU called their "key messages."

Marilyn leaned heavily against the door, as if the weight she carried were recent and she wasn't used to it yet. "I don't know, I'm pretty new. I don't want to get involved."

"Truth is," Emma said, "we're all involved, like it or not. You have a lot to gain by what we have to say. Really." The words sounded corny even to her.

"I hate this fuckin' family!" The boy's voice somewhere behind Marilyn reached a high screech before settling back into its original tenor.

"One more word out of your filthy mouth and you won't have *anything* to worry about!" the man yelled back. "You think I don't mean it, just com'ere once, you good-for-nothing runt."

"Look, it's not a good time." Marilyn swiped at the bangs she was growing out.

"Why don't you let us take you out for a cup of coffee?" Sadie urged. "We'll have you back before you know it. You look like you could use a little time to yourself."

"Hold a minute." Marilyn shuffled away from the door.

After a dozen home visits, Emma was learning to read the signs. Sadie's last comment had done the trick. When Marilyn emerged a few minutes later, they drove to a nearby diner, where, over coffee and kringle, Emma and Sadie took turns laying out the union's three key issues.

Marilyn pushed her empty plate away and fiddled with the corner of the flyer. "I don't know," she said. "I've heard some things."

"Go ahead," Emma replied. "Tell us anything." It had taken several visits for her to be able to say this.

"Well, I've heard that if the union gets in, they have to have as many coloreds as whites and that means I'd lose my job, what with me being new."

Sadie held up her hands like a cop stopping traffic. "Marilyn, no one's going to lose their job. If the union gets in, we'll all have some job security for the first time."

"That's just management bull to keep us divided and the union out,"Emma said.

"But I heard it from other workers," Marilyn insisted.

"That doesn't make it *true.*" Sadie scooped up some hair that had come loose from the bun at the back of her head. "And it sure doesn't mean management didn't spread it."

Marilyn kept her eyes and hands on the flyer, folding it into a small square. "I gotta be honest with you. I don't really care if the colored workers make less than we do."

"You think they're makin' less than you?" Sadie's voice rose slightly and her Irish lilt came out. "Guess what — whoever told you that is a big fat liar."

Whenever Sadie grew emotional, Emma tried to sound more detached. "Sadie's been at Central States a long time," she said, "but I've been there only a few years. In 1988, they decided anyone hired after that date would make a lower starting salary than people already on the job. I'm in the same group as you, Tier B. So are almost all the Black workers. They make exactly the same as we do."

"You're kidding." Marilyn's hands stopped moving.

"She's telling you the God's honest truth," Sadie said. "What else have you heard?"

"Nothing. But ..."

"Go on."

"I don't like some of the people they say are leading this thing. That Gloria, for instance.She thinks she's better than everyone else."

Saide laughed, a hearty sound Emma loved that came from the back of the throat. "I don't like a lot of people, darlin'. But let me tell you something. The gals that are leading this drive are the best people I've ever known. They saved my life. Gloria's great once you get to know her." She slid closer to Marilyn in the booth. "Want to know an important secret?"

Marilyn looked up from her flyer. Emma couldn't wait to find out herself. The waitress who came to refill their cups dawdled for a moment.

"In the long run, the best way to get anything for yourself is to get it for everyone."

"Well, the union might be the way to end everything for everybody," Marilyn whispered as soon as the waitress left. "Henderson would probably shut the place down rather than let a union in."

Someone was fanning this flame. "It's just hot air, Marilyn," Sadie said. "They can't function without this office. They've tried."

"Can I have some time to think about it?" Marilyn pushed her bangs out of her eyes.

"Sure," Emma told her. "We'll come back to see you next week. Really, there's two choices, Marilyn: We can do something to raise our pay, protect our jobs and ease the stress at work, or we can lie down and let Henderson walk all over us. And you know that's no choice at all."

After they dropped Marilyn off, Emma drove Sadie back to her apartment downtown. "Even if we get the union in, it's going to take a long time to change this insanity," Emma said. "How did the assholes get to Marilyn so fast?"

"Don't go fooling yourself. The other side is very organized. I'm sure they've got their own lists."

Emma pulled up in front of Sadie's building on Jackson Street. "Jeez, what an unhappy woman. Part of me wants to jump all over her, and the rest of me just feels sorry for her." She squeezed Sadie's hand, then watched until the older woman had walked into the building. On the drive home Emma tried to calculate how many signed cards they'd have by their target date.

***

Over the next two months, they lost a dozen people, but won over many more who'd been wavering. Emma was especially proud of her success with Marilyn Bromlich. Darnell got several Black workers to show her their pay stubs and Marilyn saw she'd been lied to about making more money than they did. She also got written up when she had to leave work early because her kid was being suspended from school.

On an impulse, Emma stood next to Marilyn and climbed onto the same bus the day she received the write-up. At first they rode side by side in silence. Marilyn

170

leaned her head forward, her face obscured by her bangs. Finally, Emma detected a muffled voice.

"You were right about the pay thing," Marilyn told her.

"Yeah."

"And you were right that they don't give a damn about family. I'm busting my ass to keep my kid from throwing his life down the tube and all they care about is their goddamn absence policy."

"I know." Emma could barely breathe.

"Maybe you're right about the union, too. Where do I sign?"

The trip home had taken three buses and more than an hour. Emma called Dean from a phone booth at the first stop and Vanessa from the second. After the last transfer, when she finally got a seat, Emma opened her purse a dozen times to eyeball her prize, Marilyn Bromlich's signed card authorizing the NTU to represent her at Central States Airlines.

That had been card #157. Now the tally was up to 164. The giant thermometer Vanessa drew was inching its way to the magic number, 200- two-thirds of the workers at CSA. Enough support to ask for recognition of the union without an election. Enough to demand an election if they had to. Enough to make Henderson take them seriously.

***

As she completed a reservation, Emma saw Mr. Henderson appear at her side and indicate she was to follow him. As she walked behind her boss, people were laying odds: suspension or termination.

"You were seen distributing anti-company materials in the cafeteria yesterday, July 5, at 11:56 a.m., Mrs. Pappas." Henderson spoke as soon as he closed the door to his office. He did not offer her a seat. The crease in his pants was perfect. Emma couldn't remember the last time she used an iron, or even where she'd stored the one they'd gotten as a wedding gift.

171

"I was on my break, Mr. Henderson."

"I don't care if you were on vacation. This is our establishment and we determine what goes on within it."

"What I passed on — not out — was a note about a meeting. It did not have one word about Central States. Your spies don't know what they're talking about." During her rehearsal with Vanessa, Emma had been cool and methodical. Now, with Mr. Henderson shaking his finger in her face, she could feel her voice getting higher and tasted the onset of tears. She tried to keep her eyes on his feet and remember Vanessa's advice to picture him in a tutu.

"Be very careful, Mrs. Pappas. Insubordination is grounds for immediate termination."

Take a breath. Take your time. Drawing a notecard and pencil out of her pocket, Emma began to write down Mr. Henderson's words. He grabbed the pencil from her hand.

"Just what do you think you're doing?"

"If you fire me, I want to make sure I have your statement accurate when I report it to the National Labor Relations Board."

Henderson slid the pencil into his vest pocket. "I didn't say I was firing you. I simply warned you about insubordination. Your employment at Central States Airlines, as you know, is at our will. I've been concerned for some time about your performance."

"My weekly stats have been above average every time." Emma delivered the line just as she'd practiced it.

"Appraising performance is about much more than statistics, Mrs. Pappas." So he had rehearsed as well. "I'm an expert at it. That's my job. You may think your job is to stir up trouble, but in fact it's to serve our customers. For your family's sake, I advise you to keep that in mind." Before she could say another word, Mr. Henderson had thrust the door open and nodded his head sideways in that direction.

For her family's sake, Emma decided not to mention the meeting to the kids. She poured her fears out in a letter to Annie.

***

Three days later Emma stood in front of her mail slot eyeing her pay envelope. They could get rid of her by escorting her out, as they'd done with Vanessa, or they could do it the quiet way, by inserting a pink slip in with her check. "Open it quickly," Vanessa had advised her, "same as ripping off a band-aid." Emma always peeled her bandages off one hair at a time.

She slid the envelope from its perch and felt its heft. Something more than a check was in there today. Using her locker key, Emma finally slit open the seal and unfolded the paper — yellow, not pink. It was in the shape of a giant check made out for $37,000 and signed "Each CSA employee."In the memo line of the check was typed, "cost of union." Laid out below, in a simulated check stub, was more detail: "union dues, cost of a strike, loss of productivity leading to loss of jobs and closing of the Milwaukee office."

This was the final paycheck before the committee planned to hand in the union cards.Henderson wasn't relying on a few blows to the gut, he'd decided to go right for the jugular.Fortunately, the committee was meeting that night. Emma shoved the envelope in her pocket and hurried to her work station. One pink slip would have been a lot easier to deal with than three hundred of these yellow scare sheets.

***

Maxine was the one who came up with the headline: "CSA's abra-ca-dabra arithmetic and hocus-pocus economics." Below that it read, "Calculate what your job

173

is costing you now." They had way more ideas for what to include than space on a half sheet flyer. After a spirited back-and-forth, they decided to focus on three things: the union pay advantage — at least $2 an hour in unionized reservation centers, the cost of docked pay and lost jobs when your kid had the flu or your dad had a stroke, and the incalculable cost of stress from living under Big Brother.

Most fun was deciding how to get the flyer out. "They spy on us when we're at our desks, in the lunch-room, walking in the aisles," Vanessa said. "They own the bulletin board. So what's that leave us?"

The answer came from all corners of the room: "The bathroom!" "The shitter." "The can."

Vanessa grinned and held up glue sticks fanned out like a bouquet. "Sisters and brothers, come and get your very own applicator." John Daitsman was already in the back designing the flyer. Each committee member left with twenty-five copies.

Over the next few days, Emma did share these esca-pades with her kids. "Henderson can control the bulletin board, but not the bathroom. Every time you walk in, there's something up in the stalls. Darnell told us the men's room is the same. And here's the beauty of it — people we don't even know are putting things up. I saw one written with letters cut out of the newspaper."

"Can we make some of those?" Sammy was ready to jump from the dinner table and grab a pair of scissors. "What do they say?"

"Sometimes it's just a few words, like 'fair pay' or 'stop Big Brother.' It could be just two people putting them up, but it could be lots more. We have no idea."

"And what about Henderson's fake paycheck?" Dean asked.

"It keeps disappearing from the bulletin board!"

***

October 20, 1993

Dear Annie,

WE DID IT!

I wish you could have been with us. Some people we never won over, we were prepared for that. And some we never tried. But lots of people amazed us. Do you remember that woman at the end of our row who always does needlework during Henderson's meetings? We skipped her in the stand-up because we didn't think she'd support it. She actually went up to Darnell in the cafeteria and said, "Where can I get one of those union cards to sign?" And that quiet guy who sits near Gloria slipped her a note one day asking for five cards. He brought them all back with signatures. Even people who resisted, little by little we learned how to get through.

Most of all, I wish you could see what's happened to the original committee members. Sadie brought her girl-friend to a committee party. Gloria and her son are going to have dinner at our house. Vanessa's been on national TV. The other day, my neighbor asked if I'd gotten a new hairdo or lost weight. "Nope," I said. "I've just learned how to stand up for myself." Me, a badass!

Two weeks ago we turned the cards in to the National Labor Relations Board. Management has the right to grant recognition to the union on the basis of the number of cards signed, and they also have the right to refuse. Henderson instantly notified the Board that he considered the effort "an illegitimate, fraudulent charade" which he would "in no way deign to acknowledge." Next step is to get the labor board to oversee an election so we can vote in the union.

So, we're planning a rally on Halloween to demand they do that as quickly as possible. You should see all the groups that promised to show up, lots of unions, the NAACP, the interfaith alliance. My grandma arranged a van from the senior center. Working Women United is bringing dozens of people (Vanessa is on their board). We met their director, Sophie Reznick. Turns out she loves what we're doing, wants to get some big-time media. Her husband's a high school teacher and he's bringing his whole class to the rally. When Max heard that, he asked the principal at the middle school if he could announce it over the loudspeaker. Sammy's beside himself because we'll have coke cans with BBs inside to make some joyful noise.

Everyone will gather right in front of the CSA building at the end of first shift, stroll up Wisconsin Avenue to that big blue federal building, have ourselves a rally outside the National Labor Relations Board. We're gonna tell them we're marching for something we thought we already had — the right to vote.

I'm sending this letter priority mail to the shelter in hopes they can get it to you right away. Because here's your part: At 5:00 pm Milwaukee time on October 31, grab some pots and wooden spoons and stand by your window with Dorey and Daniel. Shut your eyes and picture all of us. Whoop it up to whatever degree your neighbors can bear. We'll hear you, I promise.

You'll be right there with us.

Love,

Em

We Won't Let You Pollute Our Playground

Milwaukee, 1998

"Mr. Turner, Mr. Turner, you've got to come with us right now!" Kenny's nose and cheeks were bright pink. The rest of his face was barely visible, the drawstring on the hood of his parka pulled as tight as he could get it. The teen placed his palms on his thighs in an effort to catch his breath.

"Hey, guys, you all right?" Nick turned from the blackboard, where he'd been writing the Monday discussion questions.

Scherrie yanked off her earmuffs. "We're fine, but this neighborhood is definitely not fine." Her breathing was normal but her speech was speeded up, as if the story would vanish if she didn't get it out. "I was taking a short cut and I ran into Kenny at the railroad tracks and we both saw it at the same time. Oil just oozing up on the grass on both sides of the track. There was a patch of snow and it was pitch black. And then we saw puddles of it all over the grass."

The first day of freshman civics class, Nick read this girl's name on the chart and called her "Sherry." She rose to her full height and looked him right in the eye: "It's pronounced Shur—EEE. The only person at this whole school who got it right was the varsity volleyball coach, and that's because she asked."

Listening to her now, Nick put down his chalk. "And those puddles looked like oil?"

Scherrie was peeling off her outer layers: coat, scarf, gloves. "Yup. I've seen oil on the ground when my dad was working on the car. Plus Midland Oil Company is there on Hopkins. The real question is, why didn't we see it before?"

Other kids were starting to fill up the classroom. "I'll go with you right after school," Nick said. "Maybe the work we're doing on the environment is giving you fresh eyes."

"And maybe something that was already there is getting worse," Scherrie said.

Kenny had regained his composure and untied his hood. "Be sure to bring your camera, Mr. Turner," he said. "We need to document this. It's a real mess."

All year Nick took photos of his students. He'd make exhibits for parent-teacher conferences. Sometimes he put up a display just to surprise the kids. His wife, Sophie, was helping him research grant opportunities to revive the darkroom and purchase cameras the students could use. For now, the school had a couple video cameras donated by a retired drama teacher.

The thirty kids in Nick's civics class were in their third week of studying toxic sites, part of a new inter-disciplinary career program at Custer High School. The principal wasn't keen on innovation, but the program came with funds from a federal grant. Still, the teachers involved were on notice: show a positive impact on atten-dance and test scores or good-bye program.

Nick introduced this semester's project by explain-ing how, not that long ago, most houses relied on oil for heating, "I remember a really cold winter in Baltimore," he told the students. "My wife was pregnant with our first kid and I'd just gotten laid off. We had no money for an oil delivery. No oil, no heat." Nick could still remember the heavy smell of the oil the day the truck arrived, after he and Sophie had shivered and cuddled their way through two weeks waiting for unemployment to kick in.

The room was silent for a moment, until Kenny said, "Mr. Turner, is that your version of my grandpa's 'I had to walk nine miles through snow to get to school every day'?" The class roared with laughter, Nick along with them. To these kids he was an old man, one year shy of fifty.

"The oil companies stored the stuff in tanks underground," Nick said. "Most people don't use oil for heating anymore, but those tanks are still there. And in some places, oil is seeping into the land." A local environmental group had mapped all the oil tanks underground in Milwaukee. The students pored over the map and each picked a place near their homes to investigate. Every one of the students in the career program lived within eight blocks of an identified site.

"Think of yourselves as detectives, reporters, neighborhood leaders," Nick told them. "Let's see what you find."

Midland Oil was not on the list. Whatever this seepage was had to be related to an oil tank still in use.

When they walked five blocks to the site later that day, Nick saw that Kenny and Scherrie had not exaggerated. They were standing on the edge of a smelly field, covered with pools of thick muck. Overshadowing the field was the Midland Oil Company, a long building with sides laminated with rippled steel.

Scherrie ran over to the Custer Park playground next door, with Nick and Kenny on her heels. The area was pocked by similar pools that certainly looked and smelled like oil. "My little brother plays here every day," Scherrie said, jaw muscles tight. "The monkey bars and swings are right next to that slime. It feels like we're living on Love Canal."

Earlier that semester, Nick had shown them a short news clip about the environmental disaster at Love Canal. One mother wrote the principal anonymously to complain, saying her son had nightmares afterwards. Nick never found out who it was and didn't say a word about it to the class. Instead, he announced that students could do an alternate assignment in the cafeteria whenever he showed film clips. Not one kid took him up on it.

Wednesday evening, Nick drove to the airport to pick up Sophie, who was coming back from a three-day-conference in D.C. He drew up to the arrivals area just as she walked out, maneuvering her roller bag with one arm and waving with the other as if they'd been separated for weeks. Since she'd been promoted a few years earlier to head of the national Working Women United organization Sophie often had to be out of town. "I travel a lot, too," Nick would tell friends who asked how they managed. "I go to the airport and back home from the airport."

Sophie slid over for a kiss and moved back to buckle her seat belt. "Anything happen while I was away?" She always started their drive home with this question, since the time in the early '90s when Nick showed up with a shaved head. He had promised his class that whoever read and reported on the most books could give him a haircut in front of the whole school. "Couldn't you offer to catch a greased pig?" was Sophie's response.

"Actually, my sweet, a lot happened," Nick said, filling her in on Scherrie and Kenny's discovery. "You remember me telling you about Scherrie last fall? I hated that I messed up her name — these kids have to fight so hard to be seen — and I loved how she came back at me. So here she is, smart and confident. I think she's the first student at Custer to make varsity volleyball as a freshman. All the boys are smitten with her, and she can't be bothered. She's too busy making sure she's the first in her family to go to college. Told me she wants to make Black girls proud."

Nick took one hand off the wheel to squeeze Sophie's arm. "And here's Kenny, this skinny little white boy who hasn't hit puberty yet. You picture him as the kid who got pushed into his locker in middle school. He calls himself a dork but he's wicked smart. And he and Scherrie are pals, they really respect each other. Midland Oil is not going to want to fuck with them."

"Or with you, love," Sophie said. "Boy, I'm glad you made the choice to go back to school."

Nick wasn't sure he'd had any choice. When he got laid off from GE, good factory jobs were disappearing and the company was offering tuition reimbursement. He'd pictured Mr. Adebayo, the high school history teacher who changed his life. Maybe Nick could inspire a few kids as well. Elly and Jake were five and eight at the time. Now Jake was a junior in college and Elly would graduate high school in June. Nick couldn't believe these were the babies he lulled to sleep on his chest.

"I wish I had you as my civics teacher," Elly said when he told her about Midland Oil. "Our class is stuck on how a bill becomes a law. I learned that from cartoon characters."

On Thursday, Nick, Scherrie and Kenny went back to the contaminated area with six more students, the algebra teacher who taught them how to map density, and the English teacher who oversaw their correspondence with environmental groups. Under a winter sun, the oil stood out even more sharply against the snow.

Kenny and another kid began videotaping the area and interviewing the other students. Nick handed his camera to the math teacher so he could listen to the students' reactions. "It's like a horror movie," one of the white kids said. "It's unreal."

"Oh, it's real all right," Scherrie told him. The majority of students in his class and in this neighborhood were Black. Many were raised amidst disaster and low expectations. They didn't assume the system would play fair.

"I bet you don't see stuff like this in Mequon," Scherrie added. Some seniors had been inside that suburb's high school for a debate and described what they'd observed: gleaming labs, rows of computers, a gigantic swimming pool, classrooms with no more than fifteen students.

Nick handed out jars and lab gloves and directed the kids to take samples of the soil and liquid ooze. The whole class got involved. Over the following week, students learned how to examine the samples in physical science class. They worked with Nick to review the photographs and pick the most compelling. The English teacher helped them edit their video. Kids who normally shunned the library researched what oil spills do to the land, to animals, to the human body.

"Damn, Mr. Turner." Scherrie's eyebrows were scrunched together so hard, they threatened to leave permanent lines on her forehead. "This stuff can cause cancer. It can leak into the drinking water. And it's not just the kids in the park. What about all those people who walk their dogs along the railroad tracks?"

Kenny was in charge of contacting the Department of Natural Resources and inviting someone to talk to all the students in the program. "Mr. Lowe will be here February 2," Kenny said. "He's a hydrogeologist. That means he's an expert on water. He said he'd get some samples of the groundwater himself and tell us what's in them."

Mr. Lowe blew everyone away. He brought slides and pointed to a donut shape, a left-handed hockey stick and a spongy thing the students had seen under the school microscope. "Those are benzene, vinyl chloride, and cadmium," he said. "Toxins, every one of them. That means poisons. And the groundwater is full of them."

"If no one did anything," Scherrie asked, "how long would it take for the groundwater to clean itself?"

Even kids who thought they knew the answer were freaked out by Mr. Lowe's reply: "Three generations," he said. Then he gave them a quick history of Midland Oil and the problems getting companies to comply with governmental cleanup regulations.

"You young people have done a great service here," Mr. Lowe told them. Turns out he had done a little digging and found out the company knew at least a year earlier that the seams in the tank were leaking. "Management said they were in the process of cleaning it up. We already fined them, but the fine is less than the cost of clean-up."

Nick's students were scared. And pissed. "Who's in charge?" Kenny asked. "How did they let this happen?"

Scherrie went to the heart of the matter. "Does anyone give a damn about *us*?"

Mr. Lowe had one other important piece of information for them: the playground in Custer Park was owned by none other than Milwaukee Public Schools. The math teacher, who also coached the boy's baseball team, went into his files and found the memo MPS issued last year saying no baseball games could be played in that park.

"So why aren't they all over this?" Scherrie wanted to know.

For the next week, Nick turned his class into brainstorming sessions, dividing the students into three groups. One focused on how they would educate parents and students living in the area. A second strategized on a role for the media. The assignment for the third group was how to approach the school board to get the park cleaned up.

"These kids are amazing," Nick told Sophie and Elly one night after admiring and then devouring Elly's risotto with spinach and peas. "They're all in for this project, even the guy who thought his desk was meant for napping." Nick ran through their plans: A presentation for the entire certificate program. Exhibits for parent-teacher conferences and a leaflet inviting parents to see a three-minute video of the toxic site and talk about it. Everything in English, Spanish and Hmong.

Sophie was impressed that they were also contacting a local journalist. "You're nurturing some whistleblowers," she said.

The reporter wound up spending several hours with the kids, observing their planning session, reviewing the evidence they'd gathered, accompanying them to the park. That Wednesday, the article was spread across the front page of the *Milwaukee Journal* metro section. Scherrie and Kenny jumped up and down over the title, "Ooze and Ahhs: Students Find Oil at Playground."

"We got 'em!" Kenny said. "Right?"

The next day, while Nick was teaching his U.S. history class about the rise of the Klan, the phone in his classroom rang. It was his favorite secretary, calling to say Principal Odom wanted to speak to him. "He's sending someone to cover your class," she told him. "We have a visitor. Looks like a bigwig. You better hurry."

Nick grabbed his jacket and wondered if he should call his union rep.

When he walked into the office, the principal wasted no time. "Nick Turner, this is Mr. Ronald Rankin, owner and CEO of Midland Oil." He pointed to a white guy in a tailored suit and a face as red as his tie. Nick offered his hand, but Rankin kept his balled up in his lap.

"I want to know what kind of travesty our schools are involved in," Rankin said, shaking his right fist. "You had questions, why didn't you come straight to us? You would have found out we were already in the process of cleaning it up. Leaks happen — it was demonstrably not our fault. Shame on you for yanking these kids around and smearing the good name of my firm. I demand to know what Mr. Odom is going to do about it."

Nick stuffed his hands in his jacket pockets to keep from grabbing the guy by his monogrammed collar. But he also silently cursed himself. He should have had the students set up a meeting with the guy before the story came out. Rankin most likely would have put them off or fed them some PR bullshit. Now the CEO had gained a line of attack when he should have been squarely on the defensive. Nick braced himself for a second reprimand, this time from the principal. Behind his back, teachers called the guy "Benjamin By-the-Book Odom."

Mr. Odom reached out and clapped Nick on the shoulder. "Actually, sir, I'm proud of our students and of Mr. Turner here," he said. "That oil leak is a real danger to our neighborhood. It's a danger to our students and their families. You've known about it for a year and done nothing to fix it. You didn't even have the decency to warn us."

Mr. Odom must have felt Nick's shoulder drop with relief. Nick would add this moment to a list he kept of how people could always surprise you.

The principal moved behind his desk, finger poised over the intercom. "I agree dialogue is important, Mr. Rankin. Our students will be glad to set up a meeting with you, I'll have the secretary arrange it. They'll present their findings and hear whatever you have to say." Odom fixed his gaze on their visitor. "I encourage you to treat them with more respect than you've displayed here today."

Rankin, who looked to be in his mid-forties, grimaced and grabbed his overcoat. "Perhaps I'll have better results when I talk to the superintendent," he said, as he pushed past Nick and stormed out the door.

Nick brought the issue back to his civics students. "It was a tactical error on my part," he said. "Let's get in groups of three and talk about why." Afterwards all but one group agreed they should have gone to see Rankin first. They called out their reasons.

"Make sure we have the whole picture."

"Keep him from saying we didn't do our homework."

"Know in advance what his line of defense is going to be so we can prepare for how to answer it."

"We'll add it to our final report under 'lessons learned,'" Kenny said.

But Scherrie pushed back. "It may be his company, but it's *our* neighborhood," she insisted. "Why didn't he seek *us* out a year ago, after the DNR first approached *him*?"

When Nick described the dilemma at home that night, both Sophie and Elly cheered for Scherrie. "The company wants to come up with a behind-the-scenes deal," Sophie said. "The kids want justice." She moved away from the stove and stood behind Nick, arms around his chest. "It's good to put it on the checklist, babe, but don't beat yourself up about it."

Nick leaned into her. "I'd hate for the kids to lose this because of an amateur mistake on my part."

After a mostly sleepless night, Nick was sitting in front of his class engrossed in student papers when he noticed a hand snake around him and lay a bouquet of roses and a box of chocolates on his desk. He turned to find Sophie pulling him to his feet and into her arms for a prolonged kiss. "Happy Valentine's Day one day early," she said. The students hooted and cheered. Leave it to Sophie to upend assumptions about who does what in romance, as in everything else. He wondered whether this was long planned or her version of 'snap out of it.'"

"That candy is for the whole class," she announced as she scooted out the door.

Early the following week, Nick and the eight lead students on the project walked over to a conference room at Midland Oil for their meeting. The DNR hydrogeologist met them there and showed his slides. Rankin apparently had been called away on "urgent business" (Scherrie, sitting on Nick's left, drew a stick figure in a top hat hiding behind a tree marked "urgent,") but his Vice President of Community Relations was there, along with their own hydrogeologist from a clean-up company they'd hired. Kenny took detailed notes. The kids asked a lot of questions about timelines and deliverables; one of the environmental justice groups had sent them a great list of concepts and terminology.

Scherrie stood up to ask her question: "How could you know about the spill for so long without making any real steps to clean it up?"

The VP had apparently decided to play sweet rather than surly. "I know how frustrating that must appear," she said. "The problem was caused by a defect in the manufacture of the oil tank, you see, and that company, alas, put us through a lot of legal wrangling before we could get them to move. We had to cross every T and dot every I to make sure it would be done right."

Back in her seat, Scherrie kept her voice calm. "While you were crossing and dotting, our little brothers and sisters were breathing in poison," she said. "If it were your kid dangling on those monkey bars, do you think you might've had the tank checked more often and moved a little faster once you found a problem?"

Sweet turned to surly surprisingly fast. "People's jobs are on the line here," the VP said. "It's easy to make pronouncements, a lot harder to manage budgets and actually create opportunities for this community. Come back when you're old enough to understand how business really works. And get your civics teacher to do a lesson on 'defamation.'"

The kids had decided ahead of time what they would do if the meeting broke down. Within seconds, they all stood up and began a chant: "We won't let you pollute our playground. Jobs AND justice." Even though it was Midland Oil's conference room, they were the last ones to leave.

Nick took the whole team out to lunch afterwards to celebrate their performance and review their plans for the school board meeting the following night. They would be testifying before the committee that oversaw district facilities. "It's your ball game," Nick told the group. "You got all the facts. What's your take on the best way to make your point?"

After some back and forth, Kenny summed up their game plan: "We'll act as if they're on our side and hope they really are."

The committee members, seated up on a stage, had done their homework. They'd read the article and the report from the DNR. After listening to the students' presentation, they complimented them on their activism. The board president apologized several times that the school district hadn't intervened earlier. "We trusted the company would be true to their word and we were wrong," he said. "You dug in. That's what we should have done. We let you down."

"We appreciate that," Scherrie said. "But what matters to us is results. Don't ask our families to wait for lawyers or red tape or bureaucrats or the arrival of spring."

The five committee members invited the students up on the stage and shook each of their hands. They promised immediate action.

Two nights later, the school board president called Nick at home. Milwaukee city officials, representatives of Midland Oil and the school board had come to an agreement on the timetable for a cleanup. "Your kids are heroes, Turner," he said. "We'll send an official proclamation to each of them."

"What about Rankin?" Nick asked. "Is he going after us?" The guy kept popping up in Nick's dreams, oil dripping from his teeth.

"It's all good. The superintendent consulted with the city attorney. He said the issue is cut and dry: It's not defamation if it's true. Don't expect heroics. I'm sure the superintendent had a call with Rankin and talked shit about you, but he's standing behind our resolution."

The students greeted the news with whoops and a surprisingly coordinated version of the electric slide. Nick wrote a giant "133,000 dollars" on the chalkboard. "Midland Oil Company will pay not just for clean-up, but $133,000 in penalties to the state for violating wastewater and hazardous waste laws," he said. "Because of you. And that's not all. The company that's doing the cleanup promised to meet with you on a regular basis to keep you informed of their progress."

"Where's that money going?" Scherrie demanded. "Bigger salaries at the DNR or more staff to keep an eye on these suckers?"

Several students threw out ideas for establishing a community advisory council for the Department of Natural Resources. Kenny's hand flew in the air. 'We need to set up an environmental club here at school. Kids need to be part of this fight."

Scherrie spiked an imaginary volleyball. "Okay," she said. "They didn't invite us, but they wouldn't have done shit without us — excuse my language, Mr. Turner."

Nick bowed in her direction.

With her arms still raised, Scherrie made her way to the front of the room. "Now, about a public school named for a murderer of Native Americans: What do we need to do to get that asshole's name off our building?"

Feminists and Firefighters

Kansas City, Missouri, March 2004

They knew they'd have some training sessions that were all-white and all-male. The department had only twenty-one women out of seven hundred-some firefighters. When Sophie asked what percentage of the force was African-American, the chief's "best guesstimate" was ten percent. Still, she'd hoped the first group would have some diversity.

No such luck.

"All right then," she whispered to Vanessa after all twenty participants had filed into the room and taken their seats. They'd prepared for groups that looked like this. What they hadn't prepared for was the sight of all those white guys with their arms crossed tightly over their chest and scowls reshaping their faces. Likely these firefighters hadn't counted on two trainers who were both female and not both white.

On the plane from Milwaukee, they decided that Vanessa would do the welcome. "I want to establish that I'm not the sidekick," she said. They also agreed not to use their job titles, to avoid any appearance of rank.

"Good morning," Vanessa began. Her locs were carefully secured in a bun. She wore simple black pants and a soft grey sweater, her only jewelry a large turquoise bead on a piece of leather. Sophie also chose low-key, navy slacks with matching cable knit top.

"I'm Vanessa Jackson and this is my colleague, Sophie Reznick. We're looking forward to our conversation with you today. I realize you may be thinking, 'Three hours, how are we going to make it through three hours?'"

No one smiled.

"I promise you, the time will fly by, and at least some of you are going to wish we had more."

Vanessa pointed to the white board, where Sophie had written the word "SOLIDARITY" in giant red letters. Sophie wished those letters came with sound and animation, demanding attention.

"Let's start by remembering why we're here," Vanessa said, her back straight and her voice confident. "I think you all know the line in this song, 'The Union Makes Us Strong.' I think you also know that's true only if internal problems don't tear us apart." Except for one stint at the phone company, Sophie's knowledge of union operations came from her husband, Nick. But Vanessa had been an organizer with the transportation union for three and a half years. She'd sung that line dozens of times on picket lines and in union meetings.

"There's also the job you do every day — yours is one of the few occupations where people literally have to have each other's back. And clearly there's been some tensions here around sexual harassment." Every pair of eyes in the circle shifted to the floor.

Vanessa had the gift of sounding like she was just having a chat with you, keeping her voice level, never sounding preachy. "So whether it's your daily work or your power when the next contract comes up, things are going to be better if all the members of this union are on the same page. That's what we want, and what we think you want as well."

As Sophie unfurled a piece of newsprint laying out the agenda, Vanessa finished her overview. "Here's our starting place. Anyone can harass anyone else, regardless of gender. We know most people, including most men, aren't harassers. They don't engage in that behavior and they don't condone it. Yet the reality is, harassment is widespread and causes real harm. So we need to figure out together what it is and how to stop it."

Sophie's mind scrolled through a list of workplaces where she'd done trainings — from auto plants and sewer districts to fancy restaurants and high-tech companies. She thought of the women whose stories filled her head at night when she couldn't sleep. What those women wanted was so simple it hurt: Believe us, don't blame us. Stop letting people off the hook, no matter how high up they are. Get everyone to stop looking the other way when it's right under their nose.

Common sense. But so far, this group wasn't buying it. Vanessa and Sophie had arranged the chairs, each with its own writing surface, into a large circle, leaving space at the front so they could use the whiteboard and stack handouts on the front desk. "No back row to hide in and heckle," is how Vanessa put it.

But this formation wasn't stopping the hecklers, two guys who grabbed seats mid-circle across from each other. Except for saying their names, the other participants remained silent. It appeared the group had made a pact ahead of time that only these two would talk, and that they'd make only obnoxious comments.

"So are you gals a couple or what?" asked one, a guy with gray hair and a paunch who introduced himself as Christian. Sophie wasn't sure if that was his name or a declaration of his religious denomination. She wondered if she were the first Jew some of these guys had ever encountered.

The question was one of those traps assholes liked to set for straight women. If you rushed to declare your heterosexuality, you played right into their biased assumptions about gay people. If you said, "None of your business," you implied there was something shameful going on that you didn't want to disclose. Fortunately, Sophie had already been initiated in this particular trick, in her first — and clearly not her last — toxic training. In 1994, after she became national director of Working Women United and Vanessa took charge of the Milwaukee office and the local trainings, Sophie had shared her triumphs and her many faux pas — like wanting everyone to like her, or losing it and screaming at an entire group.

Vanessa nodded at Christian and kept her voice steady. "Now there's a good example we'll discuss soon — what questions are appropriate in the workplace and how do you know? When's a question friendly and when is it meant as a put-down? But first, let's work on a definition of sexual harassment."

The other designated heckler, Raymond, a blond in his thirties with a buzz cut who looked like he spent several hours a day in the weight room, clapped his hands. "That's what I came for," he said, drawing out each syllable. "I wanna learn how to excel at sexual harassment. Train me, ladies, oh, please." The rest of the group guffawed.

"Yeah," Christian added. "Train us so we can get the hell back to, you know, saving lives."

"Time out." Vanessa put her hands in a T position. "You all seem to be pretty pissed off. You've known us for less than ten minutes. What are you pissed off at us for?"

Christian banged his fist on his writing surface. Sophie hoped he didn't notice her startle. "Read the local newspaper. After the lawsuit got settled, they ran a big article, front page. Said 'It's no longer a noble profession to be a firefighter in this town.'"

"And yeah, we're pissed at you, too." Raymond sat up in his seat as he threw out this comment. "You admitted it's just a few assholes doing the harassing. So why are you punishing all of us by making us sit through this shit?"

Vanessa leaned back against the front desk. "You're right to be angry about that article. They never should have painted the whole department with the same brush." Sophie noticed at least two people unlock their arms. "But here's the problem: You knew who the assholes are, and apparently you did nothing to stop them."

The room was silent save for the sounds of the pipes pushing heat into the building.

"Remember," Vanessa added, "we're here to have a real conversation." She looked around the circle. "No punishment except what some of you seem to want to inflict on us. How about we start with some agreements: You bring an open mind. We'll listen to whatever you have to say. All of us agree to work from a place of respect."

Raymond rolled his eyes, but Sophie noticed several others nodding. One even gave a salute.

This was the largest training project Working Women United had ever done. Given the scope, they decided to have a male trainer join their team. Randy Carter, a Milwaukee organizer, would present at all the sessions while Sophie and Vanessa split the time. But Randy's baby got sick over the weekend and the last thing they wanted was to postpone. So this first day, at least, the two women were teaming up. Given how the session was turning out, Sophie was glad to have Vanessa's cool head and savvy voice.

Vanessa turned the group over to Sophie to unpack the definition of sexual harassment. A few more people joined the discussion. Over fifteen years, Sophie found similar misunderstandings and similar "aha" moments in every kind of workplace: "Oh, you're talking about behavior that's UNWELCOME and makes it harder to do your job," someone said. "So if I slip and call someone 'honey' one time, I won't get fired?"

"No one's ever called us to complain that the boss used the word, 'honey,'" Sophie said. "They call because something vicious and demeaning is going on and no matter what they try, they can't get it to stop."

To drive home the distinction between "welcome" and "unwelcome," Sophie shared a story of when Nick

195

worked at GE making cables for MRI machines with a small group of women and men. "That group told raunchy jokes a lot," she said. "Like if my husband came in grouchy, someone might say, 'Hey, look who didn't get any last night.' And that was fine with him and fine with ME. So, what set of things all had to be true for that to be the case?"

It took a lot of back and forth for the group to get the basics: those involved had to be peers, working in an enclosed area, everyone participating, and above all, having fun — no one was offended. It took even longer for them to figure out how you'd know that. A fresh-faced guy named Andy pulled on the neck of his Phish tee shirt and raised his hand. "Just ask 'em?" he said.

Sophie took a minute to mime going up to someone with a piece of paper. "Okay," she said, "please check which words I can use and which you find offensive." Christian groaned but several people chuckled.

"I get how that would be awkward," Andy said. "Plus someone might feel pressured to fit in."

"Exactly," Sophie said. "The answer here is nothing mysterious. It's all about how well you know each other. Say I really knew all of you and told you a great joke. Without thinking about it, your mind checks off who you're going to tell that joke to — assuming you remember it — and who you won't. You may decide not to share it with your elderly relatives, although frankly, that's where I get some of my best jokes." Even Christian's lips turned up a little.

"It won't be on the conversation list with your young children or your clergy. Maybe not even your best friend, because they may have a different sense of humor. The point is, out of RESPECT, you make choices all the time about who you say what to, based on whether it'll make them feel good or uncomfortable."

"And what if the person is new?" Andy asked. "How do you know if it's cool or not?"

Sophie smiled. "What do you do now?"

Andy cradled his chin in his fingers. "I guess I wait until I know them better."

"That's it," Sophie said. "Here's a little shorthand we came up with: 'Would I say or do this in front of my significant other? Would I want someone to say or do this to someone I love? Would I want to be seen on TV saying or doing this?'"

Vanessa once described for a reporter the process a lot of men go through in the WWU trainings. "They start out thinking we want them to zip their lips and stop having any fun at work. Then they realize we're talking about not unzipping their fly. They realize they already know the difference between humor and humiliation. And except for the worst offenders, they smack themselves in the head and say, 'Oh, you mean practice the golden rule? The new part they're learning is what it means to stop being a bystander."

Christian and Raymond weren't about to let Sophie off the hook. "First of all, you haven't got a clue what it's like to work in a fire station," Christian said. "We see shit that would make you puke your guts out, gruesome things. We lose brothers on the job. So we need to blow off some steam. A little hazing comes with the territory. Anyone who can't take that should go find themselves a dainty job someplace else."

Raymond nodded. The two seemed to be moving into a routine they'd rehearsed. "Plus, this is some double standard bullshit," he added. "The woman who brought the lawsuit that started this mess was notorious for telling dirty jokes. She had an apron with a big dick in front. You should hear her mouth! And then one day she realizes, because of feminazi groups like yours, she can make herself a bundle by pretending all that talk hurt her goddamn little ears."

Sophie and Vanessa exchanged a look. They had inside information, this charge was blatantly untrue.

Under the guise of "confidentiality," the department said nothing once the lawsuit was resolved, which meant the gossip mongers got to spread rumors and call them facts.

"We actually know what happened," Vanessa told them. "We can't tell you what it was, but we can clarify what it was not. So please listen carefully: The lawsuit had nothing to do with jokes of any kind. Whatever rumors you've heard flow from assumptions. And you know that old saying." She went to the white board and wrote it out in bold cursive: "To assume is to make an ass out of you and me." Chalk dust sprinkled the air.

Christian continued to grumble but didn't seem to capture anyone's attention. Sophie wished Janet, the plaintiff in the case, were in the room and could lay it all out for them. A battalion chief had gone after her for months. He showed up at her house late at night, often while drunk, describing various sexual acts he planned to engage in with her "by hook or by crook." All she wanted was for the harassment to stop, but she couldn't get anyone to pay attention. She hadn't received a dime in the settlement. What she asked for, and won, were these trainings.

The first time this woman called their office, Sophie had been working late. Janet took only a few minutes to describe what she'd gone through. The judge in the case had created a labor-management committee to select a firm. "Do you do this kind of training?" Janet asked. "If so, do you know what an RFP is? Are you on some list to get them in a case like this?"

"Yes, yes and no," Sophie told her. Janet arranged to overnight the Request for Proposal, which was due three days later. In a classic lose-lose, Janet's support for Working Women United got them in the door — but also led the management side of the committee to write them off. Still, Sophie traveled to Kansas City to make their pitch —each vendor had exactly twenty minutes. She did one role play with the union president, who insisted she do the next one with the fire chief. Later the chief told her he'd never even read their application. "I mean, feminism, firefighters, what would you know?" he said. "Then you showed up and showed us what you do. The other candidates spoke legalese and gave lectures. Your presentation was the first time any of us laughed. And after you left the room was the first time we agreed."

Now Vanessa gave instructions for one more exercise before the mid-morning break. "Sophie's passing out a large index card for each of you. Here's the assignment: Imagine you have a daughter who has the desire and the ability to do this job. She gets hired and no one knows she's your daughter. You alright with that?" Vanessa held up the index card. "Without using your name, write a few words to let us know."

"That shows you don't know shit about firefighters." Christian tossed his notecard to the floor. "Every one of these suckers would know she's my daughter."

"I'm sure they would," Vanessa said. "I bet some of you don't have a daughter at all or not one old enough to apply for this job. That's why I said 'imagine.' It's an exercise. Try it."

Raymond stretched his long legs into the circle. "What station is she in?" he demanded.

"That one, the one you're most worried about," Vanessa said. Within a few days, Sophie was sure they'd be able to name exactly which ones those were.

While the group was writing, Sophie sprayed a side wall with a special substance that allowed the cards to stick without tape. "When you're done, place your card on that wall," Vanessa said. "Then let's all walk from one end to the other and take a look."

Even Sophie and Vanessa were stunned by the responses. All but three of them had some variation of "no way in hell." More than one said, "I'd never let my daughter work around these animals."

Back in his seat, Christian kept insisting that everyone would know if his daughter showed up one day and would leave her alone. "Plus she'd be tough like her old man. She could take whatever these assholes dished out." But most of the others got the point. One more holdout unclenched his hands. A guy who hadn't said anything yet summed it up in six words. "Every woman here is somebody's daughter."

Raymond wasn't done. "How come you just worry about women? Why didn't you ask about our son coming to work here?"

Vanessa shifted the bead on her necklace up and down the leather cord. "I'm sure there are male firefighters who hate to be surrounded by porn and some who feel strongly about not taking the name of the Lord in vain," she said. "The guidelines we're promoting, know your co-workers and treat them with respect, apply to everyone. Still, the numbers speak for themselves. Most men aren't harassers, but most harassers are male. Be honest: Would any of you have said, I'd never let my son or nephew work with these animals?"

Christian and Raymond didn't move a muscle, but most of the others shook their heads.

During the break, Andy hung around until everyone else had left the room to use the bathroom or smoke a cigarette. "I want to apologize for how Christian and Raymond are behaving," he said. "You gotta understand that they don't speak for the rest of us. I mean, we didn't come in with good feelings, but you went right to the heart of it all pretty quick and we appreciate it."

When the group reassembled, Vanessa welcomed them back. "I know a session like this seems really different from what you do day to day, but actually, it mirrors a lot what happens in the station." She described the apology they'd gotten without mentioning who made it. "We understand the effort to reach out, but remember this: If you don't like something you witness, if you think it's out of line for someone to use a term like 'feminazi,' then speak up when it happens and say so directly to that individual. Someone being harassed does not want your sympathy. They want the demeaning behavior to stop. And you have a part in making that happen."

With that, she turned it over to Sophie to introduce the role play. The setting was a station with only one woman on the crew. Some of the guys welcomed her. One in particular was her mentor and good friend. But a couple were giving her a rough time and seemed intent on driving her out. The day before this conversation, between the time the woman finished her shift and arrived home, someone had called her fiancé from the station phone to say she was performing sexual favors on all the guys. Her fiancé knew it was bullshit but was ready to come down there with a shotgun — he couldn't stand knowing she worked with people who were capable of such a move.

Sophie took on the role of the woman. Someone who hadn't said much in the group volunteered to play the friend. He was attentive while Sophie described her distress about what happened. "I don't know what to do," she said in character. "The last thing I want is to cause any trouble. I just want to do my job in peace."

"So is it true?" the volunteer said with a grin.

In all the times Sophie had participated in role plays like this, no one had ever responded that way. She choked out the only response she could think of: "Thanks, mother-fucker," and stormed out of the training room, slamming the door behind her.

In the hall, Sophie gulped in air and swung her arms to keep from tearing up. Damn, she could never play these parts without becoming completely submerged. What some saw as a skill, Sophie experienced as a curse. She'd lose all the credibility they'd built up if she showed any emotion, just like the women in a job like this.

As Sophie walked back in, Vanessa caught her eye and gave two quick nods, a signal they'd agreed on ahead of time to say, "You got this."

"So, let's process that together," Sophie said. She rejoiced in hearing her normal voice. "What did this woman need? Why'd she get so angry?"

Christian didn't hesitate. "Here you've got your typical female who wants to believe she can make it in a man's world but has zero sense of humor and super thin skin. Her pal here was just trying to bring it all down a notch, get her to relax and blow it off."

But the guy who played the role shook his head. "Naw, I messed up. She needed support, she needed ... ." He looked around the room as if the word he wanted was hiding somewhere. "Affirmation. I shoulda led with that."

People debated what else this friend should have said. Should he report it to the captain? Go with her to report it?

"If you were in this station, would you know who made that call?" Sophie asked. Several people nodded. "So be this friend. What can he do?" It took five turns to get it out: talk directly to the guy making trouble. They fumbled with what exactly to say.

"Start with what *you* want," Sophie urged. "Do you feel better going to work when this kind of nasty behavior goes on?"

"Actually, it makes my stomach hurt," Andy said.

Sophie wished she could send a telepathic hug. "Then let him know it. Not to rescue some poor woman, but on your own behalf. Give the guy a chance to back off."

"So, don't let it be all on her," Andy said, cheeks flushed. "Don't let him get away with it. Let him know you'll report it if he doesn't stop." This time Andy didn't have to ask whether he got it right.

When Sophie and Vanessa came back from lunch for the afternoon session, they found the union president waiting outside the training room. "I hear you got to observe us in all our glory," he said. "Thanks for lassoing those two assholes and opening so many eyes. My bad, I should have sent someone from the union to introduce you. Not because you need help, but because we want them to know we're squarely behind you. So I'll do that now, and someone will show up each session."

Sophie felt her back muscles loosen. She made a mental note to get the union president to write up tips for other union leaders once the trainings were done.

The second session, which had its own trouble-maker and their first female participant, went by quickly. The afternoon version of Raymond came up with a few doozies: "So, this husband of yours, Sophie, does he keep a little something on the side to get his needs met?" No one laughed. Overall they met with less resistance, but they missed having someone speak as openly as Andy had.

That evening over dinner at the coffee shop in the Days Inn, they replayed the day's highs and lows. "I know you've had your share of dealings with guys like this," Sophie said. "How are you feeling?"

Vanessa pushed away the remains of her Cobb salad. "Honestly?"

"Always."

"It's like a big wave. First, I fight off images of Christian's ancestors picnicking at the lynching of one of my ancestors." Vanessa clutched the bead on her necklace. "Then I silently hum *Ella's Song* and kick them out of my mental space. I flip to thinking about the Andy's. And then I glory in the Janet's."

Sophie exhaled so deeply, the little candle flickered and the light disappeared. "We should get hazard pay," she said. "And yours should be double."

They decided to call it a night and head off to their rooms. Sophie collapsed on the bed and found just enough energy to call Nick. She'd save Vanessa's comment and her own experience in the role play to share when she got home. Instead, she rattled off a few of the day's highlights.

"My favorite part was the discussion about your work group at GE," she told him. "Most of them thought it was a trick. I mean, how could a feminazi like me live with a guy like that?"

Nick's laugh was as soothing as a caress. "Speaking of breakthroughs: Apparently your surprise Valentine's Day kiss in my class back when I was at Custer High has become urban legend. My students at Marshall want to know when they'll get to see one."

"Tell them they'll never know if it's coming, and neither will you."

Sophie could hear Nick shuffling around the kitchen. "So what do you think?" Nick asked. "Will this training stick?"

The million dollar question. "It depends. You never win over everyone, but I think our goal is doable: Neutralize the assholes, build a group of leaders who take this on, get buy-in from higher-ups. The union president and the chief are both good guys who've learned a lot already. But if either retires before they set up a real structure, it could all fall apart."

Her hotel room smelled of cleaning fluid and some weak attempt at a floral spray. Sophie told Nick about Andy. And then she described the woman in their after-noon session who was mostly quiet until they ran into her in the bathroom during the break.

"Here's what makes it all worthwhile." Sophie turned on her side and hugged her pillow to her chest. "The three of us were standing by the sinks. This woman looked at Vanessa and me in the mirror and said, 'Thank you. I love my job. And now maybe I'll love coming to work.'

Magic Monday

Milwaukee, March 25, 2013

Magic Monday. That's how Kiki felt when her second day off fell on a Monday. Two days in a row away from coding checks and feeding them into a machine smart enough to send Betty Jones' money to Wisconsin Electric and Rodney Smith's to his momma in Mobile. Monday was get-in-free day at the Natural History Museum. Sarajane never tired of that butterfly exhibit. She'd plant her little legs and stand perfectly still under a soft curtain of butterflies, then tiptoe to the edge of the room and take off for the long hallway where she could fly back and forth as long as she didn't knock into anyone.

But today — a not-magic-at-all-Monday — Kiki had to drag Sarajane to the doctor to pick up a note proving her daughter really did have an asthma attack during work hours last Monday, and then they had to go all the way down to the bank to get it in on time. Kiki didn't understand why the clinic couldn't just email the note, or why the head of the check processing department couldn't wait one more day, but People's Trust Bank didn't have a whole lot of trust in its people. "It's not up to me, Ms. Oppedahl," Dorey Stotz told her. "The rules say we need a note personally signed by the doctor within a week of the occurrence or we have to double the absence points. It's only fair to treat everyone the same, don't you agree?" That was some bullshit right there — the asthma attack "occurred" to Kiki's little girl, not to the company.

Still, if they timed it right, Kiki thought, they might be able to squeeze in an hour at the museum. She and

Sarajane would make a game of it — how fast could they run the long block from the bus stop to the employee entrance in the back of People's Trust. Sarajane was a trooper. Even though it was so cold, the hairs in their nostrils froze as soon as they stepped off the bus, she grabbed Kiki's hand and hurled herself into the race. If they hadn't been in such a hurry and the wind hadn't snatched Sarajane's good-as-new scarf and the front door wasn't so much closer than the employee entrance around the corner, Kiki might have remembered that going in this way meant they'd have to pass the bank's child care center. Whoever fixed that place up, they sure knew kids. Sarajane stopped mid-skip, mesmerized by toddlers playing with giant puzzles and blocks that looked like real bricks, the walls filled with dancing letters and rows of musical instruments. Her head whipped back and forth, but it was the easels that got her, the tangy scent of finger paint. Sarajane saw kids painting like this once on TV. Sometimes she'd pretend the refrigerator was an easel and use her finger to make big loops up and down.

"Look, Momma, paints!" Sarajane squealed, pointing to a line of easels in one corner. "Go! Now!"

Kiki tried to whirl her daughter's body to face away from the humongous glass wall. Of course, the bigwigs at the bank would want to show off this center, never mind that not one single hourly worker could afford to put their kid there. Last summer Kiki had to fill in for a day in the stockroom. In the center of the room was a set of shelves labeled "Branding," which Kiki thought was something done to cows but her friend Lalease told her meant the BS they paid people with fancy degrees to churn out just to make the company look good. The shelves were filled with brochures stacked in neat piles for customers and job applicants. One whole entire pamphlet was about the "state-of-the-art" child care center, a "Midwestern masterpiece to nurture the next generation."

As Sarajane used both skinny arms to push herself away from Kiki and turned her squeal into a holler, Kiki cursed herself for being such a stupid, shit-for-brains loser. No way to explain the rules to a two-and-a-half-year-old, why this was different from the museum, only certain people could play there, not us, never us, not even on Magic Monday, golden rule here doesn't mean sharing, means those that have the gold make the rules. Kiki would never forget the feel of her daughter's rigid body and hot tears the rest of the way up to Stotz's office.

Even though she had an assistant who was sitting right at his desk in front of her big-ass office, Stotz came out personally to see what all that fuss was about. She didn't say a word, just stood there, five feet one at most without her fancy heels, suit the color of caramel that surely cost more than three months of Kiki's grocery bill, silky blonde hair, skin that was "fair," not "washed out" like theirs. Kiki had to fight the urge to rub Sarajane's snot-filled face all over this woman, who just stood there waiting as Kiki crouched down, held her sobbing daughter with one arm and pawed through her purse with the other to pull out the doctor's note.

As Kiki hoisted Sarajane on her shoulder and pushed herself to standing, she tried to avoid her boss's face, but one glance was enough. Stotz wasn't even thirty years old, but her scowl turned her into every teacher, every landlord, every boss Kiki had ever had. Behind Stotz's "Thank you, Ms. Oppedahl," Kiki read the branding: "Loser Mom Who Can't Control Her Brat." Along with the unspoken reminder: Any more absence points and poof, Kiki's job would disappear.

Sh*t That Needs Fixing

Milwaukee, 2009-2013

Soon after her first promotion at People's Trust Bank, Dorey Stotz began keeping a list she called STNF (Sh*t That Needs Fixing). These were a mixture of things said or done to her directly at the bank: "Hey, missy, we're out of coffee, can you pick some up on your way in tomorrow?" "Ooh, this one loves to press her point. Maybe I need to press my point a little harder next time." Behavior she'd witnessed or overheard; rounding a corner: "I don't care how short she is, long as her mouth can reach my dick, we'll be just fine." And complaints she heard from other women ("I'm tired of being the only woman in those meetings. If they agree with me, what I say is 'obvious.' Otherwise I'm wrong." "Try being the only Black woman: 'How do *your people* feel about trusts?'" "Don't get in an elevator alone with Dwayne Dexter, or he'll be grinding up against you before you get to the lobby.")

Dorey vowed to do her mother proud. Growing up, Annie Stotz's story about how she and her friends stood up for themselves at work was Dorey's favorite; no fairy tales in their little household.

Still, she had been judicious about which of these issues to raise with her mentor, Leo Maguire, and which to let simmer until she had more support or more power. That April, she decided she had to do something about Dwayne Dexter. Forget sexual harassment, this was out and out sexual assault. She made her case in what she hoped was a thoughtful manner during her monthly lunch with Leo at Mo's Steak House, pointing out Dexter was a lawsuit waiting to happen and the damage that could cause the bank. She'd already seen two promising women leave because of him.

"Did he do that to you?" Leo asked. He'd just finished his own butter and was scooping hers off her plate, knowing she never touched the bread.

Dorey looked him in the eye. "No, but that's not the point. Are you saying you don't believe he could do it?"

Leo's laugh was half chuckle, half snort. Although his hair was mostly gray, he still had a redhead's ruddy cheeks. "Oh, I believe it. I make it a point never to shake the guy's hand, you never know where it's been. He's an asshole and a slime bucket. But he's also a rainmaker. Comes from a development family that's as close to aristocracy as you get in a place like Milwaukee. Uncles and brothers and cousins, up to their elbow in every major building project in this city. Sorry, my dear, but he's one of the untouchables."

"Good lord, Leo, this is 2009!" Dorey tried to keep her voice from quivering. "Are you telling me it doesn't *matter*? What if someone did that to Amelia?"

"My daughter would have her antennae up, just like you. I know you gals warn each other about him — that's the smartest thing to do." Leo waited while the server delivered his Porterhouse steak and Dorey's shrimp salad.

"But what message does it send to all the other men?"

Leo dug into his steak and speared a piece on his knife. "Look, kid, I don't mean to sound cold-hearted, but you asked me always to be direct with you. Starting out your career by instigating a complaint might clear the guy outta here a year or two before he would have retired anyway. If he put the moves on you personally, it might win you some settlement dollars. But it'll hardly win advocates to champion your career. Besides, Dexter's part of the old guard. The younger guys aren't that stupid."

Dorey waited while Leo transferred the steak from the knife to his mouth and chewed it. She nibbled at the edges of her salad as she recalled Kipp Schneider, two years out of college, cupping her butt cheek as he slid past her in the hall.

"Trust me on this," Leo said. "There'll be plenty of good you can do when you're in a position of authority here. The Milwaukee branch is the second largest at People's Trust and on track to be the most profitable. Landing a top spot here can launch you nationally. Consider these your apprentice years, time to get some calluses on your hands." He trimmed a small piece of fat from his meat and placed it on his bread plate. "Now, tell me about the new software package you want for your people."

That night Dorey stood before her boyfriend and repeated the conversation nearly word for word. At six foot one, Max towered over her. She much preferred to share this kind of news when he was seated and she was not.

"You gotta be kidding me, babe." Max smacked his thigh with his hand. "That's un-fucking-believable, the textbook definition of a corporate cover-up. You're always talking about standing up like our mothers did at the call center. Listen, I know a great guy over at the EEOC who would salivate at taking them on."

Dorey wrapped her arms around her midriff. "First of all, I'd have to convince someone to file the complaint. The woman who tipped me off told me in no uncertain terms that she needs her job and learned to take the stairs. And even if someone did come forward, you know what would happen. They'll find an early retirement package, sign some 'we'll take care of this guy but we're not saying we did anything wrong' deal with the EEOC, and that'll be the end of it. Oh, except for one little detail — Thom Luchsinger will find a way to connect me to it and deep six my career." Dorey suspected the CEO would be more sympathetic to Dexter than to her. She'd heard a rumor about him being "hands-on."

"Dorey, love of my life." Max shoved the law journals off the couch and gently pulled her beside him. "Listen, I know I talk about corporate America as if every place is a snake pit, but there have got to be better banks to work for and better CEOs. You have such amazing ideas about how to drive real change. I'm sure Vanessa or her friend Sophie Reznick at Working Women United could help you research other places. You're not a goddamn indentured servant. Just because they put you in that training program doesn't mean you owe them your loyalty."

Dorey stroked his hand. "It's the other women there I feel loyal to, especially the ones in my division, I don't want to abandon them. And I can see Leo's point. I have all these ideas, but I have to get into a position of power in order to implement them. He thinks I can become Deputy Division Head next year — that's unheard of." She decided not to mention what Leo said about the national trajectory.

"I can see what you gain." Max's hand sprawled across his mouth. He did that when he was trying to control his disapproval. "But what do you lose in the process?"

***

Five months after she got promoted to Deputy Division Head of Operations, Dorey worked on a detailed proposal to set up a Task Force on Women and Banking. She realized she couldn't tackle all the issues at once, and she couldn't tackle them all on her own. A task force would be a way to involve people from every layer of the bank, look at women as customers as well as staff. They could bring in speakers. Above all, Dorey hoped she could convince top management to conduct an anonymous survey about bank policies and culture. That way they'd have to look for some real solutions. The other bank managers in her Milwaukee Women Lead circle faced the same stonewalling. Edna Clark and Wendy Chang wanted to use

Dorey's success at People's Trust to create a similar process at M&I and Chase.

Dorey set up a special meeting with Leo in his office. Inside her binder was a twenty-page, typed proposal. It cited three banks in other cities that had done something similar and displayed pie charts and graphs showing projected Return on Investment. At Wendy Chang's suggestion, Dorey buried the survey idea in a paragraph on "data collection tools" and left out the word "anonymous."

Leo didn't even scan the two-page executive summary, never moved his eyes beyond the title page. "You're making a real impact here, Dorey. The mortgage lending program for single women is a big success. The new software packages you brought in really bumped up efficiency. You've had the least turnover in your department and promoted some crackerjack women. You know I want nothing more than to see you go farther than any woman has at People's Trust."

He nudged the proposal closer to her, a signal for her to return it to the binder. "When Bob Rawson retires as Director of Operations, you're going to see a lot more competition. Getting pigeonholed as the 'women's advocate' is the last thing you want. That proposal would be dismissed as a complaint magnet and overshadow all the positive results you're gotten here. Put it in a drawer. Later, when you're the first female Vice President, you'll have a lot more latitude. But first we got to get you there, kid."

Dorey waited to tell Max until she'd gotten a second opinion, this one from Brianna, the mentor assigned to her early on in the MBA program at Marquette. Brianna was now at Bank of America in Chicago, but visited clients in Milwaukee on a regular basis. They got together for a drink at Harbor House three days after the meeting with Leo. Dorey emailed the task force proposal in advance.

Brianna breezed in wearing a grey cashmere sweater dress and a long gold chain. She gave Dorey an air kiss, ordered them each a dirty martini, and dove straight in.

213

"The guys would just love to see you stuffed into the 'women's' slot.' They'll go after you with a sledgehammer for being caught up in special interests and identity politics. You might as well tattoo 'Feminazi' on your forehead. For now, tie a bow on that document and put it away. Wait until you're ensconced on your seat of power. Even then, make sure there are two other women and at least one man presenting the proposal as a shared idea."

The drinks arrived. Brianna took a long sip and laughed.

"You really have to learn to develop a poker face, Dorey." Brianna leaned over and touched Dorey's glass with her own. "Moving up the corporate ladder as a female is like living in a third world country. You have to learn the ways of the natives. Only when you've earned their trust can you introduce electricity."

When she filled Max in that night, Dorey didn't repeat every detail of the conversations with Leo and Brianna. "I think they both liked the idea," Dorey told him over Max's signature yellow curry with tofu. "It's a matter of timing. And power. The Task Force will have a lot more weight if it comes with authority."

Max muttered warnings about the minefield of working inside the system, but he was preoccupied with his first big case since getting a job with Legal Action: a class action lawsuit involving wage theft at a local restaurant chain. Dorey encouraged him to tell her all about it.

***

The promotions continued. So did the STNF (Lack of data by race and gender on promotions and pay. Lack of any progress outside my department promoting women or people of color. A showcase child care center that none of the hourly workers can afford. Men disregarding women's ideas until another man says the same thing, then finding the proposal "brilliant" and "original").

214

In late April of 2011, with the city finally on the cusp of spring, Dorey became the youngest candidate ever for Division Head of Operations. Two of her competitors were internal, both, men. Leo told her they had three prospects from outside People's Trust and at least one from outside Milwaukee. "I can't give you any other info," he said. "And I don't get a vote. But you've made your mark here, kid, I'll tell you that. Just keep on producing and you'll give 'em all a run for their money."

Dorey began putting in even longer hours in order to get a handle on the various departments under Operations. Max was skeptical. "Damn, Dorey, I feel like you've signed up for survivalist camp, cut off from everyone you love and everything that brings you comfort. You cancelled our trip to Puerto Rico. Your calls with your mom are like speed check-ins. And when was the last time you hung out with any of your friends? Are you sure you want to take this on?"

"Talk about double standards, Max. You've brought work home every night this week." Dorey pointed at the files heaped beside their bed.

Max set aside the article he was reading and gently pried her hands off her laptop. "Here's the thing, my love. When I work late, everyone in the office is on my side. We're all fighting to improve people's lives right now. Even if you get a top job, how much shit will you really be able to fix?"

For the first time, Dorey felt a crack in the nub of certainty at the base of her spine.

Three days later, she traveled to a Women Lead conference in Chicago to present a workshop on the women's entrepreneur program she initiated at the bank. "Of course, you say yes," Brianna insisted when Dorey checked in with her about the invitation. "Good for your resume, good publicity for the bank, good networking for the future. You can work on the train and be back the same night. No down side other than the food." Her allies at the other Milwaukee banks wouldn't be there. Wendy couldn't get the time off. Edna had decided to get out of the corporate rat race and was starting graduate school in the fall. What sealed the deal for Dorey was the chance to hear a keynote from a woman she'd written a profile on in college. Olivia Rogers was among the handful of bank CEOs who were female and, even rarer, she was African-American. Since taking that office, she'd promoted significant numbers of women, instituted a paid leave program, and launched an audit of pay procedures in an effort to end pay inequity. Dorey left the luncheon early to get a front row seat.

Olivia Rogers, whose photos always showed hair that was straightened and coifed, now wore her hair closely cropped. Contact lenses or laser surgery had gotten rid of her signature red glasses. Both changes magnified her eyes, which were inky and slightly angled and seemed to be looking right at Dorey. After laying out each of her initiatives with a series of graphics showing the positive impact on the bottom line, Rogers put her hands on each side of the podium and paused for a moment. "If you came expecting a praise song for the banking industry, you're in the wrong place," she said. "If you came looking for Superwoman, get out now. My secret is no different from any other woman who makes it to the top — find ways to put up with a lot of bullshit. There's not a racist or sexist stereotype I didn't have to push through. Grow another layer of skin. Choose your battles wisely. But once you're up there, have a clear plan of action to institute the changes you know are needed."

The audience moved from jaw drop to silence to scribbling on index cards, which were passed to volunteers and up to the moderator, a local television celebrity. "Many of these questions are a variation on one theme, Olivia," she said. "If there was so much BS, why didn't you leave for a better place?"

Olivia Rogers closed her eyes for a moment and nodded. "Where would I have gone? These problems permeate our entire industry, our entire nation. What helped was knowing I was not alone. Other pioneers were out there trying to make the same kind of changes. We had to plug away, pay our dues, keep our eyes on each other, and when we got in positions of power, find each other and work together to make change."

Dorey felt as if Olivia Rogers were sending her a direct message: Toughen up and keep your eyes on the prize.

***

The next eight months flew by, a blur of work peppered with fewer outings and more frequent arguments with Max. When she got assigned to the bank's leadership trip to Japan, Max made wisecracks about wasteful spending and carbon footprints. Alone in her office, Dorey danced around her desk. Her hard work was paying off. "You'll be flying with the big boys," Brianna told her after reading the forwarded invite. "Seeing you on the corporate jet and in high-level meetings helps normalize women's leadership at one of the biggest bastions to male privilege. This is your moment. Gird yourself."

So Dorey admired her reflection in the jet's window and vowed to tune out Thom Luchsinger's crude comments which, to her dismay, started the minute the flight began. "We're taking off!" he said. "Now all I need is a lovely lady to take it all off and wait in the back for me to land." Everyone laughed, even Leo, who was sitting beside her as she molded her hands to the armrests. "Lighten up," he whispered. "Have some fun."

The meetings went smoothly. On the last night of the trip, jet lag drove Dorey to go to bed early. The click of a doorknob woke her, Thom sashaying through the door connecting their adjoining suites. Instantly she was alert, cursing herself for not checking the lock, trying to

217

jump out of the Japanese platform bed, smashing her shin against the side as she reached for the hotel's white robe. But there was no time. Thom was already setting down the margarita pitcher and glasses rimmed with salt. He was drunk — she could smell the alcohol as he grabbed her — not sloppy drunk, surprisingly nimble, moving as she moved, like a parody of a shadow puppet. She felt so exposed. Why had she brought this nightie, purchased for Max? Now she understood why they call it a plunging neckline, Thom plunging his hand down the V-neck, pinching her nipples, oh, god, hand drifting down to her panties, fingers prodding, crude talk, much worse than the plane. She started talking fast, steady, "Stop, please. Think of your family, my Max, business rules." But nothing was working. Thom was panting against her neck, saying, "Just this once," saliva on her throat. And then blessedly, the phone rang, it had to be Max forgetting the time difference. Thom startled enough for her to lift the receiver, twist out of his grasp, keep the phone between them, pivoting as she shouted Max's name over and over, dragging the phone with her to the door between the suites, using her foot to nudge Thom out of the room. Then there was only Max's voice, filled with anxiety. "It's nothing," she said. "You woke me, it's late here, I'll call you back." She needed both hands to secure the deadbolt on that door. She never did call Max back, instead sending a two-word lying text. She never went back to bed.

On the corporate jet the next day, Dorey was too traumatized to sleep. Surely she'd have to quit her job. But Brianna's spirit accompanied her on the plane. "Remember this," Brianna had told her after her promotion to division head. "Someone in a powerful position *will* put his hands on you. You can cry sexual harassment and the powers-that-be will pay you, but he'll stay, and you'll be gone, career hopes punctured worse than an anxious schoolboy's condom. Learn when to duck, and when that doesn't work, learn to suck it up. The last thing you want to be is the girl who can't handle a bad boy on her own."

Dorey spent the entire flight pretending to be sick to her stomach and making a list of things she could control. She would tell Leo so somebody knew. She wouldn't avoid Thom altogether, that would show the CEO had rattled her. But she would limit their encounters. She would always carry a large binder to have a buffer if he came too close. For trips she couldn't avoid, she'd make sure her assistant booked the hotel room, a corner single, nothing adjoining, never again.

She'd spent five years on this journey — no way was she going to give up now. Brianna had drilled it into her that the direction in corporate America was one way: up or out. Anything she tried would end her future, not just at People's Trust, but in the banking world and who knows where else. Thom's tentacles spread far. If she was going to fulfill her promise to the women she'd hired and promoted, she had to stick it out.

Before the plane landed, Dorey made two decisions: Buy an upscale condo close to downtown, something befitting an executive. And up the ante for her chances at the VP slot by helping get the bank on a prestigious list of best places for women to work.

***

Max didn't want the condo, wasn't part of the purchase, didn't appear on the deed. But he made it clear he didn't want to fight about it, either. Dorey handed over the decorating to a firm recommended by Brianna. Once they moved in that April, she loved snuggling up with Max late at night, looking out over the Milwaukee River, listening to the occasional boat horn. They celebrated their first year there along with another career milestone: Dorey made the short list for vice president of People's Trust in Milwaukee. If she succeeded, she'd become the bank's first female vice president — and the youngest — at any branch. The decision would be announced late summer.

Max interrupted her musings with an update on his latest case. "This raid was horrific," he said, moving closer to her in the bed. "Families are split apart, kids left stranded with both parents gone, no notice to caregivers, no information on where they've taken the deportees. The only upside is the office assigned me to lead the work. To put someone just a few years out of law school in charge of such a big case, it's an amazing opportunity. And I'm working with Voces de la Frontera ..."

"Remind me who that is. I can't keep up with all your groups."

Dorey felt his arms and legs stiffen. Max propped himself up on one elbow. "Voces, Dorey. They're right around the corner from St. Rita's food pantry. The one you used to volunteer at when you first got back." Just like him to idealize the naïve girl she'd been when they hooked up.

"See, there's an example," she said. "When I get the VP job, I'll expand the bank's charitable giving and their community service. That'll do a lot more good than me dishing out food a couple hours a week. Plus, you know what they say about teaching someone to fish, the women's loan program I developed has helped dozens of women start new businesses."

"I didn't know we were keeping a tally." Max's voice dropped to a whisper.

"Listen, Max. I'm glad Legal Action sees your potential. Really I'm proud of you. But I have a lot on my mind right now."

Max reached for both her hands. "So talk to me, Dorey. You've been so busy, I don't have any idea what's going on at work."

"Work, that's what's going on," she said. "It's like a marathon, they don't just pluck you out as the winner. You have to put in the effort every day."

"Winner?" Max shook his head like a swimmer trying to get the water out of his ears. "Damn, Dorey, when did it become all about power? What happened to the passion I fell in love with?"

"Power? You bet I want power. And so do you, Mr. Serve-the-People whose dick got hard the minute you were assigned the hot case."

Dorey had been storing that one up for a long time. Still, she didn't want to turn the evening into a fight. When Max's eyes began to fill, she let him pull her close.

"Please, love," he said. "Let's call in sick tomorrow and spend the day together. The snow is gone and there might be some early blooms. We could go out to Lapham Peak. How long has it been since you took a day off?"

Their last outing flashed before her, romping with his family's Irish setter, embracing on a picnic blanket somewhere off the trail, the scent of autumn leaves burning in the distance. So tempting. But Max had no clue what it was like to be a woman in a man's world. Lapham Peak would have to wait a few weeks.

Dorey gave him a long hug. "Sounds lovely. As soon as I get over this next hurdle, my sweet. I promise."

***

Leo Maguire had loved her idea about promoting the bank and wanted to go for the biggest get, *Lead* magazine's list of Best Workplaces for Women. He asked for her help and Dorey threw herself into the task. They'd missed the 2012 deadline but used the time to study how to get high marks the following year. The story announcing the winners appeared in the Milwaukee paper in late April. Not only did it name People's Trust Bank-Milwaukee in the top tier, the article also included a quote from Dorey praising the company's efforts to move women into management positions.

Max read over Dorey's shoulder. "This is such a crock. You're always complaining they don't have a single woman in senior positions."

"That's the whole point." More and more Dorey felt like Max spoke a foreign language and needed her to translate even the simplest interactions. "This could be my ticket to the VP title. Leo Maguire just gave me a big boost."

Max carried their coffee cups to the table, where he'd already bitten into his first piece of cinnamon toast. "What bullshit magic did Maguire pull off?"

Dorey blew out a long stream of air. "I know, you're right, it *is* bullshit — but that's the way the game is played, until more of us get in there and change it. Leo's not just head of PR, he's head of the Diversity Office. His job is to get us on these lists. The one at *Lead* magazine is the biggest and most influential. I helped him write a great application. He spent a bundle on a big ad and bought the highest level sponsorship for the awards dinner."

Max wrapped his hand around his mouth as if to stifle a gag. "Jesus, Dor, I don't trust any of those guys. What I can't figure out is how they suckered you into this. Whatever happened to the bright-eyed girl who wanted to shake things up?"

Dorey whisked the business section away from Max's cup and greasy crumbs and began to clip the article with long, even snips. "We've been through this a hundred times, Max. I will shake things up, but I can only do that if I'm in a position of power."

"Fuck that, Dorey." The more Max got on his soapbox, the louder he became. "What's the point if you have to become just like *them* to get there?"

Dorey finished cutting out the article and tossed the remains of the paper into the recycling bin. Bad enough she had to defend herself every second at work, she couldn't believe she had to keep doing it at home. "Here's the point, Max. If you're a man, ambition's an asset. A sign that you're serious, that you'll work hard, that you're reliable. But if you're a woman? God forbid you should like the idea of being the decision-maker, of having an assistant after years of doing the grunt work, getting a nice office, whatever. Then you're nothing more than a scheming, climbing jezebel."

Max grabbed her hand. "I don't want to argue, baby," he said. "It's just, I miss how things used to be between us. I miss *you*."

Dorey slid away from his grasp. "You know what I think, Max? You like to hang out your feminist pedigree, but deep down, you're just another guy who wants to be the protector. You wish I was still that vulnerable girl whose dad beat her mom and whose family had to run and hide. Well, get over it. I'm not your baby. I can take care of myself, and I'm making sure I always will. Today Dorey Stotz is stepping into power."

Max jerked his head back as if she'd slapped him.

"C'mon, Maxie." She really didn't have time for drama this morning. "It's not that complicated. If you love me, show me that you're rooting for this promotion, just like I'm rooting for you to win your case. We'll have plenty of time together after that."

When she came home that night, Max was already in bed. He'd left a note on the dining room table, just three words in large red letters that looked like accusatory fingers: STNF: OUR RELATIONSHIP. Dorey planned to talk to him about it the next morning, but he was still asleep when she left early for audit prep.

Sixteen hours later, she arrived to find the closet door open, Max's side bare except for a dozen hangers jumbled together in the corner.

223

You Are the 'You'

Milwaukee, April 11, 2013

Kiki shoved her umbrella into her tote. The drizzle had started up again, but it was more like a mist, not worth the hassle of trying to stretch the fabric to fit the spoke that sprang loose in the last storm. "It's only a few blocks," she told Lalease, who was breathing through her mouth, the way she did when her blood pressure was bothering her. Lalease was busy holding on to her rain bonnet to make sure the mist didn't mess with her neatly curled hair.

At the corner of Wisconsin and Plankinton, Kiki checked the scrap of paper with the address of Working Women United. "It's across the street," she said. "Right next to that steak place." Once inside, the building looked shabby, but you could see from the spiral stairway and the high ceiling with its gold-plated doo-dads that it used to be grand.

Working Women United's office turned out to be one big room with some partitions and a tiny kitchen in the back. Kiki thought it would be empty at five fifteen on a Friday night, but the director had agreed to stay late to meet with them. The phone was ringing and a group of people were drawing signs at a big table by the door, everyone talking at once and sometimes laughing, the air ripe with the smell of fresh baked banana bread. One young boy, maybe seven or eight, was waving a just-finished sign that said, "Don't punish my mom when I get sick."

"Hi, you must be Kiki and Lalease." Kiki had expected to see a business suit. The tall woman who held out her hand was dressed in black jeans and a Ko-Thi

Dance sweatshirt. "I'm Vanessa Whitley Jackson. Really glad you could come in. Excuse our mess, we're getting ready for a rally for our paid sick days campaign."

Rally. Campaign. Paid sick days. The words sounded exotic, like something that would happen in a movie, yet Vanessa said them as if they were the most ordinary things in the world.

Kiki gazed at the posters that covered every wall, an explosion of colors and shapes and words. "My consciousness is fine, it's my pay that needs raising." "A woman's work is never done—or appreciated, or paid what it's worth." Her eye fixed on a fanciful drawing of a large animal in a silky web. Underneath were the words: "When spider webs unite, they can tie up an elephant."

That morning on the bus, Kiki and Lalease talked about what they hoped would come out of this meeting. They liked to die when they saw their employer, People's Trust Bank, in the paper for making *Lead!* magazine's list of Best Workplaces for Women. Vanessa's group might not be able to do much about the goings-on at the bank, but maybe they could get them bounced from that list. "You know they had to lie to get on there," Lalease had said. "'Bout time someone called them out."

Vanessa seated them in front of a sturdy desk that had been around the block a few times. The chairs didn't match but felt comfortable. Vanessa began with a little history of Working Women United, starting back in 1982, before Kiki was born. Sounded like they had been raising hell ever since. Kiki remembered seeing them on TV a couple times, protesting something — really, she hadn't paid attention. But now she couldn't take her eyes off Vanessa. This woman could have been a sign language interpreter, the way she waved her hands around while she talked. After calling to arrange the meeting and guessing from her voice that Vanessa was Black, Kiki had been afraid the conversation would be directed only to Lalease.

But Vanessa was so warm and interested in both of them, asking questions about their jobs like she really wanted to hear their answers. And if she was a lawyer or professor or something like that, she didn't talk like it. Vanessa could have been someone they worked with, except she seemed to know a lot about people's rights.

"So tell us the truth," Lalease said. "Can you bump them off that list?"

Vanessa's earrings, a cluster of small silver beads, swung each time she turned her head to look from one of them to the other. "Here's the problem with these lists: Everything on it can be true and the company can still be a pretty awful place to work. Some of the so-called experts don't ask enough hard questions." She pointed to the sign-makers at the front of the room. "Like, on paper they might say you get a certain number of sick days. But they leave out the fact that you lose your pay and rack up discipline points each time you use one."

"Yes!" Kiki said. "Not to mention that you have to go to the doctor's office to get a note, and pay the co-pay, even if the doctor could tell you what to do over the phone, even if you already know what to do yourself."

Vanessa went on to list a number of other loopholes, like the policies being only for managers, or only if your manager says it's okay.

"Ain't that the truth," Lalease chimed in. "That's just how they do us."

Kiki thought of Sarajane right now parked in front of the TV set at her grandma's, chewing on her hair as she waited for her momma to come home. "How about policies only if you can afford them. You should see their child care center, more toys and gizmos than they know what to do with. But it costs so much. My little girl ..." Kiki was embarrassed to feel her eyes filling up. She cleared her throat. "So instead you rely on your mother one day, a neighbor the next. You just pray they're not too tired or swamped by too many other kids." Or too drunk, but Kiki wouldn't say that, not to anyone, not even her sister who knew and tried to stop by their mother's from time to time to keep an eye on things.

Vanessa nodded like she understood exactly what Kiki was talking about. Not like the people who came up with that list.

The group at the table began to pack up their things. Kiki could hear them teasing each other about whose sign would draw the TV cameras. "Jamal's," one woman declared. "Someone needs to start listening to these children."

"I got a call from a woman who said her place won an award for having an onsite child care center," Vanessa said. "But they also have mandatory overtime. What good's it do to have your kid nearby if you don't get to see each other 'til late and you're both wiped out when you get home?"

"That may be true at the bank, too, for supervisors," Kiki said. "But for us, the big problem is mandatory *under*-time." She explained to Vanessa how five months ago orders came down from on high to cut costs. "Our division head came up with a real doozy. I can just see her at her desk, this fancy glass number, when the lightbulb popped over her head. She cut our hours to thirty-seven, just under full time, so we don't qualify for pensions and we get fewer holidays and such. Lalease was just about to make her twenty years to get vested."

Vanessa's frown transformed her whole face. "Thirty-seven hours counts as part-time? Losing that pension must be really hard for you, Lalease."

Lalease didn't have to say a word. She just fixed her elbows on the desk and sank her jaw into the curve of her hands.

"How's it work?" Vanessa asked them. "Is your schedule at least predictable?"

Kiki would have to add that word to the list she'd heard in this office, something to search for in her dreams. She shook her head hard. "Take this week," she told Vanessa. "I work first shift, that's eight to five."

"I take it lunch is unpaid?" Vanessa's mouth had remained tight.

"Oh, yeah. Forty unpaid minutes, and you get two ten-minute breaks. We don't even get a pee on their dime." Kiki was tickled to hear both Lalease and Vanessa laugh. She felt herself sit up a little taller.

"Sorry, I didn't mean to interrupt you," Vanessa said.

"Our department is open on Saturday so you have to see whether you work then and which day you get off. And most times you wind up working 40 hours — just not every week, so they can keep saying you're not full time."

Lalease lifted her head. "And then there's all the days they make you stay late ..."

Vanessa looked like someone who knew a lot about workplace bullshit, but still her eyes grew wider. She asked questions about the chain of command, scribbling names on a notepad. Kiki watched the column grow, starting with the CEO, Thom Luchsinger. When Kiki mentioned Dorey Stotz was their division head, Vanessa's jaw got all tight. She drew a little box around that name, like maybe she knew someone in the family.

"So what do you think?" Lalease asked. "About the list? Can you get them off?"

Vanessa held her pen up like an offering. "Even if you can't prove the company lied, you can embarrass them by getting publicity about how these so-called family-friendly policies leave out most families at the bank. 'How can you trust People's Trust?' — something like that. You could petition the magazine to take them off the list, and then try to get a media story about it."

Kiki's pulse was climbing so fast she was afraid she'd start hyperventilating. She looked over at Lalease, who had slumped in her chair. "We hoped you would step in," she told Vanessa.

"Actually, you are the 'you,'" Vanessa told them. "We can do a lot to support you, help contact the media, that sort of thing. But you're the ones with the power to make something happen."

She might as well have said they had the power to be trapeze artists. Kiki didn't want to see Lalease's reaction. "You don't understand. The bank isn't like anywhere else. People are scared. They just want to do their job and get the heck out of there."

Vanessa cracked a big grin. "If I had a dollar for every time someone says that. The truth is, the people in charge want you to think everyone else is too scared to move. And hope you hate each other while you're at it so no one will even try." She twisted around and pointed to the sign above her desk: *Central States workers want a union election now!* "I was part of that union drive at the call center back in the mid-90s," Vanessa said. "You're too young, Kiki, but Lalease may remember."

"You know Maxine Williams?" Lalease asked Vanessa.

"Sure do. She was one of our original committee members."

Kiki was amazed to see Lalease give Vanessa a high five. "Maxine is my cousin's sister-in-law. I heard all about it from her. Ya'll made some noise!"

"Our problems were a lot like yours," Vanessa said. "Plus, we had Big Brother. You know, 'This call may be monitored for quality purposes.'"

Kiki nodded. She worked at a call center when she was pregnant with Sarajane.

"I think CSA invented that," Vanessa said. "Anyway, it's a long story. Sometime over a nice bottle of wine I'll tell you all about it."

"But you were part of it?" Kiki promised herself she'd hear that story and remember every detail, tell it to Sarajane when she was old enough until she knew it by heart.

"I helped from the outside, they fired me before it all got going." Vanessa's hands stayed quiet, but Kiki had a feeling she'd been a leader. "Later the union hired me to help. I stayed with them a while, then moved over here to have more time with my kids. Union jobs can be great, but the hours were a killer."

Kiki hated to sound like a coward, especially in front of this woman. "It's just, they watch us like a hawk. It's hard to do anything on the job."

"I know all about that," Vanessa said. "I'm not saying it's risk-proof. But you have rights. You *are* allowed to band together to improve your workplace. And we'll have your back. One step at a time. Think about who you trust most, just a few people. Start with them."

"Don't have to think about who we trust the least," Lalease said. "That's our manager, Dorey Stotz. We have to make sure she don't catch wind of this."

This time Vanessa pressed her hands against her face, like she'd just heard her best friend's cancer was terminal. Kiki's pulse kept banging, but Lalease spoke for the both of them and said they'd make a list of five to six people to start with. They agreed to come back in a week.

Down in the entrance way, Lalease stopped to button up her raincoat. "She's right about how they want us to be too scared to move. I'm tired of them having that power."

Kiki squeezed her eyes together and thought about several names to put on their list. When she opened them, she saw the rain had stopped. They might even catch a burst of sunset on the bus ride home.

The Intervention

Maybe Tracy Chapman or the Indigo Girls could write a song about it: How many feminists' daughters does it take to screw up a revolution?

Not that Annie had done much for the movement. She'd been too busy escaping an abusive husband and trying to feed her kids. Those two were supposed to be her contribution to a feminist future: a boy who respected women, a girl who respected herself. Annie had been on a mission, especially with her daughter. Let her believe in her own power and not think she had to depend on some Prince Charming to watch over her.

Be careful what you wish for.

Annie held up her favorite photo of Dorey, captured on prom night when they were still in South Dakota and set in a bulky frame that read "2002: We Are the Future." She remembered looking through a panorama on the web of all the photos from that dance, girl after girl staring goo-goo-eyed at her date. Dorey was the only one who looked not at the guy but right into the camera, a grin on her face, one hand on her hip.

Now, Annie felt as if she'd sent that young woman into some cruel Hall of Mirrors. Dorey had gone in full of piss and vinegar to change the corporate world and came back out a decade later as a frightful distortion. When she got hired at People's Trust Bank after getting her MBA, Dorey railed about the sexism of the men who ran the bank. "This is why I want to have power," she'd say. "It'll be a different world with women like me in the driver's seat." She wound up on the fast track, where she still railed about sexism and racism, but stopped talking about how to rein in those guys, more how to outsmart them. She began using expressions like, "To get ahead, you gotta play the game."

The last time Annie tried to talk to her about it, Dorey reverted to her stock response: "You can't get rid of the old boys' club if you're not on the inside. I will shake things up,but I can only do that if I get to the top." There was even something robotic about her voice. Likely she was having the same back-and-forth with her boyfriend, Max, the son of Annie's closest friend, Emma. How thrilled they'd been when their kids got together.

When Annie raised concerns, Dorey threw out the magic words:"You're the one who urged me to dream big." Then she said she had to go, people were trying to take advantage of a blackout the night before to call off work.

This last remark left Annie doubled over, as if she'd been struck in the gut by a mis-thrown hardball. Years earlier, she and Emma had fought just this mindset—managers who saw workers as untrustworthy people needing surveillance and restraints. Since starting at the bank, Dorey kept track of what she called The Shit That Needs Fixing. Now she'd become part of it.

Still, she was dead right in accusing her mother of having a role in all this. As a child, Dorey loved to hear the story of a protest action Annie had been part of years ago at that airline call center. Now, in the long hours stolen from her sleep, Annie replayed her failure to pass on the most important lesson about creating change: You don't make it happen on your own. The success, and the joy, come from banding together with others.

Last week Max had finally called it quits. According to Emma, he was a mess. But Dorey didn't even take a day off to grieve, much less scramble to keep her relationship. "I need someone at home who's rooting for me," she told

Annie over the phone the next day. "Otherwise, just give me a vibrator and some take-out menus."

That was the shove Annie needed. Game on, she told herself. You can keep beating yourself up for your failures as a mom, or you can fight to get your daughter back.

Annie managed to convince Dorey to let her come over that Sunday morning. A storm the night before had ravaged the city and strewn the streets with tree limbs, leaving a chill wind in its wake. Annie rang the bell at Dorey's condo complex and rode the elevator with a sack of chocolate scones warm against her thigh. She'd spent hours practicing for this conversation: no sighs, no tears, no judgment.

Dorey had left the door open and was stuck to the sofa, arms tight across her chest. She had on an old Marquette sweatshirt with what looked like pesto stains on the cuff, her hair stuck up in the back as if she'd slept on the couch instead of her static-free pillow. "Look, Mom, I appreciate you wanting to see how I'm doing, but if you're just going to tell me how awful I am, you can turn right back around."

Annie swallowed hard and held out her bag of treats. "I come bearing gifts, sweetheart. Take a whiff."

"All I smell is disapproval." Dorey was holding her body so tight, she looked like she'd propel herself across the room if she released her arms.

Annie threw her coat across a kitchen chair, poured them both a cup of coffee from the machine on the counter and took a seat as close to her daughter as she dared to go. "Listen to me, sweet girl. I love you with all my heart. I'm worried about you. I don't think you're happy."

Dorey shook her head and practically spit out her answer. "You mean, you don't think I'm *worthy*. *Say* it." Annie tried to remind herself that angry was better than vacant.

"I think you're brilliant and capable of great things, Dorey. But I see you're under so much *pressure* to prove yourself to the big boys in charge." Annie prayed that naming a common villain would help. "It feels like you're always rushed, always stretched, no time for yourself, cut off from everyone who loves you. That's got to be so painful."

"Yeah. Well, here's what I think: You've lumped me in with the big boys and decided there's no difference between us." Dorey pointed her chin in Annie's direction. "Look at the programs I started, the trainings I've set up, all the women I've helped get loans. Look who I've promoted. How can you possibly compare me to Thom Luchsinger? If I were in charge, I'd never lord it over anyone the way he does, never humiliate anyone ..."

A visible shudder engulfed her daughter. Annie struggled not to gasp and reached out her hand. Dorey wrenched herself away and stayed rigid in the corner of the couch.

"Sweetheart, I *do* see what you've accomplished. I've kept every email you shared with me from someone whose life you touched. I framed a photo of that card the workers in your department gave you when you got the computer system upgraded. I know what it meant for my friend Marisol when you helped her start her business. She *adores* you."

Dorey tugged at the edge of a throw pillow. "Get it all out. I know there's an enormous 'but' you're about to hurl at me."

Annie visualized all the workers who stood up with her years ago at Central States Airlines telling her to hang in there. "It's a beautiful 'but,' Dorey. It's a, 'But those moments used to be what you talked about. You loved to create opportunities for customers and for your staff. It's what made you proud. It made you happy. I haven't seen you enjoy yourself in a really long time."

"It's hard to be happy when you feel judged every second." Dorey's voice was more disgusted than defiant.

"Please, Dor, look at me." Annie's daughter didn't budge. "I always loved how clear-eyed and resilient you were as a kid, so full of righteousness and spunk. I'll never forget you planting yourself in the doorway, telling off that nosy neighbor who wanted to know if we got food stamps. I think you miss that part of you as much as I do."

"Really, you think I stopped being *resilient*?" The throw pillow landed on the other side of the room, where Dorey had left a window cracked open. Outside the wind picked up.

Annie tried another tack. "You used to talk about wanting to make the workplace welcoming, somewhere people felt heard and appreciated. Do you feel heard and appreciated?"

The sound Dorey made was somewhere between a groan and a wail. "You don't know the first thing about it, Mom. Don't get me wrong, you and your friends were great, I love that you stood up for yourselves. But you never had to deal with the weight of making decisions that affect other people."

Despite the chill, Annie's palms were sweaty. This might be her opening. "You're right, love. Say more about those pressures. I see you weighted down by them but I don't know what they look like or how they feel."

Dorey shook her head. "It's a competition just like anything else. When Daniel wanted to join the swim team, he worked his ass off. No pain, no glory. You never made him feel bad for wanting to win the championship. Why should this be any different?"

Annie had not anticipated this line of argument about her son. "Here's the thing: Daniel didn't have to put up with all the sexist barriers you've encountered. And he was part of a team that cheered each other on. That's what

237

I had when we started things at the call center. It's the only way we could have pulled off it off. You seem so alone."

"I have the Women Lead banking group."

"Oh, Dorey, when was the last time you saw any of those women?" Again Annie reached out her hand. Again Dorey shrunk from her touch. "And when was the last time your staff made you a card?"

As if to soften the direction her questions had taken, Annie bit into a scone. Just a Sunday morning family chat.

Dorey wasn't buying it. "I know you think every worker is perfect, Mom, but let's be honest here. They're just as fucked up as the rest of us." She launched into her defense as if she, too, had practiced in the shower. "There's this young woman in check coding, Kiki. She's been late a bunch of times, and she's always got this, that or the other going on. She kept forgetting to bring in a doctor's note and I reminded her about it so she wouldn't get more points on her record. I didn't *have* to do that. Anyone else would have fired her a long time ago. So a few weeks ago, she comes in and she's brought her toddler with her and the girl screams bloody murder the whole time. I mean, people have to learn how to control their kids and have a back-up plan for day care. Otherwise there's just chaos."

Annie forced herself to chew the piece of scone. She used her napkin to wipe any horror from her mouth and keep her voice steady. "The thing is, love, I know people who could have been that mom. I came very close to being that mom. People who have no car, and have to wait for buses on those wicked cold Milwaukee days — two to get to the doctor's office and then another to work." She paused for a few seconds. "And you, sweet Dorey. You could have been that little girl."

The smallest sound, quickly stifled, came from Dorey's throat.

Annie shifted until her whole body faced her daughter. "I can imagine what it would be like to have to bring your child along because you have no daycare, and what it would feel like to walk past that spectacular child care center — the one you put high on your fix list because none of the workers could afford it — and have your kid see all the amazing toys she couldn't touch. Kind of like that doll you spotted, way back when, in the hospital gift shop."

Dorey's arms remained wrapped around her midriff but her shoulders began to sag and her body to deflate, as if Annie had jabbed her with a pin.

Annie slid a little closer. "The other day Max stopped by." She expected her daughter to protest, but Dorey merely lowered her head. "Did he ever tell you what happened when our friend Vanessa got fired at the call center after her daughter had a seizure?"

During Annie's long pause, Dorey stayed perfectly still.

"This was after we left Milwaukee. Max said Emma freaked out and insisted he wear snow pants so he wouldn't come down with a cold and trigger an asthma attack that would force her to miss work and get more absence points." Annie took a breath. "Max was eight years old. Snow pants were about as dorky as you can get, he told me. But he wore them every day after that for the rest of the winter. And once he did have an asthma attack at school, but he hid in the bathroom with his inhaler so they wouldn't call his mom."

Annie could have added the obvious: What did Dorey think they were protesting when they stood up at work? But there was no need. As she spoke, Dorey's body began to tilt to the side of the couch until she was curled up into herself.

***

Outside, bells clanged to signal that the bridge over the river was rising. Dorey could hear them. She could feel the tears and snot dripping down her face and neck. She had not died. But surely that would be preferable to the images of eight-year-old Max crouching in the bathroom stall, and of that tiny girl at the bus stop whipped by freezing wind.

Those figures reminded her of an older, black-and-white film, long buried, another girl on a frigid day, schools closed by snowfalls high even for South Dakota, playing quietly under her mother's desk in the hospital admitting office. On the way out, they passed the gift shop, and there in the window, an exact replica of LuLu, a red-headed Cabbage Patch doll the girl had cherished, lost on a bus as they escaped from her dad. The girl began pointing at the doll, ignoring her mother and the other grown-ups and some wide-eyed boy who snickered as she begged and pleaded for Lulu. And then the girl was yelling and screeching, throwing herself on the floor even though she was not a toddler, she was nearly seven years old, until her mother scooped her up and out the door, saying things the girl couldn't hear through her tears but adult Dorey heard now: "I'm so sorry, honey, the rent's overdue, the toilet needs fixing, we have to wait a while for dolls."

When she finally lifted her head, Dorey had no idea how much time had passed. Her mother had shifted them to the floor, Annie propped against the table leg. Dorey's Marquette sweatshirt was soaked with crud. So was the shoulder of Annie's crewneck.

"I made a mess, Mom." Dorey grabbed a handful of Kleenex and tried in vain to clean her mother's sweater.

Annie shrugged. "I wore an old one just in case."

"No, I mean I messed up." Dorey balled up the Kleenex and held it in the air until Annie gently pried the wad from her fingers and tossed it in a wicker wastebasket stashed under the table. "I hurt people. I hurt you."

"Humans do that, baby."

"Not everyone. Not like this."

Her mother clasped Dorey's hand. "What matters is that you can turn this around."

Dorey saw herself spinning around and around while the world stood perfectly still. Not snap at Kiki?

Sure. Get Kiki's kid into the bank's fancy child care center? Never. Walk out on Thom Luchsinger? Sure. Get another job with Thom sabotaging her at every turn? And Max? A moan came from somewhere deep inside her. She felt as if she'd been stuffed in a deep hole and had a limited air supply.

Annie put her arms around her daughter. "I don't need to tell you how much I've been missing you, Dorey. But I can see you're hurting, too. Something's happened to you." Dorey crumpled into her mother's embrace. "Whatever it is, sweetheart, you're not alone," Annie whispered. "We've got your back."

Dorey wasn't sure how many minutes passed before her sobs subsided enough to talk. She raised her head. "I wouldn't have buzzed you in if I knew this was some kind of intervention. Is there some rehab place I'm supposed to go?"

Annie lifted her daughter's chin and flashed her first smile of the day. "Not really. But I know a good place to start. Tell Kiki and the other women who work for you what you just told me. Let them know you're ready to listen."

Restoring Trust to People's Trust

Milwaukee, April/May 2013

Kiki and Lalease had done their homework after going to that women's group about the mess at the bank. Took them no time at all to make a list of people they trusted most. They talked to seven, quietly grabbing phone numbers over lunch. Every last one of them was pissed at People's Trust being crowned a "best place" for women to work. "*Flexible?*" one said. "You gotta be Gumby to work there." Another, like Kiki, was especially mad about the child care center they couldn't afford and couldn't let their kids lay eyes on. Someone in billing went on a rant about the CEO: "An award for how the bank treats women when everyone knows that Thom Luchsinger's nickname is 'hands-on?'"

Kiki wrote down every word. Lalease put a check where she'd heard the same and added one more comment, her favorite: "Hard for women to prevail when the execs are all male and pale."

People liked the idea of a petition to *Lead!* magazine to kick the bank off their list. But how to get signatures? Work was as hardass as Sister Mary Francis in Kiki's middle school. If they demanded proof you really were at your daddy's funeral, they weren't going to wave while you ran around with a paper calling them hypocrites.

Kiki and Lalease reported all this to Vanessa Jackson on Friday, a week after their first visit to the Working Women United office. This time they huddled at the big front table next to a wall of photos, people marching and singing, kids in every shot. Vanessa—she might be a grandma but her shirt said "Black Girl Magic" and her arms looked like Michele Obama's — took notes and smiled and said they did great. And then she dropped a bombshell about their supervisor, Dorey Stotz.

Actually, Kiki had noticed a change in Stotz starting that Monday morning, like some alien pod had swallowed her up. First, she stopped by Kiki's desk and asked like she meant it, "How's your little girl, Ms. Oppedahl?" She stayed put until Kiki replied. Each day, Stotz found a reason to drop in and compliment someone's work. Today she brought chocolate chip cookies from an actual bakery. But what Vanessa said raised this to a whole different level.

"I've known Dorey Stotz since she was a little kid." Vanessa pointed to a photo of her younger self with a "Union Now!" sign. "I used to work with her mom — one of the bravest women I know. She's been heartsick watching Dorey get swallowed up over there, betraying everything we fought for. So she decided to do something about it."

Kiki thought her jaw would hit her shoes. Turns out Stotz's mother had done an *intervention*, like you do with alcoholics, but all by herself. Supposedly it worked. And supposedly a big turning point was how bad Stotz treated Kiki that time she had to bring in a doctor's note on her day off, Sarajane wailing on her hip. Vanessa called the results "momentous."

"So, you believe people can really change like that?" Kiki asked.

The air around Vanessa smelled like nutmeg. "For Dorey Stotz, I think it's more a coming home than a transformation."

Lalease pulled out her inhaler and sucked in a long breath. "We could have us a philosophical discussion. Or we could get down to business. What do we want Stotz to do?"

"Fair enough." Kiki swung out of the chair and began to pace on the worn carpet. "She can't change the child care center fees on her own."

"Or the absence points."

"But she can sure change how she holds people to those doctor's notes, for one."

Lalease put her inhaler back in her pocket. "And the scheduling. Cutting our hours just enough to throw me out of the pension fund. Her fingerprints are all over that."

"I don't see why she can't put us back to forty hours."

For the first time, Lalease grinned. With her oxfords and dark clothes and tidy hair, Lalease was easy to overlook, except for the rare times she flashed those dimples.

"And what you said, Vanessa, threatening to get them off that list unless they change some of the big things — she ought to help with that." Kiki flung herself back into her chair and gave Lalease a high five.

Vanessa wanted them to say all this to Stotz in the flesh, like right then. Asked if they were okay having her come over. Fifteen minutes later Stotz stood in the doorway, wearing khakis and a tee-shirt — not a fancy I-call-this-a-tee-shirt-but-it-really-cost-$300 top, but a plain white number. Kiki'd never seen Stotz in anything but high-class suits. She looked really young, her face fresh scrubbed and puffy, like she'd done a lot of crying.

Stotz tossed her windbreaker on a chair and clung to the back of it like she might fall down otherwise. She looked right at Kiki and Lalease. "I'm so sorry," she said, her voice all hoarse. "I've been really insensitive. Please know I'm not looking for forgiveness. I just want to say, I see I've hurt you, and I want to move forward."

Kiki heard Lalease's breathing speed right up.

"The truth is," Stotz said, "if it weren't for my mom, I'd have crawled under my bed for a few weeks. She told me to focus on what I can do right now, so I'd like to talk about that. I know it won't be enough ..."

Kiki popped up before Stotz was even in her seat. She'd been thinking what to say and imagined herself all cool and sophisticated. But now she just blurted it out. "Go easy on the doctor's notes, make the scheduling fair and regular, put everyone back to forty hours. We know you don't have a magic wand, Ms. Stotz, but you do have some power."

"That list," Lalease said in one of those loud whispers bad actors use. "Don't forget about that."

"Right. We don't see how People's Trust deserves any applause unless there's some big changes, and we think you can help."

Stotz was tiny but compact, like a gymnast, not skinny like Kiki. "I can start with the doctor's notes," Stotz said, like she'd been thinking about it, too. "The management team makes the policy, but I implement it for our department. Here's one change I can guarantee: If an employee or their family member has a chronic condition like asthma, I won't ask for another note if they have a flare-up."

Kiki wasn't about to get excited too soon. "What if someone doesn't need the doctor, cause her kid has the runs and everyone knows what you're supposed to do for that?"

Stotz nodded like maybe she'd been in that boat. "We'll take all that into account. Thank you, Kiki. And the scheduling, I can work on that, too, how to make sure everyone has more notice and more regular hours."

Lalease had folded up the bottom of each page on her notepad. "No offense, Ms. Stotz, but seems like we ought to be part of figuring that out."

This time Stotz's mouth pruned up, like her I've-heard-you self was waging a little battle with her wait-I'm-the-boss self. "Let me think about a way to structure that."

"Me and Kiki could meet with you any day this week."

Way to go, Lalease! Stotz wasn't smiling, but she did say she'd meet them the following Monday.

"As for the number of hours ..." Here Stotz kind of shivered. "I don't want to sugarcoat things. Each department was ordered to find savings. We'd have to do something to offset these costs. But I promise you I'll look everywhere and I'll keep you in the loop."

Vanessa was asking Stotz about the list. "This is how we can tackle the child care center fees and the absence points, Dorey, the stuff that's out of your control. We want a petition where female employees ask *Lead!* magazine to take People's Trust off the list. Since the bank used you as a front woman, well, it would mean a lot to have your name on the petition."

"What would you do with it?" Dorey asked. The "you" changed the air in the room, like someone had turned off a fan.

"We could send it to the magazine," Vanessa said, "or we could use it as leverage with the Board of Directors. We need to do a power analysis and see what our best option is."

Kiki tried to picture herself drawing sharp-lined diagrams on an adult version of the easel Sarajane wanted so bad.

"I don't know," Kiki said. "I can hear the Directors say, 'Sure, we'll look into it,' and then do nothing for months while we sit around and pick the wax out of our ears." She glanced around to see if anyone was making a face.

Vanessa said that was a great point. "Before the meeting, we'll practice exactly what words to use and who'll make the ask. The key is to nail down a meeting date on the spot and a timeline for the changes to begin."

They still had to figure out how to get signatures without getting caught. That's when Vanessa came up with yoga class as an organizing tool. For Kiki, "organizing" conjured up those photos on the wall, huge crowds, shrieks and chants and megaphones. She never dreamed the word went with learning how to breathe.

But Vanessa did. Kiki couldn't believe this woman had done so much while raising five kids, mostly on her own as a widow. The kids were all grown now. And one daughter, Keisha, was a dancer who taught yoga.

"You told me there's a guy at the bank whose job is to get them on lists like this," Vanessa told Stotz.

"Yes, Leo Maguire. He's cautious but decent. Not like ... not like Thom Luchsinger. " Stotz looked like his name was a tiny bone stuck in her throat.

"Tell Maguire you've got a two-fer: He should hire Keisha to teach yoga classes for non-management employees. Since most of the benefits on the *Lead!* list apply to managers, this would be a perk for the others. The bank can shine as an employer who cares about wellness. Plus yoga is a proven way to relieve stress and cut down absenteeism. Keisha can teach during lunch hour so the only cost is her time, and Ms. Kiki and Ms. Lalease can use the opportunity to identify potential signers."

Stotz's face took on something resembling a smile. "That's just the kind of thing Leo would grab onto."

Lalease wasn't having it. "We got no time to change for a yoga class," she said without moving a muscle. "Plus there's no lockers."

"She's right," Kiki said. "I mean Lalease, it's a great thought, but no one will come."

"Ah," Vanessa said. "You don't know Keisha. She'll guide you in meditation and yoga breathing. No need to change clothes." Vanessa broke out in a mama smile. "I can hear her now: 'Breathe. Say it with me: Time-for-our-kids. Now exhale."

Kiki couldn't help bouncing a little in her seat. "I think that would work. You, Lalease? Would we have the petition right there in the room?"

Vanessa had it all figured out. They'd put it on the Working Women United site with an easy and confidential sign-in process. All Lalease and Kiki would have to do is hand a little slip of paper to people who looked like they were into Keisha's exercise. "It could say, 'If you think People's Trust should be a great workplace for ALL female employees, go to this website and check out the secure petition.'"

Lalease didn't say yes but she didn't say no, either. Then they had to come up with a way to get a meeting with the board of directors. Vanessa had an idea for that, too. She knew a group called Voces de la Frontera that took on a factory for underpaying workers. "Wage theft," Vanessa called it. They found an ally on the company's board. Maybe someone could help them do the same at People's Trust.

***

Stotz told them it took only ten minutes to convince Leo Maguire, the diversity manager, to sign off on the meditation classes. He was delighted with the "twofer" idea, adding Keisha to the list of women and minority contractors. They agreed to schedule it at different times on Tuesday and Thursday to accommodate the two lunch slots. Staff would brown bag it and the company would offer water and coffee, maybe baby carrots. Maguire especially liked the cost: only sixty bucks a week.

For days, Kiki worried how she'd manage in the class. First you had to figure out who should get the notes. Then you actually had to hand over the slips without anyone noticing. Lalease flat out refused to rehearse. "I don't care who sees me," she said. "I'll give 'em to every one of the three people who show up." But there were a couple women Kiki didn't trust — like that girl in payroll with the highlights who was always sucking up to management.

When they met Wednesday Vanessa's daughter came up with a solution. Keisha looked just like her mother, only taller and hipper. She walked in waving a fan of coupons. "Here's our ticket to ride — coupons for a friendly restaurant!"

Keisha put a coupon in each hand. "I'll bring one for every new person who attends. Whichever of you is there will volunteer to hand them out. We'll have two sets, one with the petition notice behind it" — she handed the coupon in her right hand to Kiki and sure enough, their slip was underneath — "and one without." Lalease got the unpaired coupon from Keisha's left hand. "This is how my mom and her friends pulled off their stand-up at the call center."

The whole time Vanessa was explaining what a stand-up was, Kiki tried to picture herself keeping straight which hand held the coupon. She decided to make a game of it and get Sarajane to practice with her.

***

When Thursday noon finally rolled around, Kiki wished she could have back every minute she fretted about people coming to the class. They had over twenty! Now all she had to do was watch people's reactions and remember "right is might," because that hand would hold the double slips.

Kiki loved how Keisha turned this sterile training room into a meditation space — "the breathing room," Lalease called it. Keisha put a bright cushion on each chair and arranged them in a circle, so they could peek at everyone's face without having to twist around. She brought a silver CD player with double disc holders. On one wall she'd strung a poster of African women dancing together under jazzy letters that spelled, "JOY." There were napkins fanned out and a big coffee pot. On one end of the table, Keisha stuck some lavender scented incense.

For the first fifteen minutes, everyone ate their lunch and didn't say much. Then Keisha used a stick that made pebbly noises to welcome the women into the circle. Without any to-do, she launched right into the breathing exercise, first demonstrating and then encouraging the women to join in, with a voice so soothing, Kiki might have fallen asleep if she didn't have her assignment. Who doesn't know how to breathe, she'd thought, but she'd never used her lungs like this before.

"Every time you breathe in through your nose," Keisha told them, "think of taking in energy and strength." Kiki watched, mesmerized as the women flared their nostrils and drank in the air, as if "energy" and "strength" were floating by and just needed to be inhaled. "Then rid your body of stress with the long, slow, emptying of your breath through your lips." A whoosh all around. "Focus on what really matters in your life." Keisha wove in little sayings in that calm, you-gotta-listen-to-me voice. "Inhale long, take in what you need: time-for-our-loved-ones. Push out with your diaphragm, send it all the way out: lack-of-control-over-our-lives." One teller started out doing her knitting and just breathing regular. By the third round, she'd put her needles down.

When the CEO wandered in, Kiki at first didn't even notice. "That's how far gone I was," she told Lalease later. "I just died when I realized it was Luchsinger. I thought we were busted for sure. Or maybe he came to get off on seeing women in leotards." But Keisha must have felt his presence before the door even opened. Moving just her hand, she hit the button on the CD player. The background music switched from Tracy Chapman to some new agey flute thing. Luchsinger stood off to the side, not saying anything, his hand on his chin.

"Breathe in deeply," Keisha said. "Go to that place of relaxation. Hold one, two, three. Good. Now a long, cleansing, breath." Nothing about flexibility or family or power. Kiki did a quick sweep of the circle. No one seemed to notice. As quietly as he slipped in, Luchsinger tiptoed out. A few minutes later, Keisha closed out the group.

"You are all worthy of joy." Quiet breath. "Inhale the affirmation of your powerful selves. Push out that which demeans you or causes you pain. Welcome to the world where you are strong. Where you are known. Where you are valued."

No one got up, even though the time was over. Keisha stood to thank them all for coming. "I've brought you a coupon for a friend's Mexican restaurant," she said. "Would someone pass them out for me?"

"Everyone seemed to go for it," Kiki said when she reported to Lalease later. "That girl with the highlights was the only one who got my left hand."

***

Today was the first time in months Kiki hadn't worn the thumb protector at work. She hated everything about that "worker's helper": the little bumps all over it like an outbreak of warts; the ugly "flesh" color that stood out on her pale hand — and don't get Lalease started on *that* word. Kiki didn't mean to chew the skin around her nails. Half the time she couldn't remember doing it, until the paper cuts started and she'd find herself bleeding on somebody's gas and electric payment.

Not anymore! The breathing lessons had already made a difference. Kiki switched her lunch hour on Tuesdays so she could go twice a week. Now, after her third session, she was beginning to feel like a pro. People were telling their friends and more new women came. Only first-timers got the coupons, so that's who Kiki watched.

"Voodoo magic." That's what Lalease called the sessions. But Kiki could tell Lalease was getting into it. This Tuesday, Kiki pretended to keep her eyes shut while she snuck peeks at her friend breathing in and out with everyone else. Lalease hadn't needed her inhaler the whole rest of the day.

***

Keisha might be growing on her, but Lalease had just about given up on Stotz. She and Kiki had a full-out fight about it on the bus that morning. "I'm telling you, she's playing games with us," Lalease said as soon as she plopped down. "I don't see why she's become your heroine."

"Why'd you go and say something like that?" Kiki felt as if the whole bus was staring. She tried to speak directly into Lalease's ear. "All I'm saying is, she did make some changes already. The medical certification, for one." Not having to bring a doctor's note if Sarajane had another asthma attack was a huge relief for Kiki. But Lalease knew that. "And for two, the schedule, she put out that survey as soon as you brought her the idea."

"Fiddling around the edges," Lalease said. "You watch, it's gonna save them money. Could've saved them a lot more if she'd listened to us in the first place."

Like Kiki didn't know that. "There's no reason she won't try to restore us to full time."

Lalease was taking up way more than her half of the bus seat. "There's one really good reason — she'd lose that big promotion. How dumb does she think we are?"

"Maybe so," Kiki said, picturing Stotz's fancy clothes and classy hairdo. "But what good's it do us if she gets fired? She has to pace out the changes."

Lalease buried her face behind a sheet of coupons from Pick & Save. "I'll believe it when I see it."

When that was the last they talked the whole day, Kiki worried Lalease wouldn't show up for that night's meeting at WWU.

***

The muffins Vanessa passed around were warm and smelled of pumpkin. She sat in the chair closest to Kiki and asked how Keisha's classes were going.

Kiki took a deep breath. "When you tell people, 'you are known, you are valuable', these women *never* hear that kind of stuff. They sit up taller and waltz out of the room."

"Yes!" Vanessa said. "And wait 'til you see our petition!"

Lalease's squeaky shoes announced her. She was ten minutes late and kept her jacket on the whole time, but at least she came, even if she sat across the table and avoided looking Kiki in the eye.

"Let's start with the good news," Vanessa said, holding up a spreadsheet. "Our goal for the petition was forty names. And ..." she slid the sheet so it lay on the table between Lalease and Kiki. "... we already hit fifty. I'll bet we have sixty by the board meeting next Friday."

Kiki clapped her hands. "Hooray! And look at this." She pulled a piece of notebook paper from her tote bag. "Martina and the other custodians don't have computers, so they made a written sheet. That'll work, right?"

Vanessa flashed a broad smile. "*Absolutely.*"

"'Do these magazines ever talk to cleaning crews?' That's what Martina asked me. She called herself a 'paper towel employee' — they just mash 'em up and toss 'em out."

Vanessa told them the Voces person found a really good board member at People's Trust, Isaac Zubrensky. "He's passionate about corporate accountability," she said. "Was on the board before Luchsinger came on and packed it with his pals. Zubrensky was ready to quit. I asked if he'd wait and meet with a group of concerned employees first. He grabbed my hand and said, 'You just made my day.'"

"That's so excellent!" Kiki said.

"How much can one director do?" Lalease asked. "'Specially if the rest of the board is a bunch of yes men?"

Vanessa ran her hand over her hair, which was silver and hugged her head. "Zubrensky can get you heard. Once you get their attention, they should act — not as much as you need, but they'll want to keep this from getting to the media."

***

Kiki had promised herself she'd remain calm and professional-like throughout the board meeting, no matter what happened. Tuesday night she and Lalease rehearsed for two hours with Vanessa. No one on that Board could say anything meaner than what Vanessa as pretend-worst-board-member-ever did. She hollered, she mocked them, she did everything but grab her crotch.

When Luchsinger tried to throw them out that Friday, Kiki didn't get splotches on her skin or anything. She kept her eyes on the chairs where Mr. Zubrensky led them, just like they practiced. Even when Luchsinger tried to dismiss her as a bad employee with excessive absence points, she imagined him wearing a teeny thong and remained perfectly calm.

Mr. Zubrensky introduced Kiki and Lalease like they were visiting big wigs. Lalease was wearing what she called her church clothes. Kiki'd never seen her in a skirt before. Kiki herself had on her yellow dress from Goodwill and the red beads Sarajane picked out.

"Thank you for hearing us," Lalease said. "Sixty-two female employees signed a petition telling that magazine the bank doesn't deserve to be on their best-for-women list. We'd like People's Trust to be worthy of trust. We'd like not to send this. But that means some change is gonna have to come." One by one, just like they'd rehearsed, Lalease went over what they called their change agenda: a return to full hours, more control over schedules, more reasonable absence policies, a sliding scale at the child care center.

Thom Luchsinger started fidgeting in his seat like an anthill had blossomed in his pants. "Now just a minute, here, Mrs. Mitchell. This is a Board of Directors, not an HR department. The idea that these esteemed individuals would waste their time micromanaging experts ..."

Dorey Stotz got to her feet in one movement. "I'm one of those experts," she said in a voice so in charge, Luchsinger just snapped his mouth shut. "And I acknowledge that I didn't understand some very basic things. The people who do these jobs, they're the ones we have to listen to. Because even if you can't imagine what it's like to wait for a bus in sub-zero temperatures with your little girl at your side, or have her walk past a room packed with toys she's not allowed to touch, even if all you care about is productivity and profits, treating people the way we have is bad business practice."

Kiki dug her almost-unbitten nails into her chair. "You go, Stotz!," she said under her breath. Stotz made the case for restoring their hours and took all the blame, and then she went on about how excellent their work was. Lalease was breathing hard, probably needed her inhaler, but Kiki knew she'd never pull it out in front of these folks.

Now Stotz was looking directly at Kiki and Lalease. "All these women want is the opportunity to do good work for us. They can be their best selves in the bank when we let them be their best selves outside the bank as well. This board, the final arbiters for People's Trust, is exactly the body to hear their concerns."

Kiki had to squeeze Lalease's hand to keep from yelling, "Hallelujah!" Before anyone could say a word, Kiki nodded at Lalease and the two of them stood up next to Dorey Stotz. "We appreciate you letting us speak today," Kiki said in her most professional voice as she gazed around the table and passed out their statement. "Here is a copy of what Ms. Mitchell laid out. We look forward to you taking action on our requests within the next ten days."

They'd prepared for everything, Kiki thought — until Luchsinger made a giant u-turn.

"I see what's going on here." He licked his upper lip, like a frog about to snatch his dinner. "This whole ruckus is attempted payback by Ms. Stotz because I rejected her sexual advances."

Kiki's gasp was loud enough to cause several heads to snap around. This guy had to be in his fifties. Everybody in the bank knew he had grabby hands. Stotz could barely say his name — no way she tried to bag him.

"I'd hoped to avoid having to expose you, Ms. Stotz. But you've left me no choice." Luchsinger spread his fingers over his heart. "Fellow directors, I went out of my way to provide opportunities for this young woman, but was horrified in Tokyo when she tried to seduce me in a vain attempt to win a promotion. I would have immediately removed her, but I resolved to give her one last chance, out of respect for our commitment to diversity."

The room went silent. Kiki wished she had Lalease's inhaler.

And then Leo Maguire rose and slowly moved to the front. His hair was thinning and mostly gray but you could tell it had started out red. The guy kept one hand in his pocket. Kiki bet anything he had a rosary in there. "Thom Luchsinger is a fine man," Maguire said. "He's been a good friend. Yet even good men make mistakes. I must correct one for you now." And then he laid it all out: Luchingser was the aggressor, made what Maguire called lewd talk on the plane to Tokyo, drank heavily at the hotel, snuck into Stotz's room and tried to assault her. When they got back to Milwaukee, Stotz had confided in Maguire. He told her to let it go.

"I failed you that day," Leo said, looking straight at Stotz. "I won't do it again."

Stotz stood still as a statue.

Kiki longed to tell her to breathe.

And now everyone was talking six ways to Sunday. Isaac Zubrensky held up his hand. "This belongs in closed session," he said. "Let's thank our guests and allow them to leave, before we take up the subject of Mr. Luchinger."

***

Vanessa was waiting for them outside the WWU office, waving her bare arms. With the sun having come out full force while they were in that meeting, it finally felt like summer was around the corner. "Mr. Zubrensky texted that you were magnificent and Luchsinger pulled a fast one," she said. "Come up and tell me everything, start to finish, while we wait for him to come." When Stotz got

257

close, Vanessa pulled her close for a hug, like she'd known about Luchsinger all along.

Stotz said very little, while Kiki and Lalease tried to recall every tidbit. "You were brilliant," Stotz told them.

Kiki was looking for the right words to say Stotz had been, too, when Mr. Zubrensky walked in with his hands over his head, like a boxing champ.

"It's big!" he said. "Full hours for everyone who wants them and departments can each work out how to schedule. Dorey's change on doctor's notes will expand to all units."

"Thank you, Jesus!" Lalease's smile stayed on so long, Kiki had to look at her twice.

Zubrensky grinned. "Don't forget to thank yourself and Ms. Oppedahl and Ms. Stotz here as well," he said.

"As far as the child care center and absence points, as you expected, it's a delaying tactic. They're setting up a task force, though they did put me on it."

Kiki thought she should be on it, too, but she didn't want to sound pushy.

"What about Luchsinger?" Vanessa was sitting close to Stotz with one hand on her shoulder.

Mr. Zubrensky started singing that song they play at baseball games, "Na-na-na-na, hey, hey, hey, goodbye."

"Fired?" Lalease asked. There were those dimples again.

"It didn't take long," Mr. Zubrensky said. "Everyone believed Leo. But Thom will land with a nice golden parachute."

"What's that mean?" Kiki didn't care if everyone else knew. She wanted to understand.

"It means he walks away with a boatload of cash," Lalease said.

"Likely, yes." Mr. Zubrensky wrinkled up his fore-head and for the first time looked like someone who might be in his seventies. "It's up to the legal department. Thom has to go, but there won't be any public shaming. He'll negotiate for big bucks and that's probably what he'll get."

Kiki crossed her arms tight over her chest. Damn. She wanted him to experience just once what it felt like to shush your baby so the bill collector wouldn't know you were home.

Stotz's eyes were all tears but her mouth was smiling. "Kiki, Lalease: This wouldn't have happened without you standing up for yourselves. You saved my life. And maybe you'll even save this bank."

Kiki tried on the words. She liked the way they fit.

The Roar of the Elders

Milwaukee, March 2021

"Feeble, frail, forgetful, forgettable." Sophie flung the words into her mask. With the lake trail cleared and the wind down, she and Nick could hear each other most of the time.

"Ask people to define 'old woman' and that's what you'll get." Welcome or not, Sophie was going to have her say. "We're either invisible or laughable, usually pitiable. Do something competent? You're mind-boggling. And oh my god, if it gets out that you're sexually active, the reaction is 'aww,' or 'eww' — mostly 'eww.' Makes me want to scream."

"I don't know, babe," Nick said, tugging Grizzly away from a frozen mound of dog-doo. "You think you may be a little oversensitive?"

She swatted at him with her giant glove, which looked appropriate for a moonwalk. "Face it, you're part of the problem. You tell people about your cataract surgery or some other ailment and you always say, 'See what you have to look forward to?'"

Nick's eyes crinkled, the only way she could tell he was grinning behind his mask and his scarf. "Uh, cataracts come with aging, love. It's just a fact."

Grizzly spied a squirrel and leaped forward, but Nick and the leash prevailed. The snow banks were so high, the little dog would be buried immediately. They'd have to scoop snow and search for black fuzz.

"So does death," Sophie said.

Nick pointed to his ears and held up his hands.

"DEATH!" she hollered. "That doesn't make it the only or main thing associated with aging. That's my point, the culture is all about *decline* and *decay*. When I went to get a fortieth birthday card for Elly, most of them were some version of 'over the hill.' Fifty-year-olds freak out that 'the best is behind us.' Sixty-year-olds start lying about their age. And seventy-year-olds? When I had my birthday party a couple years ago, the word I heard most often was *'brave.'*"

Nick looked both ways and, seeing no one else foolish enough to be out in this bitter Milwaukee cold, took off his mask. "I'm not trying to be an asshole," he said, sidling up to her and kissing her cheekbone, the only skin exposed on her face. "But I think your feelings about aging are more complicated than you let on. Why do you hate turning on your Zoom camera?"

"Ouch," Sophie said. He was right, of course. On work calls, where she was often the oldest by several decades, the lines on her face might have been cracks on a statue, so prominent did they appear to her eye. She turned on the camera only when talking with friends her age. "I never said I haven't swallowed the kool-aid. Isn't that the whole point of how oppression works?"

After every consulting trip, she peppered Nick with examples: A lead organizer in her thirties asked for suggestions for hip openers. When Sophie got on the floor and demonstrated a pigeon pose, the staffer said, "Wow, I can't believe you can still do that." Someone else used "old" as the insult for a legislator promoting a weak-assed bill. "I don't mean *you*," she said when Sophie objected. People assumed she couldn't manage the entire distance of the Women's March in 2017 and sent her on a shorter route. Each time Nick commiserated, but also brushed it off.

Now he was making a point about how people treated him and other senior members of the Milwaukee school board. "No one really makes a distinction between the older and younger folks," he said.

Sophie stopped to make a snowball. Nick ducked and twirled and would have gotten away except for Grizzly trying to lunge at Sophie and wrapping his leash around Nick's legs. They all wound up in a laughing, yelping heap.

As she scrambled to her feet, Sophie shook off the snow and the laughter. "You're just proving my point, Nicky," she said. "The older board members are all men! Did you miss the word *woman* in my rant? There's a totally different standard. We're surrounded by older men with younger wives — those guys have bragging rights. Older women with younger men? Hardly. And don't get me started on Hollywood films." She walked backwards to face him. "Name the last time you saw an older woman on a game show! There's NONE. The audience would find us 'unappealing.'"

The trail looped down toward Lake Michigan, where the sun danced on the ice. Nick pulled his mask up as a pack of high school runners crossed their path. Grizzly protested the intrusion with a series of leaps and barks.

"If I mention this little outing on a call, I guarantee you someone will say how inspirational I am. They all assumed I'd want to 'slow down.' Ugh."

No crinkle in Nick's eyes this time. "I do want to slow down, babe. This is my last term on the board. People I worked with all those years in factories, they're exhausted and their bodies are shot. The ones who can afford it, all they want to do is retire and relax."

Sophie swallowed hard. "*Of course* they do. So do most of the women I've worked with. Even so, being tired doesn't mean they don't have ideas, stories, skills, things they'd love to do. Especially if they didn't have to worry how to pay for meds and keep the lights on."

Her mind filled with images of women her age or younger who were already gone, never having the time they needed to rest and heal. "The system chews them up and then says, 'Hey, they were old anyway, you can't live forever.' And don't forget the COVID-deniers. They think all those nursing home residents were just *waiting* to croak."

As they turned their backs on the lake and slogged up the hill, Sophie slipped her arm through Nick's and leaned her head against his shoulder. He smelled of lemon soap and wet wool. "Thanks for letting me blow my stack, Nicky. Obviously, I need to find another way to raise it with the team. Any ideas?"

Nick shifted the leash to his other hand and wrapped an arm around her. "It's like everything else you do, my love. Organize. Talk with Vanessa, figure out the best way to get seen. Maybe write something, maybe a training. Link it to the work — you're always saying the opponents are trying to steal the paid leave issue and reduce it to baby care. You'll figure it out. You always do."

***

With the temperature hovering near zero, Sophie arranged an early morning walk with Vanessa Jackson inside Bayshore Mall. Five years earlier, the two of them eased out of their jobs at Working Women United and started Just Lead Consulting. Vanessa mentored Black women moving into top leadership positions, and trained women's organizations with majority white staff and boards on adopting a racial justice lens. "It's not just about who you hire, although that matters," she'd tell them. "What's your program look like? Who decides what you fight for?" Sophie advised on communications and popular education, often with national and local leaders at Working Women United.

Vanessa's kids had been haranguing her for a while to retire. "They want all my time," Vanessa told Sophie the last dinner they had indoors, just before the pandemic. "But they know I love this work. I'd be doing it as a volunteer if I retired, so why not get paid? Also, Khendon is serious about building a place in Jamaica. We need the cash." Vanessa had been with Khendon since he showed up to remodel her kitchen a decade ago. She waited a few weeks to tell Sophie about him. "As soon as he finished the cabinets, I mentioned there were a few other areas that needed handling. He stuck around."

The two women changed from boots into sneakers, left their coats in the car and took the stairs to the second-floor office area to avoid other walkers. "No eavesdropping and no masks," Vanessa pointed out. They'd each had their second vaccine two weeks ago.

After they caught up on kids and grandkids on the car ride over, Sophie sketched the basic dilemma. "I know I've been raising this 'old lady' stuff for a long time," Sophie said. "But last week something snapped. I worry I'll explode at the next comment if I don't find a way to talk about it."

Vanessa pulled off her stocking cap and stuck it in her pocket. She'd long ago cut off her locs and wore her hair close to her scalp.

"If my hair were silver, I'd gladly stop dyeing it," Sophie said with a sigh. "I'm stuck in the very bias I can't shut up about." Secretly, Sophie envied Vanessa's skin, so much smoother than her own.

In all the years they'd been friends since a neighborhood block party in the early 1980s, Vanessa's musical laugh had the power to pull Sophie out of a funk. "You and every other woman on the planet, lady. Cut yourself a break. That mess seeps way down in our limbs." As they circled the halls, Vanessa listened to Sophie's recent experiences with the WWU team. "It's a little better in the Black community," she said. "In the church, people come to elders for advice. But I still see it all the time. With this twist from white folk: If you're a person of color, in my experience, either you're invisible, or they treat you like a fount of wisdom every time you belch."

The alluring smell of cinnamon buns wafted up through the air ducts from the food court below. "Let's design an exercise for the WWU staff and board," Sophie said. "We have a long history with them, so hopefully they'll be receptive. If it goes well, we can suggest it to other groups."

As usual, walking helped them brainstorm. Sophie always carried a tiny tape recorder to capture their best and their most hilarious ideas. "Let's use the format where we assign each person a line to read," Vanessa said. "We can tee up individual emails and one of us can send them while the other handles introductions."

"I have everyone's emails, glad to get that ready."

Vanessa moved her arms briskly as they walked. "What do you think of this idea: Each comment will be something we know people say about old folks, but we substitute the word 'woman' for 'old'?"

"Love it!" Sophie paused in front of a tax attorney's office to start the tape, holding the recorder first to her own mouth and then to Vanessa's. 'I feel so womanly today, my brain isn't working right.'"

"I can't believe a woman can do that exercise."

"God, that person looks awful. She looks so womanly."

"Since you're a woman, we figured you'd want to ride instead of walk." Vanessa speeded up as she said this one.

"The applicant is a woman? This job will be too much for her."

"That legislator sells out everything we believe in. They're just female."

"Wow, you went on a hike!" Sophie thrust out her arms and then brought the recorder back to her lips. "That's so inspiring for a woman to do!"

"Don't let a woman hold that vase. She'll start shaking and drop it."

"Women like to have sex? How adorable."

"Women like to have sex? That's gross."

"Women like to have sex? That's grotesque."

In two circuits of the upper floor they came up with more than enough sayings for twenty people. That and the number of steps they'd put in earned them each a cinnamon bun on the way out.

"You do know you're giving them a gift, right?" Vanessa turned to face Sophie as they sat in the car devouring their treats "This is a great modeling of calling people in. I bet they'll need very little coaching from us. They'll hear it. And they'll make the leap on their own from personal behavior to the organizing."

***

Sophie arranged the Zoom session for March 15. They called it, "Going Over the Hill." As the participants, twenty-two in all, read their assigned statements, Sophie and Vanessa observed people's faces and sent each other private notes in the chat box. "Watching for 'aha' moments," Vanessa wrote. Half of them got it as soon as they opened their email and saw the sentence. Everyone else caught on as they listened to the others read. Jasmine, the organizer who made the comment about the pigeon pose, tipped an imaginary hat in Sophie's direction.

The tears were warm on Sophie's cheek. Before that mall walk, she might have turned her camera off, but she remembered the cinnamon-tinged moment in the parking garage. After the last person read her statement, Vanessa thanked the group for being willing to participate. "We'd love to hear your thoughts," she said. "What was most surprising or eye-opening? Was there anything you didn't understand or agree with?"

Jasmine jumped in first filling the computer screen. She brushed her hands through the shock of hair on the top of her head. "I know you've brought this up several times, Sophie, but I never heard it before. That's on me. It's just, I had no idea I'd absorbed *all* that bias. Getting us to pair these stereotypes with the word 'woman' was

267

brilliant. You think you're being complimentary and really you're reinforcing the notion of incompetence."

A woman who was fairly new to the board grabbed her phone. "I'm not multitasking, I promise. I have to delete a tweet. Right before this training, I called Mitch McConnell a doddering old fool. He's a fool, all right, but not because of his age."

Several people commented on how gender compounded the issue. "It pisses me off how much more these comments apply to older women than to men," one said. Sophie grinned as she listened to the echoes of her own conversation with Nick. "Can you imagine if Callista Flockhart had been sixty and Harrison Ford thirty-eight when they met? Never would have happened."

A staffer who was about to turn fifty put her chin in her palms. "I gotta be honest, my birthday's next month and I've been dreading it. I was hoping none of you realized it's my fiftieth. I bought into the whole shebang. Well, guess what. As soon as this damn pandemic is over, I'm throwing myself a party. And I'm starting with a toast to the two of you." She lifted her water bottle to Vanessa and Sophie.

People unmuted to holler their approval.

The board president, a Michigan woman who'd founded a local organization focused on Black mothers, raised her hand. "We'd be outraged if someone said this about people with disabilities, but we give ourselves permission to say it about older people, casually, all the time," she said. "And every time we say it about ourselves, what message are we giving our kids? Our grandchildren? This is one of those moments where you put on your new glasses and see what you've been missing. Thank you, sisters."

Just as Vanessa had predicted, the group easily turned to their policy work. The digital director and her assistant offered to review all their images of older people, as well as graphics where they were simply missing.

Someone suggested surveying network groups about how they engage older workers.

"Don't forget to look at language," Sophie urged. "I have a pet peeve about the word 'aging.' Every single person is aging, even babies, the minute they leave the womb."

People threw out ideas on possible blogs and decided to do a piece on grandparents taking care of grandkids or an adult child with a disability. "We need to lay out what older adults need, but also show them as vibrant people who give as well as receive care," the board president said.

"My grandmother," Jasmine added. "I want to do a story on her and the home care worker, Aquilina, who comes in every day. My grandma worries because the agency pays Aquilina so little, and Aquilina tells me all the things my grandma's taught her:how to crochet, how she survived Jim Crow. They sing each other's favorite songs."

**

Nick was waiting in the kitchen rolling out dough when Sophie got off the Zoom call. "I heard it all," he told her. "I learned some things. Like the word 'doddering.' I wasn't sure what that meant before."

Sophie lifted up the canister of flour and mimed scooping some out to toss at him.

"Seriously, babe, that was magnificent. I heard the roar of the elders." Nick placed one hand on the dough and the other on his heart. "On this pizza crust, I make you a solemn promise that I will stop contributing to the bias. I will embrace my age." He grabbed a dishtowel to brush the floury print off his shirt before folding her into his arms. "Just remind me, what was that sex part again?"

Acknowledgements

Ellen Bravo

Years ago my father tried to convince me to abandon the life of an organizer. He ticked off the downsides: no money, no security, powerful people going after you. "Look how much you sacrifice," he said.

"Ah," I told him. "You're forgetting the joy — the enormous satisfaction of watching people stand up for themselves, the friendship and love, the ever-growing community, the delight of being present when people grow their power and bring about real change."

Larry and I have spent more than five decades as organizers. In good times and bad, we've especially cherished the moments when people grasp that oppression isn't normal or inevitable, that change is possible and that they can be part of that change.

Standing Up shares many moments like these. While the stories are fictionalized, all are inspired by experiences we've had and people we've worked with. As the characters slow down, stand up, form unions, make good trouble, we hope they'll entertain and enlighten, make you laugh and make you rage, encourage you to love deeply and to keep finding ways to fight for justice.

We also hope our stories will help counter the notion of "the voiceless." The author Imbolo Mbue describes the oppressed as the "deliberately unheard." We're proud to elevate these voices, sparked by people who led us and moved us and brought us joy.

In our tales, you will see white organizers continually grappling with issues of racism, urgently, often clumsily.

271

They recognize over and over, as Heather McGhee says, that racism costs all of us. That defeating it is the only way to win.

You'll see people who have the capacity to change. Even the most evolved men need to learn about sexism. Even someone caught up in the rat race may be able to remember their values and take a new path.

We've tried to share insights into how those in power wield that power and various ways to upend them. Our hope is that *Standing Up* will nourish those already in struggle and spur new generations of activists. We'd love to see it lead to a host of "stand-up's" in workplaces across the country.

Huge thanks to Tim Sheard and Hard Ball Press for getting these stories out in the world.

Thanks also to the many people who read the drafts and gave us feedback and encouragement along the way. Full-throated appreciation to my writing group, Rachel Ida Buff, Patty Donndelinger-Bogyo and Jennifer Morales, whose wisdom and suggestions strengthened every story. Much love to the morning community of writers who give new meaning to "writing-adjacent" — Rinku Sen, Rona-Lee Fernandez, Cielo Cruz, Christola Phoenix, EunSook Lee, JoAnn Blingit, Jyotsana Uppal, Makani Themba, and Juhu Thukrai. Undying thank you's to my nearest and dearest, my twin sister Lynne Bravo Rosewater, and friends Barbara Deinhardt and Zohreh Emami, whose love and support and confidence make everything possible.

Gratitude to Jane Fonda for the idea of the feminist's daughter turned monster manager. I would have loved to see Jane, Dolly and Lily do the intervention, but I hope readers agree Annie does a pretty good job.

Special shout-out to our sons, Nat Miller and Craig Bravo Miller, who inspired the various children you meet in this collection. Their love and laughter and skill at making fun of us kept us going through the pandemic.

Above all, we thank the extraordinary people — the real-life Sam's and LC's, the Rosa's and Vanessa's and more — who inspired these characters.

Larry's wonderful stories were the spark for this book. In 45 years of marriage, we've raised two sons, conspired in the fight for justice, co-written a training for high school students on sexual harassment, been each other's sounding board, first reader, editor, cheerleader and best critic for every kind of writing, from songs and poetry to blogs, articles, and books. This book is our first collaboration on fiction. Can't wait to add "book talks" to this list.

Larry Miller

It's been a joy to have spent over 45 years as a co-conspirator with Ellen Bravo in fighting for equality and justice. While these 23 short stories are fictional, they are all based on real events and people that we came to know. Our combined interactions in communities like Tulsa, Atlanta, New York, Baltimore, Chicago and Milwaukee have allowed us to stand alongside amazing workers, activists and champions for human dignity.

My life as a community and union activist and as an elected school board member has rewarded me with friendships and comrades who are forever in my heart.

While this book provides me the opportunity to tell some of the stories I have experienced, Ellen has done the heavy lifting of the writing and editing. We have truly collaborated, but the credit is all hers. She is the love of my life and I could not have come this far without her.

Title from Hard Ball Press

A Great Vision: A Militant Family's Journey Through the Twentieth Century, Richard March

Caring: 1199 Nursing Home Workers Tell Their Story, Tim Sheard, ed.

Fight For Your Long Day, Classroom Edition, by Alex Kudera

Good Trouble: A Shoeleather History of Nonviolent Direct Action, Steve Thornton

I Just Got Elected, Now What? A New Union Officer's Handbook, 3rd Edtion, Bill Barry

I Still Can't Fly: Confessions of a Lifelong Troublemaker, Kevin John Carroll

In Hiding – A Thriller, Timothy Sheard

Justice Is Our Love In Action: Poetry & Art for the Resistance, Steward Acuff (author), Mitch Klein (Artist)

Legacy Costs: The Story of a Factory Town, Richard Hudelson

Love Dies – A Thriller, Timothy Sheard

The Man Who Fell From the Sky – Bill Fletcher, Jr.

Murder of a Post Office Manager – A Legal Thriller, Paul Felton

My Open Heart: 1199 Nursing Home Workers Tell Their Story

New York Hustle: Pool Rooms, School Rooms and Street Corner, A Memoir, Stan Maron

Sixteen Tons – A Novel, Kevin Corley

Throw Out the Water – Sequel to Sixteen Tons, Kevin Corley

The Union Member's Complete Guide, 2nd Edition, Updated & Revised, Michael Mauer

The Lenny Moss Mysteries (in order of release) – Timothy Sheard

Made in the USA
Monee, IL
26 March 2022

93194200R00166